The Green Door

Hazel Mattice

ISBN: 978-1-7351054-0-6 (SC)
ISBN: 978-1-7351054-1-3 (e)

Part I

"The whole course of human history may depend on a change of heart in one solitary and even humble individual...For it is the solitary mind and soul of the individual that the battle between good and evil is waged and ultimately won or lost."

M. Scott Peck

1

Valley City, North Dakota
December 13, 1975

"Each of you is assigned to an individual warrior," Chief of Seraphs, Michael told the guardians arriving at the Catholic hospital nursery.

A guardian glanced around the empty corridor. "When are they scheduled to arrive?"

"They are here." Michael pointed beyond the glass to the bassinets side by side in the nursery. Five infants wrapped in blankets: three pink, two blue. The infant on the end yawned with a tiny squeak.

"That's your keep," Michael told Amael, the guardian at his side.

Amael eyed the baby. "Doesn't seem much of a warrior."

"God is particularly pleased with her," Michael said. "See how she reflects His love? Her spirit glows with His fire. To protect this gift, she must grow to be resilient and brave."

Amael observed a few minutes more. "Perfect love casts out fear. To love like a child, wholly and unconditionally against the rage and hatred is what this fight desperately needs."

"Godlike," Michael said. "Risky and terrifying."

Amael gave a nod. "His love never fails. In terrible days, she'll have the power to overcome."

On alert, Amael hovered alongside the infant warrior until they reached her home.

The caregiver mother was a beautiful woman by human standards. Hair flowing to her waist in a shiny platinum cascade. A paisley silky shirt with large sunflowers, white cloth belt, and bell bottoms completed her outward appearance. Inwardly, she possessed a strong spirit and a searching soul.

The newborn's family met them at the door. Two children trailed behind their father, crowding around the baby. The girl looked up with large eyes. "What's her name?"

"Rosemarie Grace." The mother smiled warmly, handing the infant warrior to her human caregiver father who gazed at her for the first time.

No real threat. A boy, five years old, emerged from the kitchen, his eyes shadowed with rebellion. "Where's the baby?"

"Sit down and I'll let you hold her," the father said.

The boy reluctantly complied. The baby squirmed in her brother's arms. He looked away, passing off an air of boredom. The infant warrior grabbed his pinky, and the brother gave her a startled look. She gazed right back with innocence. His features softened briefly before he thrust his chin in the air.

An ally. Amael sighed.

Suddenly, a heavy wave of hatred emanated from the shadows.

A destroyer.

Amael watched the creature's every move. Dark forces like this one were subject to humans.

The protective brother and the sister with the big brown eyes felt the dark presence. Children were sensitive to their world, and didn't mess around with something terrifying as the malevolent shadow.

It moved behind the warrior's mother, tendrils curling around her.

Amael waved his arm. "Be gone."

Quickly as it arrived, the force of evil disappeared.

Destructive shadows were easy to scare, especially in the spirit world. The environment to raise a warrior appeared adequate. A hard-working father, an innovative mother, and good-hearted siblings.

Except.

The Almighty's love, soothing balm to the deepest wound. The infant warrior glowed with divine adoration, inviting lonesome and hurting souls and those of a darker nature.

Given a chance, The Dragon would eat the baby alive.

Amael stood watch.

2

Halloween 1980
Welcome, North Dakota

"Our House" played on the fireplace radio. Our actual house, a four- story once-upon-a-time hospital, was home.

There were five of us Mattson children. Three brothers, one sister, and me, Rosemarie.

My older brothers' rooms were on the fourth floor. The nursery for my baby brother. On the third floor, yellow and white-striped wallpaper, tall windows around and a Peter Pumpkin Eater-light switch, Josie's and mine.

"Trick-or-treating is for kids." Josie twirled the phone cord around her finger.

"You're twelve," I said, pulling on my sister's arm. "Come on, I can't go by myself."

"Twelve and a half." Josie popped her gum. "Steve will take you."

Music boomed from down the stairs and I took them two at a time, sailing into my brother's arms. "Hooray."

"Whoa, Rosie." He hoisted me up and replaced the lid on the record player.

"Who's the Queen of Hearts?" I wrapped my arms around his neck.

"Juice Newton."

"Josie said you would take me trick-or-treating."

"She did, huh? All right, but only if you promise not to be a nuisance."

"What's a nunesance?"

"Not nunesance, silly. Nuisance." Steve set me down by the door and a giant green bowl full of candy. "Wait here while I grab your costume."

I stuck my nose in the candy bowl and took a deep breath. My Labrador Retriever, Chester, pushed his nose in alongside me.

"Hey, keep your schnoz outta there," Steve said, handing me a plastic mask. "It goes for your mutt too."

"I don't want to be Sally." I frowned at the Peanuts' character, neither good nor bad and horribly forgettable. "Josie's not going. Maybe she'll let me be Lucy."

Steve rolled his eyes. "Everyone hates Lucy."

"Not me." I hooked a finger beneath the rubber band, pulling the plastic mask over my head. "Please?"

"Rosemarie..."

"Why can't I, though?" I stuck the tip of my tongue through the tiny mouth hole.

Steve handed me a plastic pumpkin. "Because babies get last dibs."

"I'm not a baby." I tugged on his arm. "Tommy's the baby."

Steve pulled a Batman mask over his face. "Let's go, baby."

It was a mild fall evening. Dried leaves crunched beneath our feet, swirling warm bursts of air around us.

Trick-or-treating consisted of walking, walking, and more walking. Kids flew past us up and down the streets. My face grew hot and sweaty beneath the mask. At a sudden rustle of leaves, I rushed Steve.

He brushed me off. "Don't touch the threads."

A boy and a girl in werewolf costumes trotted toward us. I drew closer to Steve. We weren't allowed to wear scary costumes. They pulled up their rubber masks: Dennis and Stacey Wilson. Werewolves suited them. They were mean, selfish, and I couldn't wait until they were gone.

"You make it over to Howard's?" Dennis asked.

Steve glanced in his bucket. "Not yet."

"We have. Twice," Stacey said.

Steve winked at me. "I have to take my baby sister around."

"Ditch her and come with us," Dennis said.

"He can't, Mom said." I reached for Steve's hand.

Dennis pulled his mask back on. "We've been to almost every house in town and it's only six. The way I see it, we can make it to all of them twice."

The full moon lit up the next house. Branches from the yard elms shadowed the second-story window. "It's him," Steve said in a spooky voice.

"Who?" Stacey whispered.

My heart stopped, then started hammering in my ears. "Yeah, who?"

"You know." Steve gave me a fearful look. "Him. Old Man Water. Only you pronounce it like Grampa says water, *Warter.*"

"Oh yeah, right." Dennis nodded slowly. "Old Man Water."

"*Warter,*" Steve said. "He's a miser they say. Wouldn't give a penny to save a reverend's life. His son is in the cemetery out of town. Seven years old."

Two years older than me. "How'd he die?" I shivered.

"In a fire. Lit a candle and forgot about it. His room was ablaze by the time the fire department got there. They managed to put it out, but couldn't save him. They say the room mysteriously glows red ever since."

I looked up at the second story window. A red hue flamed the room. I turned and ran.

"Rosemarie, come back. I didn't mean it," Steve called.

"She's gonna tell," I heard Stacey say.

And Dennis laughed. "Yeah, but did you see her face?"

Back at the house, I sat with Mom in the entrance. She gave Steve her usual quiet lecture about me being the little sister to watch out for. After 'the talking to,' Steve rubbed my head. "Sorry Rosie." Mom let him finish trick-or-treating. "Only the last two houses you missed," she said.

At the door, Steve paused. "You should have seen Rosemarie go. For a girl with short legs, she runs like the wind."

I could tell I wasn't supposed to hear, but I did. And I beamed.

Steve said it, so it had to be true.

I woke up in the dark, alone. Fear raised fine hairs on my arms. Where was I? In our cargo van. I looked out the window. The Thompson's were having a Halloween Party.

I'll go in and...The house next door was Mr. Water's. I sat back in the van seat and shut the door.

Calm down. Go inside.

I squeezed my eyes shut, terrified to see the red glowing room and Old Man Warter in the rearview mirror. Two more times I tried to get out of the van before finally I sank in the seat, defeated.

Don't be afraid.

Later, Mom retold the story to the rest of the family. "Steve forgot her."

"I'm sorry, Rosie." Steve rubbed the top of my head.

At bedtime, the branches of the elm outside our bedroom window scraped the pane. I pulled the covers over my head. Josie hadn't come to bed yet and I couldn't stop thinking about Old Man Warter.

For a girl with short legs, you run like the wind.

A surge of power flowed through me and I sat up. Old Man Warter was no match for me. I was too fast for him, and the van was no big deal. Sure, they forgot about me, but even alone I had me.

Special. Born for such a time as this.

A smile tugged my lips in the dark. I lay back down, peace settling over me as I drifted to sleep.

3

On our way home from Walsky Grocery we saw him hunched over in the grass along the broken sidewalk.

The boy's carrot top hung low between his shoulders. "I was riding my bike around the park and they jumped me. They said my bike was payment to be their friend."

"Billy Lane and Donny Gild aren't anyone's friends," Anne Clark said. Victim-expert, beat up by school mean girls for "stinking up the joint" two days after the city shut their water off. "Nothing worse than being a redheaded new kid."

School jerks didn't take summers off.

"Doesn't help your mom is the school janitor." Shelly Vanguard got all her gossip from her mother, neighbor to my mother. The pair shared coffee and what Mom called, the local scuttle.

He looked up, his face a map of freckles. "Or a pudgy cabbage patch doll."

"If you can't say anything nice, don't say anything at all," Anne said in her sing-song voice.

"You like Hot Tamales?" I shook the box of candy.

"Sure." He held out his hand.

"My name is Rosemarie Mattson." I poured him some. "What's yours?"

"Greg Hamill." His eyes were fixed on me.

"Anne's poor," Shelly said. "Her and her mom live off food stamps and the thrift store. I know your mom moved in next to our house, and your parents are divorced."

Greg pulled his hand away from me. "So?"

Shelly tightened her ponytail. "My dad's the vet. Your mom's cat Marvin ran away. I helped her catch it."

"My mom likes the cat better than me," Greg said, glancing at me. "What about you?"

"I have friends. Good ones." I shoved the box into my pocket. "You want to come over to my house tomorrow? It's the biggest in town. On the…"

"I know where you live," he said. "Pastor Brady lives in your garage apartment." The back alley, a two-stall garage with an upstairs apartment was a temporary home for our pastor and his wife while the parsonage was being renovated.

"You're gonna need friends if you want to survive school," Anne said. "Probably full-body padding too. It's full of all kinds of 'em."

Greg pushed to his feet. "All kinds of what?"

Anne sniffed loudly. "Bullies. They're like sharks. They can smell fear."

"We're playing Shark. My mom said we could have hot cocoa. Plus you'll need to bring my bike back." I offered him the handle bars.

Greg took a step back. "The blue's not bad. I don't know about the basket, though. Flowers are for girls."

"I'm a girl, it's a sunflower, and the bike's a loaner."

Greg took the handle bars from me. "Who's all going?"

"Me, Shelly and Anne."

"I'll be there," he said, got on my bike and rode off.

4

A hint of sunrise on the morning sky and we were awake. The TV static turned low, we waited for five o'clock and the best part of the weekend: Saturday morning cartoons.

The chimney supplied a large fireplace on all four floors including the basement. Behind the TV on the top of the hearth, yellow wooden Dutch shoes with "Mattson" painted in black.

Shelly spent the night and brought her latest toy: a Fisher Price houseboat. Mrs. Vanguard was what Mom called frugal. I couldn't remember the last time Shelly got a new toy. I loved Fisher Price and wasn't about to complain.

Shelly plopped down on the bean bag next to me in the basement. "When is Anne coming?"

"Whenever her mom drops her off," I said, puffing up the beanbag. Anne never spent the night. Her mom's new boyfriend didn't let her. If she wasn't home by six she was in for it.

"And what's-his-name?" Shelly asked.

"Greg." I sank down on the cool leather bag. "I never gave him a time. I guess whenever he shows up."

She crossed her arms. "I still can't believe you invited him."

"He's good," I said, listening to the beads settling around me. "He didn't want a bunch of girls helping him. Didn't cry. In fact, he almost seemed—annoyed. Like he thought he was something special."

"He's a boy."

"Who needs us," I said. Shelly was the first friend I made outside my family. She was loyal and fierce, but made up her mind about people straight off. If they didn't make the cut it was eye-daggers the entire time.

"He's definitely a boy," Shelly said.

"Yeah, he is," I said. "You know what this calls for."

Shelly's eyes lit. "A story?"

"Yep. A tragic one," I said, recalling a tale from Bernard Evslin's *Heroes, Gods and Monsters of the Greek Myths*. Each story tucked away in my heart. "Once upon a time, there was a dryad named Echo. She had a beautiful voice and all the woodland creatures begged her to sing and tell stories. The goddess of love, Aphrodite came to Olympus to get the local scuttle from her."

"Like my mom and your mom."

"Right?" I leaned forward. "Except there was one teensy weensy problem."

"What?" Shelly sat up.

"Echo was a chatterbox and always had to have the last word. One day, she was walking in the woods and saw the god Zeus with a river nymph. Echo ran to tattle about it to Aphrodite. That's when Zeus' wife stomped through the forest looking for him. Echo told Hera that Zeus was in Olympus looking for her."

"Why cover for him?" Shelly asked.

"Perhaps it was for the blue sapphire ring Zeus gave her from his own finger."

"Were they friends? Did she know she would be rewarded?"

"Not sure. Anyway, doesn't matter. When Hera came back, she saw the ring and was what Mom would call 'madder than a wet hen.' She cursed Echo, 'to never be allowed to say anything but the last words said to her.'"

"Poor Echo." Shelly clamped a hand over her mouth.

"Totally. Echo wandered about the wood, wallowing in misery when she came across a boy."

"Oooh. Was he cute?"

"The most. A boy she could love. Echo forgot her sorrow and danced toward the boy. He asked Echo if she could show him the path out of the woods. Echo said, 'out of the woods' and the boy asked her why he must repeat everything."

"Let me guess, Echo said, 'repeat everything.'"

"You got it. After a few more tedious attempts, Echo tried to steal a kiss. When he pushed her away, she tried again. Once more, he knocked her to the ground. On her knees on the path, arms wrapped around his legs, Echo tried to beg, but she could not."

Shelly rolled her eyes. "What a loser."

"She loved him. The boy was nothing but an arrogant..."

Rosemarie.

"Anyway, the boy called 'farewell' to Echo, and all she could say was farewell back. The boy disappeared." I drew a breath. "When he was gone, Echo was sad. Now she prayed to Aphrodite a desperate plea to, 'make her disappear along with her love.'"

"Oh." Shelly tucked herself deeper in the beanbag.

The TV screen flipped to the American flag, and the National Anthem began to play.

"Okay, part two next time," I said.

"You know, Greg's brother, Rich plays football."
Shelly's attention reverted to the TV. "He's the coolest
guy in Derrick's grade."

An image of her cocky brother popped into my head.
"Totally." I yawned. "Your brother is lame."

"So?"

"So so suck your toe all the way to Mexico." I stuck
my tongue out at her.

"When you get there cut your hair, stuff it down
your underwear," Shelly said, pushing messy bangs
away from her eyes. "Rich is super cute."

"He was outside Dairy Queen on the benches with
his buddies drinking beer. He gave me the creeps."

"Beer drinking gives you creeps."

"No. He's plain old obnoxious with nothing better to
do than..." I stopped. Shelly was my best friend, but her
mom was queen-bee of talking too much. I didn't like
Rich. Not one bit.

Quiet.

Shelly got the last word. "Hopefully Greg doesn't
completely suck."

Greg and Anne showed up before lunch. We pulled all
the basement furniture in a circle. The floor was the
ocean, and the chairs and couch were dry land. Being
the new kid, Greg was the shark. If any of us even
stepped foot on the floor we were toast.

"No place to hide in open water." Greg glided in front
of us.

Shelly hopped from the couch to the chair. "Sharks'
emission of light is camouflaged by counter-
illumination, making sharks invisible to predators and
prey."

Greg's eyes widened. "Wow. I didn't know."

"I read it in *The Weekly Reader* in school." Shelly crossed her arms over her chest. "The mouth is on its underside so it can eat krill easily."

"I bet the light is their lipstick," Anne said, jumping from the chair to the couch, one foot in the water.

Greg touched her arm, making a ferocious eating noise. "You're out."

Phil Collins' voice boomed from the radio. I sang along, "Say my name, say my name."

"Paperlate," Greg said.

"What?"

"You keep singing 'say my name,' but it's actually 'Paperlate.'"

"Nuh uh." I pushed his shoulder.

"Yah huh." He pushed back.

"I call timeout." I grabbed the cassette player from the hearth, flipped the tape over, and pushed 'play' and 'record' at the same time. When the song finished playing, I pressed rewind and play. I held up a shushing finger when Shelly's mouth opened. After several rewinds and pressing of the play button, I realized Greg was right. "I had no idea. Here this whole time I thought it was 'say my name.'"

"I used to, too," Greg said.

"Guys, time to eat," Mom called from the top of the stairs.

"Race ya," I said, and we took them two at a time.

Mom dished up Swedish meatballs, mashed potatoes which Dad said "put hair on your chest," and peas. Steve and George were at Grandpa's farm. Josie was going through a no-eating kick because of a boy, and Tommy ate with Mom in the kitchen.

Greg dug into his potatoes. "You're smart. For girls."

"Mommy hamsters eat their young because if people pick them up, the momma doesn't like the way they smell," Shelly said through a mouthful.

Anne grimaced. "Man, we're eating."

"Which comes first, the chicken or the egg?" I reached for my cup.

"I don't get it," Anne said.

"You don't get anything," Shelly said. "Frogs."

"Frogs come before the chicken and the egg?" I made fork marks in my mashed potatoes. "Nothing bad can be said about frogs."

"I got one." Shelly leaned forward. "A wasp paralyzes a caterpillar and lays eggs. The eggs multiply until the caterpillar is infested." Her eyes grew wide. "The caterpillar is alive the whole time."

"Gross." My stomach rolled with the image.

Shelly paid no mind. "It only takes a couple boys to..."

Anne reached over, spilling her cocoa.

Shelly leapt to her feet. "Anne."

Anne reddened. "Sorry. I'll get a napkin."

"Greg, your brother is here," Mom called from the entryway.

I walked Greg to the door. Rich was in his hot rod car with a bunch of girls piled in front and back. He unrolled the window, "Hey girls, there he is. Alice the fag," a name sure to get my mouth wash out with soap. "Get in the car, Alice."

One girl said, "Maybe they'll make a man out of him."

"You're way cooler than him," I told Greg. No way was I going to ask why Rich called him Alice. No way.

"I don't care." Greg rubbed his arm across his nose, turned and trotted away. "See ya, wouldn't want to be ya."

"We're doing the same thing next Saturday."

Greg reached the car. "Cool."

"See ya," I said with a satisfied smile.

5

Late Friday afternoon, I lay in the grass in the park. The cool breeze brushed my arms, raising goosebumps. The sound of car engines in the distance broke the silence.

"He's good, right? Greg, I mean," I said.

Talk less, listen more, said the still, small voice inside me.

"Yes, I know. I feel he is though." I pondered this a minute, a wave of sadness washing over me. "Rich is mean to him. Definitely a..."

Fake.

"I wish he had a good family. Like me." Mom never yelled like the other kids' parents did. Dad and the boys were out at Grandpa's farm where I wanted to be. Steve said I was too little. Didn't help that I was a girl. Josie, the oldest, looked out for the rest of us. Two years old, Tommy followed me around, but I didn't mind.

Yes, it's good.

"What is it?" I asked.

No answer.

"I feel it too. Like I should freeze time or something. As though to remember everything now. Because it's about to change. Do you..."

"Who are you talking to?" Greg's voice came from above me.

I bolted to a sitting position, brushing fresh-cut grass from my pants. "You scared me."

"Sorry." He plopped next to me. "My mom is a big fan of Alice Cooper."

"I don't know who she is."

"He." Greg gave a humorless laugh. "Alice Cooper is a rock star. I play the guitar and sing."

"Good. I mean, about playing the guitar. Not about being called 'Alice,'" I said. His eyes were distant, his face, drawn. "Are you tired?"

Greg yawned. "I didn't sleep good last night. Something was scratching under my bed. It would stop, then chewing. And scratching again."

"Probably a mouse. I bet you couldn't hear a mouse chewing."

"I looked under the bed." Greg glanced over at me. "The dead man looking back was no mouse."

"A ghost?" I looked around as though expecting to find one. I didn't believe in them, but Greg's expression said he did. "What did it want?"

"What do any of them want? Some play tricks. Some don't know they've passed on. Some are hateful in death as they were in life."

A shiver rolled up my spine. "Were you scared?"

"Heck no. Ghosts can't hurt you."

A blue car pulled up alongside the pavement and a man got out. He had shiny black hair, like a raven. The woman in the passenger seat gave a slight wave. She was beautiful, with pixie-like features, and a soft mouth painted pink.

The raven-hair man made his way over to us. "Hey kids. I'm looking for Dairy Queen. Can you point me toward it?"

"No." Greg grabbed my hand and pulled me back.

His smile twisted. "Come on now, son—"

"I'm not your son," Greg said. "If you ever come near me or my friend again, I will call the cops."

The man's hands flew up. "No harm, no foul."

"Come on Rosemarie." Greg dragged me further away.

The man hesitated, turned around and headed for his car. Sunshine reflected off his hair in a sheen. I bet he lived off carrion like the raven itself.

Greg's gaze followed mine as the man got in the car. "What do you think?"

I straightened tall. "He gives me the creeps."

"Same."

The car pulled away from the curb. The woman looked back at us. All life was gone from her eyes, replaced with a rather serene look. Like a prop of some sort. Or maybe she was empty. No, not it either. More like in her own body, she was—

—trapped.

6

No one in Welcome, North Dakota, we knew had a real tree.

Not even Pastor Brady.

Snowsuits, hats, mittens, scarves, and thermal boots donned, we spent the morning tromping through the snow alongside the tree row at Grandpa's farm outside town. Above us, sun dogs, a reminder if we thought it was cold today wait until tomorrow. We picked the smallest evergreen in the snow-drifted field. Before Steve fired up the chainsaw, there was one last thing to do:

Dad prayed for the tree.

Back at the house, the Christmas tree reached the nine-foot living room ceiling. Andy Williams sang "It's the Most Wonderful Time of the Year" on the record player.

The tree was trimmed with lights, garland and every decoration from today and Christmas past. Family, relatives, and friends filled the living room.

Mom and Mrs. Vanguard talked over coffee while we kids decorated. Grandma Degner brought hand-knitted stockings to hang over the fireplace. Grandpa Degner talked with Dad and Uncle Kevin in the den about the weather and the economy's down-turn. Tommy played toys on the floor. Josie and Mom's sister, Aunt Jane, bustled about the kitchen, preparing goodies.

There would be sugar cereal for breakfast in the morning. Kipper Snacks and Lifesaver story books in our stockings. Josie started Snow Ball cookies, what Shelly's mom called Mexican Wedding Cakes.

Lutefisk on the stove said Dad would be a happy man Christmas morning. I tried it once because he said, "It'll put hair on your chest." I didn't mind the taste of the buttery cod as much as the texture, fish jelly- like substance sliding down my throat.

Christmas Eve tradition: big kids go outdoors for a game of Duck Duck Goose. Josie stayed inside to bake cookies, make hot cocoa and Russian Tea. Tommy did whatever I did.

Steve reached for his jacket. "Come on, Rosie."

Easy choice. "Coming." I beamed.

The winter moon hung in the sky above, reflecting off the deep snow. A hoot of an owl broke frozen silence.

"Duck." Steve tapped my head. "Did you see someone moved into the house across the street?"

"Don't tell Rosemarie." George ducked his head away as Steve came closer. "She'll invite them over to play shark. Especially if they're losers. She draws 'em like a magnet to metal."

"Hey." I moved my head away as Steve called me duck. "My friends aren't losers."

"Rosemarie," Steve said in his firmest voice. "Trust no one unless they give you reason to." He tapped George's head. "Goose."

It was on. Around they went until Steve slid into George's spot.

"Purple duck," George said, patting Tommy's head. He reached me, tilting my head back. "Ugly duck."

My eyes instantly welled with tears. "Nuh uh."

"Just say duck, George," Steve said.

"What a baby." George pushed me. "We were fighting over the clicker this morning and she left the room."

My bottom lip quivered. "Fighting's stupid."

"Speaking of stupid, I'm done this baby game," Steve said. "I'm starved. You hungry, Tommy?"

Tommy got up and pulled at my arm. "Romarie."

"You guys go. Take Tommy with you. I'll be right in."

Steve reached the porch, and called, "Rosemarie, you have company."

Greg made his way toward me. Features shadowed by the moonlight, he took long steps through deep snow. The sag of his shoulders and long face pierced my heart.

"Want to make snow angels?" I asked.

"Sure." He dropped into the snow.

"Are you really very sad?" Puffs of frost emerged from my mouth into the starry sky. "It must be awful."

"You know there's no reasoning. Nothing good will come of gathering information about it."

"Come on, you can tell me." I carefully pushed off my angel.

"My mom got another cat," he said, getting off his own.

"How many is that?" I brushed the snow from my legs.

"Ten."

Ten cats in his trailer house couldn't be good. Litter and cat food, and the smell, and... "What are you doing tomorrow?"

He blinked. "It's Christmas."

"I know, silly," I said, making my way toward the house, every window lit with festive decorations and holly. "What I mean is, do you open presents tonight or in the morning?"

"I didn't see any presents." Greg's shoulders sagged. "Last year, my mom gave me a hat and gloves in a grocery bag. No tags. A little worn. I think they belonged to my dad."

"You want to come here for Christmas?"

His eyes widened. "To your house?"

"Yeah. Your mom too." I bit my tongue before inviting Rich.

He gave me a suspicious look. "Why?"

"It's a time of year when we should help people. Be tireless, forgiving, and defenders of friends." I reached the porch steps and stopped. "And, because I like you."

That's how you do it.

Greg studied me like a bug beneath a microscope. "Makes sense I guess."

Matching black outdoor lanterns hung on either side of the front door. "My living location is important," I said. "I love it here."

Greg stood alongside me. "The only thing better would be in the country."

A gray sports car pulled up to the front sidewalk. Steve would have called it, "A dumb ride for North Dakota winter." Anne got out. Her mother's boyfriend watched her the entire way from the street to our front door. Tires spun and the car roared away.

In the entrance, we stomped our boots and shed our winter clothes.

At seven, Anne was my prettiest friend, freckles and smooth skin. Today, her appearance said it all: dirty face and stale cigarettes emitting from her grimy dress.

Looks like her mom forgot about the water bill again. "I'm glad you're here," I said, reaching for her hand.

Anne smiled, her beauty shining through the dirt. "Me too."

A mixture of nutmeg and peppermint floated through the air. Shelly's mom and mine were visiting by the fireplace. Shelly hurried across the thick yellow carpet to us. "Hi Rosemarie."

"Take Anne downstairs," I said. "We'll be right there."

Shelly took her by the hand. "Want to play Barbies?"

Anne's eyes lit. "My favorite."

Greg's eyes were on the knitted stockings hung by the fireplace. I admired the blue angel with a gold halo, mine. Grandma Degner made her way over with a red stocking. Stitched in front was a Wiseman sitting on a camel. "Merry Christmas, Greg."

Greg held it up. "It's got my name on it."

Grandma patted his arm. "Yes, well Santa knows all of Rosemarie's friends."

One day looking at some old Polaroids, I came across one of Mom wrapping presents. I leaned over and whispered in his ear, "Santa's not real."

"I know," Greg whispered back.

Aunt Jane made her way over with an array of goodies: cookies, divinity, yogurt-covered pretzels and Chex mix. "Wash your hands and you can have some."

"In a minute," I said, took Greg's hand, and pulled him toward the basement stairs. "First I want to show my friends my paper doll collection."

George grabbed a sugar cookie from the tray. "Greg doesn't want to see your dumb 'ol dolls."

"Does too." I stuck out my tongue.

7

Walsky Grocery

"How is your keep?" Michael asked Amael.

"The warrior has four siblings: Josie, Steve, George, and Tommy," Amael answered. "Her earthly father, Darwin is a successful farmer, respected and liked by everyone in the south. Her mother is an empathetic woman, Brenda. Rosemarie has a big house and plenty to eat. Birthday parties like royal feasts. She treats those less fortunate, Shelly Vanguard, Anne Clark and Greg Hamill as kings and queens..."

Greg Hamill rounded the isle, reaching for a jar of peanut butter. "Hey Rosemarie."

"Hi."

"Shopping with your mom?"

"Yeah."

"Me too." He held up the peanut butter.

"Greg?" a female voice boomed from two isles over. "Get the lead out."

"Gotta go." Greg stopped in his tracks. His mouth fell. A blond giant, thick muscles chiseled like steel, stood directly before him with an easy smile. His companion, over seven feet tall with long, silky black hair, six- pack abs and a Native American complexion. He wore a bright red pair of wrestling tights and a stern look.

The boy broke into a wide grin. "See ya, Rosemarie."

"See ya."

The angels waited for the seer to move on.

The Dragon slipped into the grocery store, savoring the memory of terror on the Queen of England when Michael Fagan broke into her bedroom in Buckingham.

The first thing he noticed was the child.

She was at the end of the isle with a daydreamer look and faraway smile, like honey. Didn't appear to have a bad thought in her head. Too easy.

The second thing, the guardians.

"Sounds like Rosemarie is growing in grace and beauty," Michael told Amael.

Blah, blah, blah. Typical seraphs, pouring over lives of souls beneath them. So what if she was made of sugar? A far more interesting topic: the earthquake and volcanic eruption at El Chichon, Mexico, killing thousands.

The Dragon was more worthy of conversation. He'd been the one controlling Carlos the Jackal in France terrorist attacks. The mastermind behind the potassium cyanide-laced Tylenol capsules in Chicago. Not to mention the Lebanese militia murdering Palestinian refugees in West Beirut refugee camps.

"She loves everyone," Amael said, wings fluttering.

Love? He shuttered. An old magic spell could destroy the cure in bitter, envious, lustful targets until their souls were ground to dust. However, the real stuff in a reckless goody-two-shoes would spread to another loser. And another, until...

He couldn't take it anymore. "Are you kidding me?" He burst forth. "A combat guardian to babysit?"

"There's no room for you here, Dragon," Michael said.

"Come on." He slithered behind the child's mother. "The largest robbery in New York history took place. All you care to discuss are tea parties for fools. What about seven hundred thousand demonstrators in Central Park protesting nuclear weapons—"

The guardians moved the family further down the aisle.

"You better run." The Dragon swiped the shelf, knocking a whole row of cereal boxes to the floor.

Rosemarie's older sister folded her arms. "Steve! George! Clean it up or I'll tell."

Steve held both hands up. "I didn't do it."

"Me either," George said. "How come Rosemarie never gets blamed?"

"Because Rosemarie's not dumb." Steve pushed him.

George pushed back. "She's dumber."

"George, clean up the cereal," their mother said.

"Steve started it." George glared at him.

She pinned George with a cold stare. "You finish it."

George cleaned up the boxes, a sliver of dark anger slipping inside him. He trailed behind his family.

Alone, dark thoughts focused on the girl, Rosemarie. The Dragon couldn't get close enough to do proper damage. Not with combat guardian- surveillance. Sticky sweet and obedient, Rosemarie would make a lousy puppet. Family members: a brother willing to take a punch from his own sibling. Sister, the mom when their mother was preoccupied...he chuckled, realizing the perfect way to take her down a notch.

8

February 1, 1985

It was crazy cold. Snow drifts covered the top of our six-foot deck. The weatherman said the cold wave was a result of a polar vortex moving further south, attached to a high pressure system. Frigid temperatures kept the furnace running like a rabbit and us kids inside.

Not Mom, though.

Every night after supper until around eight o'clock, she went out with Shelly's mom, Mrs. Vanguard.

Wintertime was my favorite.

Dad wasn't in the field and got to be at home with us.

I pretended not to notice the way he ran to the window right after Mom walked out the door. His grumbling at the sound of her car in the back alley close to eight. The dash back to his red velvet chair in the den to prop his feet up and grab the newspaper. Like he wasn't really spying every evening since Christmas.

"They go to secret meetings," Shelly told me one day we were in the basement playing with my new Barbie home and office.

"What kind of secret meetings?" I asked, brushing Barbie's hair.

Shelly shrugged. "I don't know. They're always talking real quiet. Hard to make it out, but maybe about a boyfriend."

My belly rolled. "Not my mom. My parents never yell or fight. One day, I saw them by the upstairs bathroom kissing. And they weren't kissing like Grandma and Grandpa. They were going..." I held an imaginary head, opened my mouth and rolled my tongue around, making all the mushy noises.

"Gross Rosemarie." Shelly set Barbie at her desk. "I'll bet Narcissus kisses like a movie star."

"Narcissus was a self-absorbed fool."

"Did Aphrodite make Echo disappear?"

"Yes, but she was mad about what Narcissus did to Echo. She cursed him to 'Fall in love with someone who wouldn't love him back.' Narcissus was oblivious to spells and curses, and quickly became annoyed with wood nymphs and Dryads falling in love with him everywhere he went. He despised their love. 'They aren't worthy of me,' he decided."

"Did he ever find love?"

"He came to the bank of a river. In the water was the most beautiful person he'd ever seen. Nymph or river god. He was enamored and unable to look away. The more he stared, the deeper he fell in love. He reached out, but the water rippled and the object of his affection disappeared."

Shelly's eyes were wide. "His own reflection."

"Narcissus said, 'Will she never come out?' A voice said, 'Never come out.' When he heard Echo's voice, Narcissus promised to stay with his reflection forever. Echo repeated, 'Forever.' Narcissus stayed there. Leaning over the water, he watched his reflection. Day after day, he begged it to come out. Until his legs grew into the river's bank. His hair became tangled and leafy, and he turned into a flower called Narcissus."

"What about Echo?"

"It's been said that you may come across her if you ever travel to those woods. Call a certain way and she'll answer you."

Don't let her be you.

"Leave me alone," I shouted, waving a hand by my face.

Shelly's head came up. "What is it?"

"It's nothing." Please let it be nothing.

It's not nothing.

It was late March before the cat was out of the bag. Our moms held secret meetings at Janette Brown's house every night. Until one night, my mother came home late, and said, "I've been saved."

"What did you need to be saved from?" Dad asked.

Mom said, "I'll tell you at supper."

Supper was served. Over Dad's favorite meal, steak and mashed potatoes, Mom told the family all about it. Josie was the next to get saved. Steve and George didn't say much. Tommy was too little to understand.

When they got around to me, I answered, "God lives in me." The universal roll of the eyes and groans around the table had me climbing on my chair, spilling my water glass. "But He does."

"Yes Rosemarie, everyone knows you're perfect," Steve said. The edge in his tone caught me off guard, and the wind slowly left my sails.

He's scared.

George rolled his eyes. "You're such a klutz."

"Am not," I said, sitting down.

"Kids." Mom mopped up the mess with a rag.

"Here I thought you had a boyfriend." Dad let out a laugh and dug into his potatoes. "I even told Pops it was only a matter of time before you'd leave me."

Dad got saved after that.

9

March 11, 1985

Mikhail Gorbachev was elected General Secretary of the Communist Party of the Soviet Union. A step to end the Cold War.

The war with the dark neighbor had begun when the doorbell rang.

"I got it," I said, flying to answer it. It was dress up day and we were rock stars. Shelly, Anne, Greg and me. "About time you showed..."

The raven-hair man from the park stood in a long, black coat.

"I..." I stumbled back, catching my foot on the rug and landed on my butt.

He laughed. Not a real laugh.

A half inch taller, the woman from the car stood next to him. She wore a long fur coat and winter gloves, her dark hair tucked beneath a woolen hat. "Is your mother home?" Her gaze searched the living room.

"Mom," I said, fixing my eyes on them. "Someone's here to see you."

Mom joined me in the entryway. "Duane and Mara. Do come in. This is my middle daughter. Rosemarie, this is Duane and Mara Sim. They moved into the house across the street where Mr. and Mrs. Brown used to live."

"Hello." Mara Sim flashed a half-smile that didn't reach her eyes, continuing to survey our living room.

"Hi," I said. "Did you find Dairy Queen?"

Bird man—Duane Sim—gave me a blank stare. "I beg your pardon?"

"You know, the park," I stammered, glancing at Mara Sim, who was clearly of no help. "You remember."

She gave me a vacant stare. "I'm not sure what you're talking about."

"Aren't you funny?" Duane said.

"But..."

"Come on in and sit down." Mom gathered them toward the couches alongside the fireplace. "Would you like coffee or tea?"

"Tea for me please, thank you," Mara said.

Duane held up his hand. "None for me."

They moved into the living room and the doorbell rang again.

It was Greg in a plaid shirt, suspenders, and pleated pants.

I pulled him inside. "You look perfectly fabulous."

"Duh," he said, glancing at the Sims. "What..."

"We're downstairs."

Shelly and Anne didn't disappoint either. They arrived in Sunday dresses, long necklaces and high heels. My pink dress was new. The long dangly necklace I chose was the one Dad got Mom for Christmas. The wedge heels were tall and perfect.

Tommy grabbed a corner of my dress, and stuck his thumb in his mouth. "Silky."

Greg motioned upstairs with a tilt of his chin. "What are they doing here?"

"I dunno." I handed Greg a stick of deodorant. "Since you're a boy, you get Mitchum."

"He's bad news," Greg said.

"Mom is probably trying to get them saved. She talks about it to everyone who comes over. About the recession, being born again, and the end of the world." I handed Shelly and Anne Tickle roll-ons.

Shelly eyed the deodorant. "When is the end of the world anyway?"

"When everything is ready," I said, pushing the record player volume- knob to high. "Now let's rock out."

Antiperspirant microphones in hand, we belted out "Sweet Dreams" with the Eurythmics, and danced to "Eye of the Tiger." Chester ran around, Tommy trailed behind, reaching for his tail.

"We better turn it down or Rosemarie's parents might get mad," Greg said between songs.

"Nah." I dropped to the couch. "Dad took Steve and George to Grandpa's farm. My mom is cool."

"I can't imagine the creepy neighbor is cool," Shelly said.

Anne sat next to me. "We should start a secret club."

"Creepy Neighbor Club," Greg said.

"Keep Kool Kids." I pushed sweaty hair from my forehead. "All start with 'K.'"

Shelly held out both arms. "Ooh, goosebumps."

Chester let out a bark. Greg tucked the record into the sleeve. "We should have animal names."

"Let's see." I tapped my finger against my chin. "Greg's an owl."

"Anne is most definitely a cat," Shelly said.

Anne leapt to her feet. "Shelly's a fox."

"Lion." Greg put his hand on top of mine. "When you make a move, we follow."

"Seriously?" I glared at him. "I'm not manly or cowardly."

"You're brave," Greg said. "We'll call you Lady Lion if it helps."

Shelly put her hand in. Anne followed, and me again until we formed a close circle. "One, two, three," I said, and we broke hands.

10

Coca-Cola introduced New Coke. Keep Kool Kids tried it from the enclosed sun porch while watching Duane Sim across the street. He was mowing the lawn. Back and forth. Forth and back. Stopping occasionally to push his cap down with a gloved hand.

I popped the top on my soda. "He fusses with the yard because it makes him look good to other folks in town."

"Probably a moocher. One of those who attends church potlucks for the free food," Greg said from his post.

"Rocket Man" played on the mantle radio. Shelly brought Cabbage Patch Dolls. A blond one and black one.

"This boy Cabbage Patch is rad, Shelly," I said. "How come your mom is buying—"

"I'd rather be watching cartoons," Anne said, fixing the dolls around the table. "We're missing Scooby-Doo."

"—all these new toys." Weird. Anne never interrupted. A dark thought popped into my head. Maybe Shelly's mom got a new job and Anne knew about it. Shelly probably told her on the way over.

Shelly smacked her lips. "Oooweee, that's sweet stuff."

Indignation burned like fire in my belly. Shelly was my friend first. We hadn't even met Anne until last year.

Greg scowled at the can in hand. "I can't believe this was preferred by taste-testers. Must not have much for taste buds."

Anne reached for the boy Cabbage Patch, knocking over her can. "Oops."

"I'll go ask your mom for a towel." Greg tossed his can in the garbage.

"I don't like it." I poured the rest of mine in Chester's dish. He lapped it happily.

"Me either," Anne said, and took another swallow.

I glared at her. "You're saying that 'cuz everyone else is."

Rosemarie. Really?

"I didn't mean it." I twirled my necklace and sang, "...things bring me back again."

Greg returned with a towel. "It's 'Til touchdown brings me round again.'"

"So?" I pushed his arm.

"Suck your toe." Shelly pressed her nose against the window. "His wife, Mara, is a nurse. They have two kids, Erica and Sonja. Erica is older, thirteen. Sonja is eleven."

Greg mopped up the sticky mess. "What does he do?"

"Maybe he's really nice," Anne said, sitting on the floor. "We don't really know anything about him."

"He is really nice," I said. "It's really quite weird how pleasant he is. His wife hangs on his arm and every word like he's King Tut."

"Mom didn't find much on him," Shelly said. "They came from Medora. Used to work for the musical."

"Why'd they quit?" Greg asked.

"Health reasons. At least, what they're telling people. Mrs. Sim has high blood sugar."

Greg's eyes were dark. "You're sitting ducks, Rosemarie. You and your house. Next time he comes over he'll bring his kids."

"I don't think he knows what's wrong with him," Shelly said.

Anne held a tea cup for a Cabbage Patch Kid. "He knows *something's* wrong with him."

Cold hands of fear took hold of my gut. "He doesn't think about it because he wouldn't be able to live with himself."

Sure enough, the Sims brought their kids the following Saturday. Shiny, black hair and pale skin, Erica and Sonja sat close to the TV as possible without getting sucked in.

Keep Kool Kids played war at the pool table and watched them.

Tommy made his way over with his new Tonka truck. "Vrrrrrrooooooooooom."

"Give it to me." Erica took a swipe.

"No." Tommy pulled the truck to his chest.

Quick rage flashed in Erica's eyes. She took a step toward Tommy. I was off the floor and next to my baby brother before you could say, "Suck your toe."

"Hold on now…" Anne caught her big toe on the carpet, landing on Erica.

Erica pushed her. "Get off me."

"Leave her alone," I said, fists clenched at my sides. "This is my house. Don't forget it."

Chester growled low in his throat.

Erica backed away. "Fine, I didn't want the baby's toy anyway."

We returned to the game. Shelly said, "Easy enough."

This time.

Something dark and evil wanted to destroy me, my family, and friends.

And it was right here in my house.

11

Michael Jordan played crazy good basketball. April 30, 1985, Erica and Sonja Sim parked themselves in front of the TV to watch him accept the NBA "Rookie of the Year" award.

Shelly brought her backpack of toys. Strawberry Shortcake and her Berry Happy Home. We gathered in a circle. Greg got Purple Pie Man. I passed out bags of peanut M&M's and cans of pop.

Erica stared at the yellow bag. "I don't like peanut M&M's."

"Too bad." Shelly popped one in her mouth. "They're our favorite."

"I got Oreos in case." I pulled the package out.

Erica grabbed at the cookies. "I'll take those."

"Say 'please.'" I held it away from her.

She folded her arms across her chest. "Keep your stupid candy. I'll get twice as much when I get home."

Chester gave a bark. I handed him a cookie.

Shelly reached for her backpack. "Erica and Sonja, want to play with us?"

"We should play pool," Greg said, pulling her toward the pool table.

"Let's Go Crazy" began to play.

Erica inched closer to the screen. "I can't hear the TV."

"I got it." Anne dashed toward the stereo, Mountain Dew in one hand and M&M's in the other. Chester stepped in her path. She pitched forward, spraying soda all over Erica. "I'm sorry."

Erica jumped to her feet. "Klutz!"

"Here, let me help you," Anne said, attempting to brush her off.

Erica couldn't have moved any faster if Anne were a snake poised to strike. "Stay away from me, you jinx."

"Let's go, Erica," Sonja said. "This party is stale."

"I guess she didn't want to play," I said after they left.

Greg picked up a pool stick. "Did you see their toys? He-Man in particular? Heads are gone. Arms missing. Unless you want Strawberry Shortcake's 'berry happy head' decapitated, I wouldn't let them play with yours."

"So not cool," I said. "They're pigs."

Anne tossed her empty can in the trash. "Don't play with pigs or you'll get dirty."

12

Keep Kool Kids met on the balcony overlooking my garage. Chester and my shadow, Tommy, joined us. Shelly brought a backpack full of Care Bears.

"Fox, what do you got?" Anne asked.

Shelly pulled out a notebook and flipped it open. "I made a list."

The Neighbor:
Hates snakes
The sight of his own blood

"What about the sight of his own blood?" I asked.

"He hates it," Shelly said.

Anne shivered. "I don't like blood either."

"Yeah, but he likes other people's blood. Sonja got a cut on her hand. He watched it ooze totally fascinated. Then he got a papercut and freaked out. Like wet-your-pants scared."

We took in the information, and huddled once more around the tablet.

Reads the obituaries in the paper
Mows yard
Checks weather
Checks news
Laughs at us

"Wait. Again, how is this any different than anyone else?" Greg asked.

Shelly squinted up at him. "He's a copy-cat."

Anne danced Good Luck and Bedtime bears on the railing. "Soar like an eagle, don't cluck with the chickens."

"He'd like to destroy everything good." I swallowed hard. "Including us."

Greg folded his arms. "So why doesn't he, Lady Lion?"

"Because he can't," I said, rubbing my belly. "He needs us."

Don't forget.

13

Keep Kool Kids rode bikes to the park. The sun twinkled between the leaves on cottonwoods that held song birds in chorus. We downed cans of Mountain Dew and skipped rocks.

"Greg and Rosemarie, sittin' in a tree," Shelly sang off-key. "K-i-s-s—"

"Nuh uh." My cheeks burned. "I checked out snakes since the neighbor is scared of them. They are predators that ambush or sneak up on prey."

"What do they eat?" Shelly asked.

"Mice and rodents. Nothing too difficult so they can preserve energy. They camouflage themselves under sand or leaves. Hiss, huff and puff. They even flop over and play dead with their tongues hanging out. If they bite you, you'll only bleed a little."

Anne shrugged. "Avoid getting bitten. Not scary at all."

Greg grabbed a stone. "I suppose this will be our last summer together."

My stomach took a dive. "Why?"

"Because we're almost teenagers."

"In two years. So?"

Shelly tightened her pony-tail. "So so suck your toe..."

"Yeah, yeah." I waved my hand at her. "But what does it have anything to do with it?"

Greg's eyes twinkled. "Next summer, I'll be thirteen. Probably even have a mustache. I'm not going to have time to hang with a bunch of girls. Unless they have a car and license to drive."

"Stacey Wilson and Katie Marsh are dips." I propped my hands on my hips. "Hang out with them over my dead body."

Greg chucked a stone across the water. "Speaking of dips, Erica and Sonja are at your house pretty much every day. Might as well move in."

"There's my mom for you. People are her mission," I said. "They'll move on."

Greg arched a brow. "Are you sure?"

"Of course I'm sure."

They're going nowhere.

Mara Sim's high-pitched laughter floated up the stairs. Duane's low voice rumbled as the adults carried on what my folks now referred to as a PW—Powwow.

Erica and Sonja stared at the TV. "The Power of Love" music video with neon sign Uncle Charlie's in the background.

Keep Kool Kids played cards. Tommy sat next to me, sucking his thumb. Chester lay alongside him. Something landed on my head. "Ah, get it off!" I jumped to my feet, swiping at my hair.

Greg looked up from his cards. "Whatcha got, Rosemarie? A spider?"

"I don't know." I sat back down. We started passing cards again. A piece of popcorn flew across my line of vision.

"Hey you guys, did you throw this?" I held up the popcorn.

The Sim girls giggled with their backs to us.

After a few more popcorn pieces, Sonja said, "This is lame. I'm bored."

"You got those demon possessed Cabbage Patch dolls?" Erica asked.

Shelly blinked. "Demon possessed?"

"Yeah. Some kid put hers on a shelf and there was a loud crash. When she ran in to see what happened, the doll sat in the middle of broken plates, and said, 'You didn't play with me. You didn't put me to sleep. That's why I broke the dishes. I'm not a doll. I'm the lord of Hell.'"

"We read about it in the *Enquirer*," Sonja said, her eyes fixed on the TV.

My heart roared in my ears.

"They're trying to scare us," Greg said, heading for the stairs. "Let's get out of here."

14

The Sims were at our house again. Keep Kool Kids found solace at the park.

Shelly took the swing. "Mom said Mr. Brown served them an eviction notice. Then Duane Sim chased him off the property. When the cop showed up, Duane told him someone was peeping in his windows."

"My mom said they haven't paid rent for three months," Shelly said.

"They'll have to leave town for sure," I said.

Greg hung from the monkey bars. "He doesn't have a job. Ten bucks says he'll worm his way into your house."

"No way, Jose." I spewed Mountain Dew, wiping my mouth with a forearm. "My parents are nice, but not that nice." Oh yeah? What about Pastor Brady and Karen? Grandma, when she broke her hip last winter?

"Shelly, did your mom tell you what they were going to do?" I tossed the empty can in the trash.

"She hasn't heard." Shelly kicked her legs, swinging high.

"Then nobody knows," I said.

"They're staying until they find a place," Mom said. Two trucks full of boxes arrived at the back door. Steve and George trailed behind Mom.

"How long will it take?" Steve asked.

"They aren't staying in my room," George said.

"Why our house?" Steve asked.

Mom smiled, looking through him rather than at him.

"Earth to Mom," George said. "Come in, Mom."

Steve followed her around real close. "A month? Two?"

"Until they find a place," Mom said, a far-off look in her eyes. "Six months."

Six whole months? An uneasy feeling settled in my stomach.

"Isn't that special?" a loud voice bellowed.

It turns out there was a boy Sim, Malcolm. He'd been living with his grandma. Raven hair like his dad, Malcolm was fourteen. His obnoxious laughter was pretty much everywhere. Maybe even his grandma got sick of him.

Erica flopped down on our gold sofa. "Look, Malcolm we have a couch."

We?

"Isn't that special?" Malcolm said.

"There's a basement," Sonja said.

Malcolm sat next to Erica. "Isn't that special?"

I scowled. "You already said that."

The three Sims exchanged glances before bursting into laughter.

"Church Lady," Malcolm said.

"Who's that?"

"Man, have you been living under a rock?" Malcolm asked.

Erica sat up. "What an idiot. Let's go downstairs and watch TV."

They ran toward the stairs, pushing each other. In one big commotion, they pounded down, each Sim yelling louder than the last. "It's better than our old house."

"We don't even have to sleep in the basement."

"Our room is upstairs at the top."

Our? I didn't like the way this was sounding.

"Where's their furniture?" Shelly asked when we were alone.

I sighed. "I didn't see any."

"They're real jerks."

What an understatement.

15

Keep Kool Kids showed up after lunch to bring me peanut M&M's, *Myths and Legends of the Greeks*, and listen to my lament.

We met outside the back door. "Sonja hasn't said a word since she moved in. She sits and organizes stacks of *Teen* magazines. Erica coddles her, waiting on her every unspoken whim like she's a worker bee and Sonja's the queen. Malcolm is loud and obnoxious. I avoid him like the plague. When he comes in the same room as me, I leave.

"Josie gets her own room. Mom says seventeen is old enough. Meaning I'm moving out of the Peter Pumpkin-Eater room."

Silence followed, the weight of the news sinking in.

Josie called, "Rosemarie, where are you?"

Drawn faces, Keep Kool Kids picked up their bikes and slowly rode away.

I waved. "See you tomorrow."

The first full day with the Sims was relatively uneventful. Storm clouds rolled in during supper time. I shared my new room with Sonja Sim on the third floor. The smallest and closest to Mom and Dad. One bed for her against the wall, mine across from it.

The sky outside my window had a strange greenish hue. The center, pale yellow. Wind gusts carried the scent of rain. I closed the window.

One by one, Keep Kool Kids called to say they couldn't come over.

Artists sang "We Are The World" on TV for the famine in Africa. Michael Jackson and Stevie Wonder were in front.

I found a yellow spiral notebook from school, and ripped out three pages of math problems. On the front, I wrote "Rosemarie's Diary" with a black marker. Keep Kool Kids wouldn't miss a detail of the situation.

Seven tornadoes were spotted in Welcome.

Sonja made no attempt to unpack. She sat in stony silence on the top of her bed. I asked if she wanted to play with toys. She responded with silence.

"Do you like reading? I do."

Her expression didn't change. Maybe she was mad.

"Must be tough to move," I said. "I'm sure it will be nice when your dad finds a house."

I waved a hand in front of her face. Anger would have been something. It was as though she felt—nothing. Oh, well. I dragged my bean bag next to the fireplace, and plopped down with *Myths and Legends of the Greeks*.

"*The Silver Bullet* comes out Friday," a voice thundered.

Malcolm.

I focused on the page. "What?"

"Wasn't *It* a Stephen King book?"

My eyes lifted. "You read?"

"Ah, no. I'm waiting to watch the movie," he said, laughing. It was loud, obnoxious and fake.

"Of course you are. Don't you have something to do?"

"Too much." Another phony, dark hoot burst from him.

My mind willed away the oaf standing over me.

Erica called, "Malcolm, come here. I want to show you something."

Another minute ensued before he left.

Finally. I returned my attention to my book. If Echo could talk to him and Narcissus wasn't cursed, they would have a chance for love. Maybe.

If he really knew her.

The rain started at five-forty in the morning. Pitter patter on the window turned to a steady stream. No one knew about the Sim status. At least, the kids didn't. I suspected Mara didn't either. Dad might, but appeared to be in denial. Which left Mom and Duane, the only ones with a clue. The Mattson children asked the questions:

Why are they here?

How long are they staying?

Who's in charge?

Since the Sims moved in three days ago, there was an unspoken directive all enquiries immediately cease. I couldn't wait to talk to Keep Kool Kids. I didn't care for conversation filters.

Duane Sim.

Duane moved about room to room stealthily. Crept in private places to catch us doing something wrong. He wandered into the room I shared with Sonja. I guessed him to be the reason for her cold disposition. His reverent aura, a ruse.

Beneath it, hatred boiled. I was being sized up. He knew I was on to him and wanted to be sure I knew it too.

Malcolm Sim.

All day yesterday, he wandered around our house. Pestering, poking, and provoking to gain attention. Negative or positive, the reaction didn't seem to matter. In fact, he preferred drama. He reveled in the fact we were prisoners in our own home. There was deep envy and something else I couldn't put my finger on.

Fake.

But what was to be done?

It was gloomy outside. The atmosphere inside, darker still. Duane moved about the main floor with a superior air. He wore a sweater and blue jeans like my dad. His five o'clock shadow, closer to nine o'clock. A beard similar to the picture of Jesus hanging above the fireplace mantel. My dad he was not, and most definitely not the Messiah.

Who was Duane Sim really?

A cloud settled over an already oppressive afternoon. I snuck down to the basement, escaping his vigilant eye and derisive demeanor.

Malcolm entered the basement.

Tommy's arms came up around Fisher Price houses, towns, and people. Malcolm laughed and moved away, proud to terrorize without a touch.

He made his way toward Steve and George. My brothers acted like he was invisible. He set a course for my corner.

"Leave her be," Steve said without looking up from his card game.

Malcolm retreated.

"When are they leaving?" I asked Mom.

"It's a seller's market," Mom said, and when I asked what that meant, I got the look of silence.

Skies cleared. The earth was warm and muddy beneath my feet. I pushed my bike through the soft track in the back alley, waiting for Keep Kool Kids. I didn't ask Mom if they could come over. I was dying for the Sims to move out. Then Keep Kool Kids could hang at the house instead of the park. Nothing wrong with the park, but I wanted my house back.

Duane Sim hauled Josie up by the scruff of her shirt. "You're listening to Satan, Josie!" Bulging muscles rippled beneath his shirt as he hoisted her with ease. Josie was crying, but not in a sad way. She shouted back. It was apparent by the volatility of her voice and fire in her eyes, she was furious.

I was frozen in shock.

He didn't notice me as he shook my sister. I'd never witnessed such an event. Josie was the nicest of us all. She helped with Tommy. Cooked, cleaned, and remembered our birthdays when no one else did. Didn't complain.

Wait until Mom finds out. I swiped my kickstand, turned, and stopped.

Mom stood next to Duane, her dazed gaze on Josie. She did nothing.

Dad came down during Saturday morning cartoons and lost it. He threatened to throw the TV in the trash if we didn't march out directly and clean the yard.

I'd never seen my dad quite so furious. Unnerved, I snuck up to my room for *Myths and Legends of the Greeks.*

"Back by popular demand," Mara said outside my door.

I hid behind it.

Mara handed Malcolm a six-pack of pop. "Coca-Cola Classic. Out with the new, in with the old."

"Yes," he said, popped a top and chugged it down.

Mara laughed, high-pitched and phony.

Now I know where Malcolm got it from.

He belched. "Where's the Cheetos?"

"I forgot them."

"Rule number one, Mom. Never forget the chips." He opened another can. "The Pig has us on clean-up patrol."

"The Pig?" she asked.

"Darwin Mattson."

Anger boiled inside me. The nerve. How dare he call my dad a name?

"Here you go," Mara said. I peered through the crack and watched her hand Malcolm the toilet brush and cleaner.

"How 'bout let's not and say we did," he said, downing another noisy swallow.

"Oh, Malcolm." She giggled.

I began to hate the sound of laughter.

Malcolm had names for all of us. I was Piglet. He had a sound for Josie. Whenever she walked past, he muttered it beneath his breath. It wasn't coherent, but something to do with the bounce of her walk.

Sunday was the Lord's Day. Mom, Dad, and Josie took naps. Steve and George played Monopoly. Erica played too, until Steve caught her cheating. He kicked her out of the game. Erica started to cry, but it was no use. There were no second chances for cheaters. Steve and George went outside to toss the football around when Malcolm showed up. He kicked the Monopoly board and it went flying. Stole Tommy and my snacks and threw them at Sonja.

I hid in the world of fantasy. C.S. Lewis' *The Silver Chair.*

Icy fingers of fear danced up my spine. The pages of my novel blurred out of focus. Malcolm was outside my door.

There was no adult supervision anywhere in the vicinity.

16

Keep Kool Kids jumped on bikes and rode to the park to see who could swing the highest. Ride the merry-go-round longest without getting sick. Hang from the monkey bars, feet not-touching the ground until we were sure our arms would fall off.

I shared the notebook minus the part Duane Sim pinned my sister against the house by the scruff of her shirt. They would want to know how fast my dad kicked them out. I would have to tell them the part about my mom being there.

Shelly unzipped her backpack, and pulled out four sticker books. She handed each of us one. "My parents are getting a divorce."

"A divorce?" I echoed the horrible word. "That explains all the toys."

Shelly passed out sheets of stickers. "They said they grew apart."

"Maybe they'll get back together," I said. "Like *The Parent Trap.*"

Shelly wiped her sleeve across her nose. "They fight all the time."

Greg scratched and sniffed the Strawberry Shortcake sticker. "It's scary how nobody stays together these days."

"What do you think will happen?" I asked.

"She'll move away," Greg said.

Shelly's eyes welled with tears. "I don't want to move."

"What will Keep Kool Kids be without the Clever Fox?" Anne asked.

"What can be done?" I picked a puffy sticker for my book.

Greg had the last word. "Nothing can be done."

17

August 2, 1985: Delta flight 19—casualties, 137

August 12, 1985: Japan Airlines flight 123—casualties, 520

August 22, 1985: British Airtours flight 28M—casualties, 55

August 25, 1985: Bar Harbor Airlines flight 1808—casualties, 8

August 27, 1985: Shelly Vanguard's parents' divorce—casualties, unknown

Erica answered the door. "Your freaks are here, retard."

I didn't like Sims answering my door. They didn't belong in my house, and shouldn't be opening anything.

"The KKK," Malcolm said. "Who knew you were racist, Piglet."

I glared at him. "What are you talking about?"

"Where's your white hood?" he asked, clearly enjoying himself.

Chief Emotional Energy Officer, Duane, was nowhere in sight. Stellar at showing up out of the blue to assert dominance or plain old make us kids feel bad. But when Malcolm roamed about, loud and out of control, he vanished.

Keep moving, Rosemarie.

We reached the basement and Shelly turned to me. "Only forty miles, according to Mom."

"It might as well be a hundred," I said with a sigh, handing her a package topped with a red bow. "It's a going away present."

Shelly tore it open, and held up the Compact Disc "Don't You (Forget About Me)." "How did you know I got a CD player?"

"Your mom told me." I pressed play on my tape player, and "Only time will tell" began. "This is my new favorite song."

Anne handed her a stuffed homemade picture frame. "I didn't have wrapping paper."

We gathered around the photo. It was the four of us the first Christmas Greg came to my house.

Shelly gave Anne a big hug. "It's perfect."

Greg brought his cards for a game of Texas Hold 'Em. The Sim kids came down. Popcorn flew past us followed by snickering. Next, raisin bombs. After a pile of snacks surrounded us, it stopped.

"Finally," Greg said.

"It's gotten worse since George exploded on Friday," I whispered. "Yesterday, they threw raisins for over an hour."

Shelly moved away the next day.

I wrote her a letter. She wrote right back. It was the last time Anne came over. Shelly's mom wasn't around to keep an eye on her. Now who would make sure she was fed, lice free, and treated like a human being?

"She seems to have an invisible top shirt..." Sonja's off-key singing came from the basement.

"It's touch." Greg's response was clear and didn't sound one bit put out.

I raced down the stairs. "That's our thing."

Greg jumped to his feet. "Hey, Rosemarie."

"Don't have a cow, Rosemarie." Sonja gave me a smirk.

Upstairs, I laid into Greg. "If you like her so much, why don't you marry her?"

He blinked. "Okay, well I was going to ask you if you wanted to go for a bike ride, but I can see you're busy having an episode."

"I'm tired. Maybe next time."

Greg lingered at the door. "Call me if you change your mind."

"Don't look at me like you expect me to disappear."

"Promise me you won't."

"I promise nothing counts." I crossed my heart.

18

The wreck of *RMS Titanic* was discovered.

George was obsessed. "Doomed from the start, Rosemarie, but completely avoidable."

The problem: the bulkheads were not capped at the top. Any system claiming a ship made of iron to be unsinkable didn't make sense to me.

George never listened, and I kept my comments to myself.

"Their demise was total disregard for multiple iceberg warnings," George said with a sigh. "Not to mention lifeboats for only half the passengers."

Even still, only seven hundred five souls were saved.

"The 'chickens' were saved," George said, reading my mind. "Fear- based individuals took their sweet time returning the boats. They were terrified of being swamped."

Would he have done any different? Would I?

"In the end, only eight percent of third-class citizens survived," George said.

But did it matter, first class or third? In the words of Dr. Seuss, "A person's a person, no matter how small." Rich or poor. Male or female. Woman or child. Mattson or Sim.

We were moving to the country. The place next to Grandpa's. All of us, Sims included. They hadn't found a place that didn't cost an arm or leg.

"What if they never do?" I asked what no one else dared.

Dad said, "Ask your mother."

Mom said, "We'll see. Stop asking."

I waited until she was taking a nap to ask the Sims. The worst they could say is that they didn't want to talk about it.

Mara gave me a worried look. "How will we move Mother's magazines without damage?"

Duane's laugh said, *Aren't you the fool?*

Okay, then. He had no intention of leaving and she had no clue.

19

The country house was thirty miles southeast of Welcome, and two miles south of Grandpa and Grandma's.

Sonja and I got to ride in the back of one of the moving trucks. She sat right on the pile of precious magazines. She was what Mom called, big boned. Malcolm called her Chubby Checker. I didn't think the name had anything to do with the sixties singer, but everything to do with chubby. I didn't think she was chubby. I did think Mara would kill her for smooshing the magazines. Why the lid wasn't on the box, I had no idea.

"Those are your mother's. You're going to get it." I grabbed her arm.

She pulled away. "Quit it."

"Suit yourself." Not my fault if she wanted to die young.

My mind wandered to the country house ten miles away. We spent summers there when school was out. October trees of red, gold and yellow greeted us as we pulled into the yard. A familiar haunt, I couldn't wait to explore the fall woods.

Malcolm and Erica got out of the truck and started horsing around. Erica was thick and boy-tough. They didn't rough-house like Steve and George. More, a fight to the death. I sat frozen, watching them punch and choke each other.

"Who sat on the magazines?" Mara's voice shook.

Yikes. I tore my gaze away from the wrestling match. Maybe Sonja would tell on herself so I wouldn't have to.

Sonja cut me a twisted look. "Rosemarie did."

Mara glared at me. "Those were my mother's."

My mouth dropped open. "I..."

You won't win.

Sonja grabbed a box. "Where do you want me to put them?"

"You're a doll," Mara said.

They headed for the house.

Let it go.

The sun peaked between tall cottonwoods adorned in their fall splendor. Not even the Sims could detract from this perfect place. I turned to Tommy. "Hey, buddy. Want to make a fort?"

Tommy's eyes sparkled. "Yeah."

"Okay, soon as we empty the truck." I jumped out.

Sonja returned, grabbing the closest box to the tailgate. "Ahhh."

"What happened?" Mara asked.

Her bottom lip quivered. "I smashed my finger."

Okay, that was totally fake.

"Why don't you go inside and take a break," Mara said.

"Thank you, Mommy." Sonja flicked me a triumphant look.

"Well?" Mara gave me a glare. "Get to work."

A teepee from a fallen log was the perfect way to spend the first afternoon.

We discovered an old trunk. A place for my notebook, a box of superballs, and four stuffed animals. Mickey Mouse, a cat from the Thrifty store, a bear missing an eye, and the blonde Cabbage Patch Shelly gave me.

"Rock Hudson is gay," said a voice outside our teepee.

"Go away," I called from inside.

Malcolm entered the tent. "For all you dummies, Hudson was in the movie Giant. He got aids from having too much sex."

Never before had I heard so much about Hollywood or sex than in the last two weeks living with Malcolm Sim. Neither did I care to talk about either. "Okay, now go away." I managed to keep my voice even, hiding the unease creeping inside.

Malcolm grabbed the edge of the quilt hanging over the sticks we set up against the fallen tree. "What are you freaks doing out here anyway?"

"Playing," I said. Go along with it or something bad is going to happen.

Chester gave a warning growl.

"Get your mutt away." He took a swing with his foot and missed.

Tommy got between Malcolm and Chester. "Don't kick him."

A sly grin slid across Malcolm's face. He hauled his foot back.

"Your dad is looking for you," George called, shuffling toward us through thick leaves.

"See ya, wouldn't want to be ya," Malcolm said.

When Malcolm left, I turned to George. "He should come with volume control."

"More like an on off switch." George hocked a huge loogie, turned and spit.

So gross. "One thing's for sure, we'll have to find another location for our fort. This one's been compromised."

George's brow lifted. "Has he kicked Chester before?"

"No."

"Let me know if he does."

"George?" I asked. The thing about George, there had to be a reason you asked anything.

"What?"

"What's KKK mean?"

George's eyes narrowed. "Why? Who wants to know?"

"No one. Something I heard."

"I'll tell you when you're older," George said.

"I guess." Another of his tricks: act like I wasn't worth the truth. Didn't matter anyway. Hard to have a club with one lonely lion.

20

Halloween and no sign of my brothers or the adults. The Sim kids were always there. Roaming around, wild and loud. In the world of Dr. Seuss, they were Thing One, Two and Three.

Malcolm pulled out a carton of milk from the fridge. *He should not be here when your mother is not.* I couldn't have said it better, Fish in the Pot.

He broke into song. "Johnny is missing, he is very saaad. He is missing for a very special reason."

The made-up jingle must be about the kid on the back of the milk carton, Johnny Gosch. Malcolm's beautiful singing voice was often used to chant our nicknames or turn every rock song into a dirty one. To Malcolm, everything was about people doing dirty stuff and girls wanting "it."

"Have you seen my mom?" I asked him.

He took a drink of milk straight from the carton. "Rawr."

I don't know which was more disturbing, Malcolm having his own language, or me understanding yes, yipe. No, rawr.

"My dad?"

"Rawr."

"Is that all you can say?"

A smile. "Rawr."

At last, Josie walked into the kitchen. My knees buckled with relief. "Where have you been?"

"Buying these," she said, holding up a stack of masks.

They were the ones we wore in Welcome six years ago, but I wasn't about to burst her bubble. "Where's the costumes to go with them?"

"Um..." Josie crossed the room to the drawer, pulling out a box of garbage bags. "I'll cut holes in these. Sit Tommy down. We'll eat supper and go." She flattened a black bag on the countertop.

"I'm not hungry," I said, poking at the hotdish. Josie wasn't much of a cook. Besides, I planned on eating a lot of candy. I had to save room.

"I don't care. You have to eat all your food and drink your milk or we don't go."

"I don't like milk," I said. "Mom knows and doesn't make me drink it."

"Mom's not here." Josie worked the scissors across the plastic bag. "Obey your elders."

Tommy reached for his glass.

"Don't drink it," I whispered. "Malcolm drank straight from the carton."

He pulled his hand back.

"Unless you do what I say, I'm not taking anyone trick-or-treating," Josie said.

My hand flew out, knocking Tommy's glass over. "Sorry," I said, got up to grab a rag, spilling mine in the process.

"Rosemarie Grace. What are you doing?"

"I'll get a towel." I reached for the milk.

"No don't—"

But I did, knocking over the rest of the carton. "Oh well." I threw the empty carton in the trash. Mopping up the mess, I smiled at Tommy. He grinned back.

Josie scowled. "That's the last of the milk, Rosemarie."

"Sorry." I pressed my lips together. She left the room.

Goodbye Halloween. "I won't do it again," I said. "Please. It was an accident."

Josie returned from the pantry with a box of powdered milk. "No problem."

"Okaaay."

Josie held up the box. "I'll mix up glasses of this."

My heart kicked in my chest. "I'll tell."

"Go ahead." Josie's eyes narrowed. "In the meantime, no Halloween."

Tommy started to cry. "I want candy."

"Drink your milk." Josie set a glass of the muck in front of him.

I reluctantly held my hand out. Josie passed me a glass. "Now if you hurry up about it, I'll even let you sit in the front seat."

"Really?" I never got to sit in the front. The fake milk was daunting. I plugged my nose, downing the entire contents before coming up for air. I did it! I let go of my nostrils. The after-taste was rotten. Some residue snuck up the back of my throat and into my mouth. My belly rolled. "I think I'm going to be sick."

"Don't be such a drama queen," Josie said. "Get your costume on and let's go."

I didn't get to sit in the front after all, but in the back between Erica and Malcolm. Josie's boyfriend and his mullet showed up last minute.

He tugged up the collar of his jean jacket, giving me a bored look. "Who are you supposed to be?"

"Lucy."

Malcolm smiled at me, warm and friendly.

A surge of warmth formed inside and I smiled back. Maybe he was human after all.

21

Mikhail Gorbachev informed President Reagan he would accept on- site inspections as part of a comprehensive ban. Route 66 was removed from the United States Highway System from Chicago to Santa Monica. The border between Gibraltar and Spain was officially reopened after being closed since 1969. A decision by Spain to garner support. Boris Becker won the men's Wimbledon Championship.

Thanksgiving, Grandpa and Grandma arrived for dinner dressed in their Sunday best. Around the large dining room table we gave thanks. Grandma read from her Bible. "Everything created by God is good, and nothing is to be rejected if it is received with thanksgiving."

Table conversation was minimal.

The Sims copied everything we did. Dressed the same. Ate the same way. Said the same things. Imitation was the sincerest form of flattery. Except, I didn't feel flattered. They were trying to mock us. Be us.

Duane ate in cold silence, and left when finished. His posture was dominant, almost reptilian. I looked around, but no one noticed except me. A few minutes later, my mother excused herself.

Grandma and Grandpa went home. Stuffed like the turkey, I couldn't wait until the dishes were done. C.S. Lewis' *The Last Battle* was calling my name.

Sonja was sitting on her bed when I got there. The room I shared with her was in the basement. A large space where Sonja hung a clothesline in the middle to separate my side and hers.

"Hi," I said, crossing the room to my bed.

"Want to play Barbies?"

Silence.

"Let me know if you change your mind." I rolled to my side, feeling beneath the bed for my book. I pulled out *The Magician's Nephew*. Nope. *Silver Chair*. Book after book until I found it.

"Chubby Checker, Chubby Ho," Malcolm sang, entering our room.

Erica was behind him. One on one, the Sims were tolerable, barely. Together they were explosive. If I was quiet enough, I could slip out unnoticed.

"Piglet?" Malcolm said.

Erica threw a pillow at my head. "You slow or something?"

Malcolm bounded toward me. Self-preservation kept most people from doing anything stupid or life-threatening. A trait he did not possess. I didn't put it past him to kill me.

Next thing I knew, Malcolm sat on me. Before I could utter a word, he smothered me with the pillow. I couldn't breathe and pounded my fists on the bed. Chester gave a loud bark and the pillow was gone.

Malcolm stood and hooted. "You should see your face, Piglet."

Get out of here.

After dinner, we went to the shelterbelt for a Christmas tree. When we returned, Mara carried a plastic tote to the living room. "Look, Rosemarie. All the decorations since I was a little girl. Would you like to help me decorate the tree?"

Since she was a little girl? Her dark eyes were expectant. Compassion welled inside me. She was a kid once, like me. "Uh, sure."

"Afterward, I'll show you how to make Russian Tea."

Test her spirit.

I'd test it later. It was Christmas time and I was needed.

22

September 1986

The Nintendo Entertainment System released seventeen games including *Duck Hunt* and *Ice Climber*.

"We don't have time for nonsense," Dad said.

Three days later, Mara showed up with a new system and *Super Mario Bros.*

Rules applied to the Mattson household. That Sims didn't follow rules was putting it lightly. They were lawless. Around them, craziness thrived. When the adults were working, it was every man for himself. Or herself.

Bathroom usage was tricky. No lock on the door, it burst open followed by the sound of laughter. It was Malcolm. Always Malcolm, although Erica and Sonja weren't beneath getting a chuckle.

"Privacy is a real challenge for you, huh?" I said, hiking up my pants behind the door.

He wanted access whenever and however. No rules to prevent him from doing what he felt like. Pee quick or don't pee at all.

Hiding places were difficult to find. Malcolm had the knack for exposing them. If he thought you were actually trying to hide from him, it was worse yet.

Sonja loved to give the silent treatment.

Erica loved to be whoever suited her at the moment.

Dad said the thing about cattle, they know who was good for them and who wasn't.

Cement was poured into the old barn. Stanchions were added. A separate building for a milk house. There was even an office with a phone. The door to the office was green.

"I got it off the old Benson place," Dad said, he and Steve cutting into the milk house wall to fit the bulk tank.

"I like it." I ran my fingers over the pea green surface.

"His wife's favorite color. It was taken from the bathroom," Dad said. "The girls will do the milking. Boys have bad tempers."

Malcolm was infuriated. He wasn't allowed to drive a tractor either. Or truck. All he could do was haul in hay and fill corn hoppers.

Twenty-head of Holsteins arrived. Milking commenced four in the morning and at the same time in the afternoon. The girls assigned to the task were me and Sonja.

Chasing cows in the dark was a sleepy task, and I could barely keep my eyes open. Sonja prepared the milkers and the wash station. Sonja wasn't a morning person. She wasn't really a night owl, either. There was really no time in the day where she didn't dwell in disdain. Mostly, she hated the farm, the Mattsons, me...

...Sonja just hated.

Each Holstein locked in its stanchion, the only sound in the barn was the swish of the milkers.

"Do I hear happiness in here?" Malcolm hauled in a load of hay.

Go along with it, or he'll mess with you. "No, Mrs. Hannagan." I liked the movie *Annie* too. The first five times. The thing about Malcolm, if something was good once a hundred times was better. He loved quoting every line.

"Sunny day..." he belted out the theme song to *Sesame Street*. It didn't matter he was fourteen, way too old to watch the show. He'd seen every episode. "Hallelujah," he said, switching to his loudest voice.

A warning to the rest of us: Duane was close. This meant Erica and Sonja had to stop wrestling with each other and get to work. Malcolm would stop talking, joking or laughing. Me, I was supposed to stop— existing.

He came through the door and stopped at the end of the alley, reading my thoughts.

I offered a silent apology for a swear word earlier when a cow stepped on my foot. It was better to be caught in the act of wrongdoing and take a deserved punishment. His cold demeanor made me feel worthless. Bad.

It was nothing compared to his own kids. The way he lost it on Malcolm yesterday for sassing back could be measured on the Richter scale. It made me feel sorry for Malcolm.

Sort of.

Back at the house, I changed clothes and reached for *Harriet the Spy*, a bag of peanut M&M's, and a can from my six pack of Mountain Dew I kept beneath my bed.

Malcolm burst in.

Go away. I pushed my nose further in my book.

"Ever heard of knocking?" Sonja said, not getting off her bed.

Malcolm disregarded the clothesline of defense. "What you up to, Piglet?"

"She's reading her dumb book," Sonja said.

Malcolm tore the book from my grasp. "There's no reading in Jonestown."

"Hey." I leapt to my feet.

Malcolm held it out of reach. "Want it, come get it."

"Give it back." I took a swing.

"Over nine-hundred murdered, a bunch of them were kids."

"What are you talking about?" I made another swipe.

"They worshiped him. He had sex with all their wives and daughters."

Oh right. Jonestown. Malcolm was the expert on tragedy. He also thought everyone was having sex with everyone else. I didn't know enough about the cult to know if it were true. I certainly wasn't going to ask.

"They gave the kids poisoned Kool-Aid," Malcolm went on, enjoying the sound of his own voice. "The parents offed themselves afterward."

"Other people should have called the cops to have their kids taken away."

There's no reasoning, Rosemarie.

"Some did. Government took the children away, but didn't know what to do with them. So they sent them back."

23

Milking cows made me famished. The thought of a snack made my mouth water. My tummy rumbled. My mom would grab something from the house if asked. She always did. I headed for the milk house office.

The door was shut.

Malcolm said, "My dad and your mom are in there. They're going to homeschool us."

I stopped. "How come?"

"Because of sex education."

"Whatever, I'm glad. I hate school." The bullies and the cliques. Shelly wouldn't be there. I wasn't sure if Anne would be either. School at home was looking pretty good.

Malcolm eyed the office door. "I'd like to be a fly on the wall in there."

My gaze followed his. "Why?"

"Why do you think?" Malcolm grabbed the sink, thrusting his pelvis against it.

Note to self: don't ask Malcolm. Anything.

The chain broke on the gutter cleaner, and the world came to an end.

At least you would think so from the way Duane lost it. Erica ended up against the wall by the scruff of her neck. The worst, breakfast would be delayed.

It was me and the Sims. Since the move, it was always me and them. I couldn't get away from them. I couldn't get away from oatmeal, either. No pancakes or sausage. Mom must be on a sugar kick again. No cold cereal. Not even Cream of Wheat.

Sonja wrinkled her nose. "Gross."

"I hate oatmeal," I said. "I'm going to ask my mom if I can have something else."

Sonja sat at the breakfast table. "She went to town."

I picked up the serving spoon from the pot. The oatmeal came with it in one big pile of jelly. "Ugh. Gag me with a spoon."

Mara walked in. "Pretty ungrateful, I'll clue you."

"Mara." All the blood drained from my face.

Mara scooped a heaping lump of oatmeal in a bowl, and gave it to me. "Eat up."

My mouth went dry. "Seriously?"

"If you sit and talk about it, it'll be the rest of the pot."

I guess it was true what Malcolm said about his mom. She was a kid like the rest of us.

"Yeah, Rosemarie," Sonja said.

Malcolm pushed my back. "Good luck, Piglet."

How many spoonfuls of oatmeal does it take to get to the center of a bowl? It turns out a lot. Alone I sat, working away at the cold mush. Mara wanted to read magazines. She made me sit on her bedroom floor to keep an eye on me. Cheeks stuffed like a squirrel, I spent the morning choking down cold, flavorless oatmeal.

Mara drove me to school. First day in my life I was tardy.

The next day, oatmeal was back. Same ending. Mara's room on the floor.

Oatmeal was served most often.

I didn't realize how many days this went on until I showed up to school, and Josie said, "Wow, you're not late."

Saturday morning, Steve loaded us in the van for ice-skating. "Don't worry Rosemarie. I won't forget you this time, even if we have to wait until you're done eating your oatmeal."

The tears were quick and unexpected. They streamed down my cheeks, and my nose started to run.

"Whoa, Rosemarie." Steve held both hands up. "What did I say?"

Before I could answer, Mara walked in. "Steve, your mom is looking for you."

After he left, Mara scowled at me. "I don't think the tears are necessary," she said. "Go get your breakfast."

24

The Dragon slipped beneath door cracks, slithering from room to room. It reached hers.

Rosemarie.

Even asleep, embers burned bright.

Separating Piglet and her friends was a powerful move. Getting the human caretakers to isolate her in the middle of nowhere with fakes, choice. But none of this stole her hope.

He slunk next to her while she slept. Awake, she wouldn't allow him near her, but asleep—

Suddenly, a powerful force shot him across the room. Cowering in the corner, The Dragon looked back. Amael stood alongside Rosemarie's bed.

Cursed seraph. Piglet must be something special to the Enemy.

What was one girl compared to worldwide violence? South Africa invaded Angola, riots and protests continued.

Mexico City earthquake killed nine thousand. Famine in Ethiopia. Rioting at housing estates in Brixton, London and Liverpool. Volcanic eruption in Armero, Colombia, killed twenty-five thousand. Hurricane Gloria. The bomb dropped by Philadelphia police containing C-4 and Tovex, destroying fifty-three houses.

The cure.

The Achille Lauro hijacked by Palestinian terrorists. The attack on passengers at Rome and Vienna airports. A car bomb in Beirut, Lebanon killed forty-five, injuring one-hundred seventy-five others...

Putting the cure inside a child was stupid. So be it. God-like fire in a human would be her destruction.

The Dragon slipped out, calling forth the origin of the domain, Asmodeus. To another room and a grown boy who didn't sleep. An earthly father who paid him no mind unless he was doing something bad. Malcolm needed attention more than favor. Asmodeus whispered words of dark lust in Malcolm's ears to make Rosemarie question nobility. Give her something to talk about. Or rather, not to.

And ultimately steal her innocence.

Feet planted apart and hands at his sides, Amael said, "Slick snake. He wormed his way into their home. The caretakers are often working." A pause. "She's a curious little warrior."

Michael's stern gaze was on the sleeping Rosemarie. "Almost reckless."

Amael frowned. "She's often left alone with them."

"Her grandmother prays for her," Michael said. "An ally will lighten her heart. The Almighty will provide such a friend."

Amael saluted him. "Holy is the Lord God Almighty, who was and is and is to come."

25

A trip to Welcome and a stop at the library shed light on Jonestown.

The librarian, Marlene McDaniel, wore an ugly gray sweater and her brown hair short. She looked up at me through cat eyeglasses. "Hi Rosemarie. How did you like Bernard Evslin's book on Greek mythology?"

"Good. My grandma bought me my own copy when she was on vacation."

"How nice."

"Do you have anything on Jim Jones?"

She removed her glasses and they hung on her neck by a chain. "Let's take a look."

I picked three of the resources she advised and sat on a chair by the window.

Jim Jones promised his followers an island to live out ideals. A place of fulfillment. Pamphlets promised paradise and a land of milk and honey. There was not enough food when they arrived. Jones confiscated passports. Bridges were burned with outside families and they were stuck. Malcolm watched too much TV, but he was right about the Kool-Aid.

Amy Grant's "Love of Another Kind" on my tape player, I crawled into bed early that night.

He was there, disappearing in the darkness. The world between dreams and reality.

We watched *Back to the Future* on our new VCR. Marty McFly cranked up the amp, strummed the guitar, flying back with "Back In Time."

"Mom is going to buy me that vest," Sonja said, standing on her head.

Malcolm stared at the TV screen. "She'll have to find one in quadruple X."

He never. Stopped. Talking.

On my bed, *Harriet the Spy* in hand, I planned my exit strategy before things got wild.

Erica entered the room, knocking Sonja down. "Get her."

"Get off me." Sonja reached back, slapping her. "What are you doing?"

"Farting on you," Erica said.

She screamed, but it was no use. Her cheek pressed against the brown carpet, Sonja didn't stand a chance.

Malcolm joined in, letting a long one rip. "Two against one."

"Malcolm, Erica? Where are you?" Duane's voice came from upstairs.

Their eyes met in horror. In a flash, they were gone.

Pregnant silence followed.

I didn't pester Sonja with a lot of questions. I figured she was humiliated enough. Better to give space to recover from her horrible siblings.

At last, she spoke, "Last night Malcolm was sitting on your bed, watching you sleep."

"What for?" I admired my new jeans in the mirror.

"I pretended to be asleep." She turned the page of her magazine. "He was playing with your butt."

26

I felt awful. My throat was scratchy, my head hurt, and the green door was closed.

The unspoken rule for the milk house office: if the green door was shut, we weren't to open it.

"Just the two of them," Malcolm sang to the tune of "Just the Two of Us."

His never-ending obsession and innuendos about sex now included our parents: his dad and my mom. He was wrong, of course. I only wished they'd keep the door open to prove it.

After cow chores, I changed clothes, and crawled beneath the covers.

Sonja was on her bed reading magazines and listening to her latest Amy Grant tape.

Morning rolled around and I couldn't get out of bed. When Sonja saw the state I was in, she ran. "I'll get your mom."

What felt like an eternity later, Mom came in. "What's wrong, Rosemarie?"

Duane was behind her.

What does he want? I quickly wiped my face with the back of my sleeve and sat up. "I don't feel good."

"We don't go by what we feel but by what we know," Duane said.

"I know I'm sick," I said, wishing I could vanish.

Mom touched my forehead. "I don't know, you do feel pretty warm."

"She has the symptoms of being sick," Duane said.

Uh. What? "When I swallow, it feels like ground glass." I reached for the roll of toilet paper next to the bed. "I use this to spit in."

Duane's eyes narrowed to slits. "Then you're faithless."

"Maybe you should gargle with salt water before chores," Mom said.

"I'm too sick for chores."

Duane shifted forward, pulling *Heroes, Gods and Monsters of the Greek Myths* out from beneath him. He held it up, eyeing Mom. "Too sick for chores?"

"Is this what this is all about?" Mom asked. "So you can read?"

My eyes burned hot. "No. I'm really sick." Silence. "I mean, I know I feel really sick. Greek mythology is classic. There are no dirty parts or swear words," I said. Duane's criteria for reading material.

"Greek mythology teaches false gods." Duane's voice was hard.

"Yes, but I don't worship them."

"What would God think if He were here and you were reading such books?"

It's a trap. "He'd be mad?"

His expression was victorious. "That's right, he'd be mad."

"I feel like God doesn't mind the books. They're full of good stories."

Duane stared straight ahead. Mom cleared her throat. "Do you have other books like these, Rosemarie?"

"On my bookshelf where they've always been."

Duane didn't budge. Mom got up and searched my shelf.

"What are you doing?" Claws of fear clenched my belly. She never touched my books before.

Mom began pulling novels.

"Look," I said in a happy voice. "Two of those you gave me for Christmas when we lived at the house in Welcome."

Mom withdrew three more.

"Not *The Great Divorce*." White-hot tongs of despair ripped my soul, tearing the flesh from my bones. "C.S. Lewis is a Christian."

My beloved characters. This must be how Echo felt. Maybe if she hadn't talked back she'd be okay. Narcissus got what he deserved, but must I earn my place? Was there a god to punish and reward? There was, but I suspected His reprimand was gentle.

Duane stood and made his way out. Eyes glued to him in rapture, Mom followed with my books. Duane was evil. My mom was a slave. If only Dad had been there.

Tears spilled down my cheeks.

Sonja's eyes were etched with horror. "Rosemarie..."

"Go away," I said, flipping to my side. "Leave me alone."

Several minutes of silence followed before the door clicked shut.

I was dismissed from afternoon chores and the following morning chores. A needed break from the cows and the Sims. Mostly the Sims.

The fever lifted three days later. I wrote Shelly a letter about what happened. The oppression and injustice. The manner in which Mom was being handled. The sneaky way Duane made sure my dad didn't know. Miles between us allowed a safe place from judgement. Shelly was my best friend. I wasn't disloyal.

It was returned, stamped in red letters, "No such number. Return to sender."

I was crushed by the censorship of my bookshelves. Reluctant to return to the scene of the crime, I took a crack at Josie's famous Snow Ball cookies.

I took the tape player from the living room, slid in *Unguarded* by Amy Grant, and spooned dough onto the cookie sheet.

Crack.

I stilled. Someone's ankle. I set the spoon down and searched the area. No one was there. Not like anyone would be spying on me. Flour and sugar can't get you in trouble.

The cookies didn't turn out. Too much flour. I followed the recipe to a T. I returned the tape player without being caught. Try again tomorrow.

The following afternoon, I baked Snow Balls after church instead of the usual nap before chores.

"Where are the pecans?" Josie asked, taking a bite of a warm one.

"I don't like pecans." I rolled a cookie in powdered sugar.

"You can't make Snow Balls without them, goofy."

Christmas vacation provided me time to try it with nuts. They turned out "okay" according to Josie. I still didn't like pecans. Tomorrow I would do my own thing: chocolate chip cookies.

Sonja tried one. "Too much flour."

"Let's see you take a shot at this." I threw the spoon into the sink. It missed her head by an inch.

She jumped back, glaring at me. "You better get back to naps or I'll tell."

"Go for it," I said, even as my heart kicked up.

After she left, I tried again. Too much vanilla. There was tomorrow. Forget the nap. I wouldn't give up. I tiptoed back to our room a half hour before cow chores. No point in interrupting her sleep.

Sonja was curled on her bed. Waves of sorrow emitted from her side of the room. Her mom sat alongside her, stroking her hair. "Your dad said you might as well be listening to rock music."

Unguarded was clutched in Sonja's hand. "One song. He can't judge a whole tape by one song."

Mara chewed her lip. "I know, I'm sorry."

Duane. He was always watching. Or maybe it was Erica spying on me. I let out the breath I was holding. Mara's head shot toward me. "Do you mind? We are having a private conversation."

Not like it's my room. I kept silent backing out, pretty sure it was my fault.

27

The unspoken contract we made would be the first of many.

Our shame was vast. Embarrassment isolated us, and we didn't talk about the indignity we were forced to endure. Silence was secret and welcoming, didn't expose or humiliate.

Dust particles floated in the early morning light Christmas Day in the loft above Grandpa and Grandma's barn. Momma Cat moved her kittens, leaving a single runt behind.

My cousin, Gloria, held the tiny ball of fur against her chest. "Momma Cat is smart, Rosemarie. Bet she comes back for him."

Gloria was four and innocent. The runt, small and weak. My bet was she didn't. I took the kitten from her and returned it to the nest. "We better get back."

Her eyes lit. "Grandma said she would start the ice-cream. Maybe it's ready."

"Maybe," I smiled back.

Snow-capped trees and fences aligned the tracks to the house.

"Christmas is the best." Gloria rubbed her nose on her coat sleeve.

Christmas was the spirit of shame. Where dust from the haymow clouded visions of sugarplums. Aroma of spiced cookies, cinnamon, apple pie, forgotten by the trace of sour sweat and smelly farts. A terrible picture to paint for Gloria.

"Christmas is cool." I drew the edges of my jacket.

"Why do you say it like that?" Gloria asked.

"Like what?" The moon hung behind a thin layer of haze. "Hey, look at the wolf moon."

Gloria reached for my hand. "Does it make people werewolves?"

"No, silly," I said, some of the weight leaving my shoulders. "It means the moon is the brightest it will be for a while."

We reached the house. Lively conversations hummed throughout the kitchen. Braided rugs were scattered across the wood floor. Grandma unrolled lefse with a stick against the stove. The aroma of vinegar and fish wafted through the air.

Aunt Jane looked up from kneading dough. "Don't track snow in the house, Rosemarie."

She wasn't usually grouchy. Must have to do with Uncle Kevin. "They're going through a rough patch," Mom said when I asked why he didn't come. "Will they get a divorce?" I continued, and at "divorce" I got the look.

"Take your boots off, girls," Mom said.

"Is the food ready?" I kicked mine off. "We're hungry."

"Hallelujah," Malcolm said behind me. He stomped the snow from his boots in the entrance. Mistletoe hung above me. My stomach rolled with the morning's eggs. He will kiss me. House rules. This morning, he ordered me to wash my private parts and get the udder balm ready. The ride to Grandpa and Grandma's was the reason for pants. We stopped for Aunt Jane and Gloria. Malcolm took the back seat next to me. A Christmas dress was easy access.

Gloria popped a piece of dried apple in her mouth. Josie tweaked her nose. "Those are for the bread."

"Can I help make Christmas bread?" Gloria asked.

"If you wash up," Aunt Jane said.

Gloria picked up a frosted gingerbread man from the counter. "Rosemarie said Momma Cat moved her babies because Daddy Cat wants to kill them so Momma Cat goes into heat. Heat means she gets babies in her belly," she said, and took a bite.

Silence, loud as a train whistle, followed.

"Rosemarie Grace Mattson, what have I told you about telling Gloria stories?" Mom's tone said I was dead. "Both of you, upstairs. Don't come down until I call you."

You didn't make Mom ask you twice. Gloria started to cry.

"Let's go." I reached for her hand.

In the spare room, we lay side by side on the quilted poster bed.

Gloria sniffed. "You don't like me anymore."

Staring up at the ceiling, all anger drained from me. "No, you're good, but you shouldn't have said that."

"Does Malcolm think you're in heat?"

Slick, hot fingers of fear played across my neck. I didn't answer.

"He touched me, too." Gloria dragged in a hiccupping sob. "If we tell your dad, he'll make him stop."

"Maybe." I sucked in a breath to voice the question haunting me. The one I teetered between every day. Each hour. Minute. "But if we tell and it doesn't?"

Our eyes met in a silent promise. One that said we wouldn't talk about it again.

Not even to each other.

28

The first day of Sunday school for fifth graders at Welcome Lutheran Church was in the classroom at the end of a long hallway.

The teacher, a tall, slender woman with riotous hair the color of wheat said, "Hi. I'm Pearl Frank, and this is my son Victor," in a loud voice. He was plain-looking with flaxen hair, and the only other kid besides me.

"I'm Rosemarie," I said, smoothing my damp hair. "How old are you?"

"Eleven."

"Me too."

I had trouble focusing on the lesson. I stared at Victor instead. He didn't look away, as though he liked me back.

The next Sunday, there were three logs of real wood with a fake fire in the center of the room. "Hi, Rosemarie," Victor said.

"I hate cows," I said. Pearl leaned back and laughed. I liked the sound of it. "I thought we'd have a picnic," she said.

"Thank you, Mrs. Frank." I didn't know what fried fish sandwiches had to do with the Bible, but I was famished.

"Oh, pshaw." She laid a hand on my arm. "Call me Pearl."

The fish sandwich was delicious. I downed it quickly.

"You want another one, hun?" Pearl asked.

"Yes, please."

"What do you suppose it would be like to share a fishwich with Jesus?" Pearl took a bite of her sandwich.

I didn't know, but I knew exactly how I would feel. Like I did right then, important.

We finished our sandwiches in silence.

The Franks were friends of my Grandmother's. Pearl invited our whole family over to her farm New Year's Day. Grandma drove and I could hardly wait to get there.

Treelings lined both sides of a long, winding driveway. At the end, tucked behind a hedge of thick evergreens, a castle on a snow-covered hill. Victor and his brother Oliver ran down it as we arrived.

Sonja watched from the window. "Running? Who does that?"

"People excited to see you." I pushed to get out. Not even Sonja could damper my mood.

Ice-skating was on the agenda. Hot cocoa afterward. Outside, a fire with S'mores and Russian Tea. Inside, logs on the fireplace and built-in bookshelf. They even had a copy of *Myths and Legends of the Greeks*.

Victor walked in wearing full cowboy gear: blue jeans, cowboy boots and a button-down shirt.

"I like your pearl buttons," I said. "Are you a cowboy?"

Victor stood tall. "I will be one day. I'm going to own my own cattle ranch."

My eyes returned to the row of books. "Psyche redeemed herself by overcoming every obstacle in her way."

"Huh?"

"In the story of Cupid." I ran a finger over the spines. "Impossible odds can't compete with true love. She achieved a status more than human. Did you know Cupid means love and Psyche is the Greek word for soul?" He's going to think I'm a silly girl.

Victor studied me. "Which is your favorite?"

My mind went blank. "I..."

"Victor, we're headed to the barn for a game of b-ball," Oliver said.

Victor turned to me. "You coming?"

Easy choice. "Yes."

29

Josie was graduating. I had mixed feelings about it. It was like having your mom leave home. We were going over to Franks after yard cleanup. An outing I did not have mixed feelings about. Horseback riding and a bonfire were on the schedule. I baked my first cake. It flopped.

Mom was on another no-sugar kick. In spite of being "magically delicious," Lucky Charms were out. Oatmeal it was, but I managed to down it in record time. I shoveled in the sludge, barely noticing as it slid down my throat. A shower and my favorite sweatshirt, I was almost ready.

"Can I use your hair dryer?" I asked Sonja.

She cut me a look. "Since when do you care about your hair?"

"Can I?" I eyed the magazine her dad would kill her if he saw.

"Yes." Her tone said this time was alright, but don't ask again. One that usually made me feel bad, worrying all afternoon. Not today. Madonna sang "Crazy for You" on the clock radio. Hairspray until kingdom come and I was ready to go.

"You're going to the Franks," Sonja said. "Victor's there."

I reached the door. "He is a Frank."

"You like him." The light came on in her eyes. "You love him."

"So what? He's nice."

"He's ugly." She picked up the latest issue of *Teen Bop.*

"He's cool," I said. "See ya."

"Here you go. Sheldon is perfect for you." Victor handed me the paint horse's reins. "Doesn't need a saddle."

"Thanks." I used the fence to get on, making a wild grab at the reins.

"Hold on with your legs, Rosemarie," Victor said. "You have ridden before, right?"

"Yes," I lied, hoping the horse was gentle and slow.

Sheldon was not gentle or slow, but took off at a quick pace.

"Whoa." I pulled back on the reins until they were over my shoulder. I gripped with my legs, spurring Sheldon into a trot. The gelding responded with little direction. After several minutes, I discovered a new love: horseback riding.

Back at the barn, Victor said, "Good ride, Rosemarie."

"Thanks." I patted Sheldon's flank. "I sort of lied about being able to ride. It was my first time."

Victor nodded, his lips curving in a smile. "I know."

"You knew? You said Sheldon was gentle and slow."

"I believe what I said was 'Sheldon is perfect for you.'"

I was unable to hold back a foolish grin.

At the bonfire, Malcolm and Erica inhaled hotdogs.

"No more," Victor said, making his way through the group. "Rosemarie hasn't had any."

The tips of my ears warmed. "Thanks."

Malcolm thumped Victor on the shoulder. "Want to throw the football around?"

"Maybe later." Victor reached for a stick.

Erica grabbed the ball. "Let's go, Malcolm."

After they left, I said, "Jim Jones sold imported monkeys door to door, and made enough money to open his own church."

"Jonestown?" he asked.

I reached for a hotdog. "He held church services in his home as a kid. Most of them were funerals for dead animals he killed. Followers gave him their stuff and money. Even their kids. Everyone had to call him Dad. He claimed to be God. In the end, most of his followers were forced at gunpoint to drink cyanide-laced grape punch."

Silence ensued.

Firewood gave way with a snap, sparks flying. "Did you know hyenas have been known to kill people?" I said. "They're opportunistic and prey on healthy targets along with the weak. They're nocturnal, which means they hunt at night."

"I know what nocturnal means."

"Right," I said, realizing I liked him better than anyone. "Only one starts the chase, but more end up on a kill. One time, a zebra and her baby were torn apart and devoured by thirty-five hyenas in half an hour."

Victor squinted at me. "Why do I get the feeling you aren't talking about animals or Jonestown?"

"Not everyone drank the Kool-Aid." I took a bite of my hotdog.

"Yeah." Victor wrapped his with a bun, pulling it from the stick. "Some were scared out of their minds and shot while running away." He downed it in three large bites and wiped his mouth with his sleeve. "I think I'll join the football game. Want to?"

His kindness was my humiliation. I would die if I saw repulsion in his eyes rather than favor. I wasn't good enough for him. Not good enough at all.

"Rosemarie?" Victor waved his hand in front of my vision. "Let's go."

Easy choice. "Okay."

30

Two miles. The distance between Grandma's house and ours. I rode my bicycle. Sonja insisted on coming. She rode Josie's old yellow bike and didn't say a word the whole way. She didn't love my grandma. Rather, it was a chance to watch Soap Operas.

We reached the yard. In the big picture window, Grandma was wearing pastel pink pants with a matching jersey and a frilly white shirt. She met us at the front door and wrapped me in a hug. "Grandma loves you, sweetheart."

Our green pickup pulled into the yard. Steve was home from North Dakota State University for the summer. George rode shotgun. Erica and Malcolm were in the back. Malcolm's loud voice called, "Hi Grandma."

She was my grandma.

Mine.

In the basement, Grandma had books of all kinds.

Nothing on Greek mythology. Some were about animals. I read up on beetle larvae that latched onto a frog's face, sucking all but the bones. The worm always won. Even if a toad managed to get one in its mouth, they threw up. The worm then turned on the frog and ate it.

There was a wall of romance. Historical and inspirational. Romance interested me even though Mom said it was sappy. Sonja was boy-crazy. Echo definitely lost her head and pride, groveling at the feet of an oaf.

I didn't care about looks or money, but imagined a friend. He would know me. The real me, a quiet spirit. A creative mind. Passionate inside. For such a boy I would overcome impossible obstacles. A fight to win true love, achieving a status more than human.

To match.

I recognized a few from our own collection at home. Grandma's branched out to Harlequin. I pulled one from the shelf. The cover made my face get hot, working its way down to my insides until I felt my entire being on fire. A muscular man with black hair had a beautiful blonde woman in his arms. My hand trembled and I looked up.

I was alone.

A page or two couldn't hurt. For kicks.

Are you sure it's a good idea?

Time became meaningless until I heard Grandma's voice. "Rosemarie."

"Coming," I said, my eyes going from the novel in hand to the bookshelf where it belonged. I couldn't leave it. I wanted to finish it and read it again. And again.

"Rosemarie, we're late for chores," Sonja said from the top of the stairs.

Without another thought, I slipped the book in my jeans and pulled my shirt down over it.

Rosemarie. Really? Stealing? The quiet voice was unsettling.

"I'll bring it back," I said out loud.

"You'll bring what back?" Sonja descended the stairs.

"Nothing." I pushed to my feet. "You ready?"

Her eyes burned holes through me. "Yes. It's already three-thirty."

Oh boy. There was nothing Sonja despised more than being late for chores. The silent ride back was punishment for not coming when she called. Didn't matter. My mind was on the book hidden beneath my shirt, and the torrid scene.

I couldn't wait.

31

August 1987

I found him by a spigot outside the milk house where water dripped.

Mr. Toad.

Unbeknownst to anyone but me, Mr. Toad hopped happily through the green weeds created by moisture. I crouched down and watched him blend in. He was unable to be detected until a hop. He knew I wasn't a threat.

A secret friend.

My new favorite song by Tiffany "I Think We're Alone Now" playing, I drifted to sleep. I woke to a wet bed and hid the evidence underneath.

When I returned from chores, Mara was in my room, holding the wad of bed sheets. "What are these?"

Shame rolled over me in a fresh wave. "I was going to wash them."

"Why are they wet?"

My eyes fell.

She glared at me. "Answer me."

"Lay off Piglet, Mom." Malcolm pushed the back of my head. "She can't help it."

"Now I have to wash sheets," Mara said. "You should have told me right away instead of hiding it."

"Praise the Lord from whom all blessings flow," Malcolm sang on the way over to the barn that afternoon.

One good thing about Malcolm, he talked so I didn't have to.

"Me and you are the best team, Rosemarie."

Me and you. "Right."

Like Mr. Toad, he seemed to know instinctively when I was good for him and when I was dangerous.

Mr. Toad hopped across the cement toward the weeds. "What the heck?" Malcolm lifted his foot.

"No don't—" I rushed him.

Too late. His foot came down on Mr. Toad, grinding him into the dirt. "Hey Rosemarie, you should take a look at this. Bet he doesn't have the guts to do that again."

And we're back to being a monster.

My heart broke in the heat and sunshine. Malcolm the vulture, soaring for hours until a perfect time to descend on an exposed target.

For Nocturnal Enuresis. I shoved the prescription in my pocket.

It was a rather hot day at the Frank farm, eighty-five in the shade. For July not bad. For a foot race, downright miserable.

All the boys, plus Erica and I were racing. Sonja sat in the van. She didn't say why. She also accused me of being a show-off. I didn't care. Winner was first to reach the end of the driveway.

We lined up. Malcolm and Erica shook their legs.

Erica flicked me a glare. "Rosemarie, this is a serious competition."

"I know, you invertebrate."

"Let her run," Malcolm said. "Rosemarie sucks at sports but she's fast."

Victor glanced over. "Ready Mattson?"

"You're going down Frank," I said.

Victor shook his head. "In your dreams."

"Get a room," Malcolm said, loud enough to be heard in the next county.

I blushed and looked away.

"Mark, get set, go." Mara brought her arm down. We were off. The boys sprinted ahead of me. Not a problem. Eyes focused on the winding road, I was running for me.

Erica slowed down halfway.

George disappeared.

Malcolm faked a sprained ankle.

Oliver was at least four strides behind. Victor, my only competition. He wasn't taking it easy because I was a girl. He wanted to win as badly as I did.

Tommy was at the end, shouting, "Go, Rosie."

I pushed for all I was worth across the twine string, circled back around, sucking air.

Tommy jumped up and down. "A tie!"

"We match." Victor smiled just for me.

My heart leapt in my throat. "Yeah." I leaned down, placing both hands on my legs to catch my breath. *Clunk.* The pills slipped from my pocket onto the dirt road.

Victor picked up the bottle and handed it to me. "Here you go."

"They're not mine. I mean, I don't really need them," I said, feeling my nose grow. I shoved the pills back into my pocket. Stupid. He'll never like me now.

Victor's eyes were on me. "No one can make you feel inferior without your permission."

"Eleanor Roosevelt," I said.

We match indeed.

32

Dire Straits' "Money for Nothing" played on the stereo while we played basketball in the barn. A handicap was tailor-made for me and my irrevocable incapacity for dribbling.

Fall leaves and the smell of burning firewood permeated the early afternoon breeze.

On our way back to the house, I grabbed Victor's arm. "Hear that? A coyote. I'll bet he's calling to his pack. They form them in the fall, for better hunting. Did you know they can run forty miles an hour?"

"Only you would talk like they're fantastic," Victor said.

We walked a few more steps, and I said, "Echo."

Victor looked over at me. "What?"

"She's my favorite in Greek mythology."

He whistled. "Man, you have a good memory."

"I talk too much."

"I don't mind."

"You don't count." My cheeks grew warm. "I mean, to people I shouldn't. I even talk to myself. A sort of—imaginary friend."

Victor sliced the ground with a stick. "Or guardian angel."

"I need one," I said, and clamped my hand over my mouth.

Victor pinned me with a serious look. "Apparently you do."

"Yeah, funny. My family is pretty good."

I stood by the fire, dreading going home to the Sims, Malcolm mostly. "I get these urges," he said, like he couldn't help it. Something was terribly wrong with him, and now something was wrong with me.

Victor didn't say much as he built the fire. I rehashed everything I said. Did he think I was too talkative? Boring? I should have let him talk more.

"You're quiet, Rosemarie." Victor tore open a package of marshmallows. "Focused on your shadow?"

"My shadow?"

"You know, like when you worry you said too much. What to do or not to do. How you should have or shouldn't have handled something."

My eyes grew wide. "How did you know?"

"Everyone does it. Especially you." He turned his marshmallow over the fire. "It's only a shadow of you. It can give you wisdom if you recognize it. Make it work for you, not against you."

I straightened and took a deep breath. "Shadow work."

"I like it." He nodded. "Shadow work."

The green door was shut.

"Guess who?" Malcolm said with a devilish grin.

"They're discussing work." There was nothing going on. He was bad for even thinking there was. My mother wasn't Mara. She loved my dad. No one told her what to do, and a kicked dog she was not.

Malcolm grabbed my shirt. "Let's see those."

I pulled away. "Let's not."

He took a lunge at my breasts. Sonja came around the corner. Malcolm took off like the devil himself were after him.

Humiliated, I turned away. Sonja said, "I'll go get your dad."

I waited for my dad on a square bale at the end of the stanchions.

Duane strolled out. Contempt radiated from his muscular form. Like I was an inconvenience. A bug to squash. He stared at me for an eternity.

Then, "What did he do?"

My eyes fell and I shrank back in horror. "I...nothing."

Silence, invasive and probing, followed.

At last, "Did he touch your breasts?"

"Yes," I managed, and scurried away like a mouse with a cat on its tail.

33

"It makes you look stocky." Mom's description of my Christmas present from Grandma. Next to her five-foot-eleven willowy figure everyone looked stocky.

"Okay." I swallowed back tears, smoothing the dress with shaky hands. It was lipstick red and tied at the waist with a bow. The skirt was right above my knees. My generous curves filled the bodice perfectly. I didn't look stocky at all.

"Your blue V-neck sweater with the black slacks will work," she said.

"Okay."

After Mom left, I donned her choice and studied my reflection. The shoulder pads made me feel like a football player. Pleated slacks were alright, but black against light blue, an overall failure. The outfit did nothing to accent my thick brown curls and plentiful curves—oh who am I kidding—stocky stature. The Franks were coming to our house for Christmas dinner. There was communion to follow. I couldn't let Victor see me in a frumpy outfit.

The sweater-slacks getup was fitting for the photograph with the Sims on the stairs. "People have problems" became "Succeed together" with the click of a button.

After pictures, everyone disappeared.

By some Christmas miracle, I managed to slip upstairs to the bathroom without being spotted. I slid the bolt in place and exchanged the sweater and slacks for the Christmas dress. I returned to the group as the Franks were arriving.

Miracle number two, Mom didn't say a word about the dress. We sat at the same table. Broke bread and drank wine—grape juice—together. It was as if she didn't even notice.

Miracle three, Steve was home from North Dakota State University on Christmas break, and drove us to the Christmas Cantata in Valley City. I sat next to Victor. He leaned forward, talking to George in the front passenger seat. To my immense disappointment, he didn't give me a second look. Proof my Christmas dress changed nothing.

I imagined it playing out differently.

Tonight I was his Christmas wish. His usual façade for my brothers' sake would be replaced with admiration. The cowboy boots I wore weren't warm or practical. He would know any girl wearing boots with a dress equaled him. He would notice I curled my hair and put on make-up. A little lipstick to match the dress. His lips would brush my cheek, and...

"Rosemarie." Steve's voice broke into my thoughts.

"What?" I said, rather irritated.

He waved a hand in front of my face. "Wake up or you'll get left again."

A blast of cold air brought me back to reality. The van was empty. Victor stood alongside the sliding door, exhaling frosty puffs. "You go on, Steve. I'll wait for her."

Steve clamped his hand on Victor's shoulder. "Thanks, man."

I slid across the bench seat and got out. Victor shut the van door behind me. Toe to toe, I'd never been this close to him. I wasn't going to move until he told me to.

"Rosemarie." He was only three inches taller than me.

"Yeah." I stood my ground.

His gaze dropped. "Nice boots."

"Thank you," I said, breathless.

His eyes lifted and caught mine for an eternity.

At last, I motioned toward the church. "Shall we go?"

"When you've kissed me."

My heart thundered until I was certain he could hear it. Did he say...? And then I was being kissed. A hundred times I've imagined him kissing my cheek or even my forehead. His lips, cold at first, awkwardly trembled and bumped against mine. Mine were no better. He stepped in. I kissed him back.

All too soon he lifted his head. He appeared a bit dazed, silly even.

"I love you," I said, the words tumbling out. Not at all adequate to explain the rush of emotion and the way I felt about him.

His eyes took on a shine and he grabbed my hand. "Come on."

Huey Lewis was right. The power of love was curious indeed. Probably cruel too.

But I hoped it might just save my life.

34

Sunday afternoon we watched *Return of the Jedi*. Mara made popcorn. I think her favorite thing about movies, aside from the approval of her children. As for me, I finally understood Malcolm's fascination with watching a movie a bazillion times. Luke's desperate plea, "Father, help me. Please." And the look on Darth Vader witnessing his son being destroyed. The way he took action against the...

At once, all the breathable air was sucked out of the room. Duane stood in the doorway. "Mara," he said, her name on his lips a curse.

Without a word, she followed him out the door.

Malcolm grabbed the clicker, turning the volume up three notches.

Sonja's eyes darted toward the door. "Shut the TV off."

My palms grew sweaty. Mara was getting it for letting us watch a movie. I didn't know why Malcolm thought he was exempt. I'd seen Duane scream at him.

Mara returned. She slunk over to the TV and turned it off.

Feeling her humiliation, we retreated in silence. The way Mara acted like a kicked dog infuriated me. What was Duane going to do if she didn't go in her place? Give her the silent treatment? That happened on a daily basis anyway.

He even had my mom and dad shunning her at whim. She'd been reduced to housekeeper and babysitter. Even those tasks were supervised.

I imagined a different ending.

One where Mara stood up to him, held her ground, and gained freedom.

Freedom for me came in an announcement.

We were selling the cows. All of them. A semi pulled into the yard. After the last cow was loaded, a burden lifted and skies cleared. The green door and the secret it kept were gone.

I showered and went for a bike ride, monster cookies tucked in the basket. Chester trotted alongside me. We reached the black top, and looked both ways before crossing the road.

The tree fort was vacant. The cookies, delicious. Chester ate most of them. He made three circles right, three circles left and laid down next to me in a sigh. I withdrew the latest Harlequin I "borrowed" from Grandma. A feeling of unease overshadowed me. I ignored it. Grandma read them too. And I was going to return it.

At the rustle of grass, Chester lifted his head. A rabbit came up. Chester bolted from the fort in one giant leap.

Without looking up, I said, "Get 'em, Buddy." I was on a juicy part. A few more pages and I'd head home.

Gears shifted in the distance. The screech of tires much closer made my heart stop. I stood, looking out toward the commotion. A semi barreled down the road.

Chester was in the ditch.

I scrambled down the ladder and jumped on my bike. Reaching Chester, I saw the rise and fall of his chest. He was still alive! Whimpering and torn up, but definitely still breathing. I rushed over.

"Here boy." I reached down. "I'm sorry. Are you..."

He growled.

"Chester?" I went to smooth his hair.

He turned and snapped. The pain was surprising. I looked down at angry red teeth marks. That can't be right. "You bit me?"

Chester snarled, licking his lips.

"But I love you." My heart cracked, hot tears streaming down my cheeks. "You wouldn't hurt me when I love you so much."

Bared teeth told me not only would he hurt me, but tear me apart given a chance.

Back home the news was on. Mount St. Helens erupted, disappearing in a cloud.

Mom talked to the vet about putting Chester down.

"No, don't hurt him." I flew in a rage at her. "Don't touch my dog."

George grabbed me by the arms. "Get ahold of yourself. We can't have another nuisance around."

Malcolm gave me a look of pity. "When it's your time to go, it's your time to go."

Without another word, I fled to my room, and flung myself across the bed. I didn't want to think about how Chester tried to bite me. That he wanted to hurt me. I wept brokenly for my friend and confidante.

My protector.

35

A trip to the library yesterday revealed Mount St. Helens erupted May 18, 1980. Nine years ago. There hadn't been a letter from Shelly. Anne's phone rang busy. I ran into Greg at Welcome Pharmacy. After an awkward "hey" he turned his attention back to his mother refilling a prescription for Ritalin.

Controlled reality took precedence over old friends. Back home, Josie parked the van. I marched to the house for confession and the truth.

"...How many tax dollars is Welcome public school losing every year? And teaching your kids at home? Unheard of," Mom was saying in the kitchen.

"Who said this?" Dad asked.

"Fred Demit."

I slowed down. "How come you said Mount St. Helens happened this May? It doesn't make any sense."

"I didn't say it happened this year," Mom said. "Where did you get such an idea?"

"It was on the news. The one playing when Chester died." I searched my brain for details of the report.

"Chester's death was pretty traumatic. There was no news on," Mom said.

"What are you talking about? Of course there was. I know it because when the vet was here, I thought—"

"Rosemarie Grace," Dad said gently. "The vet never came to the house. We brought Chester to Welcome."

"—the ash looked like snow." I remembered the vet right in our living room.

Duane put his hand on my forehead. "You okay, Rosemarie?"

I couldn't wait to tell Victor. "When are we leaving for the Franks?"

Mom and Dad exchanged glances. Dad thrust his chin forward. "We aren't going over there."

Fear wrapped me in a cold embrace. "What do you mean? We've been planning the ice-skating party for weeks."

"We'll talk about it later," Mom said.

"When's later?" I hugged myself and began to shake.

Duane cleared his throat. "Smurfs are New Age."

If he'd grown a second head, I couldn't have been more confused. "What?"

"Mickey Mouse and Smurfs are New Wave. There will be no more in this house."

"Wait, did you say New Age or New Wave?" I asked.

"New Age," Mom said.

Slowly, the pieces fit into place. This was Duane's doing. I felt it in my bones. He put my folks up to canceling the party. To punish me.

The room dimmed around me. "Why aren't we allowed to go to the Franks New Year's party?"

"They joined the Catholic Church," Dad said. "Catholics don't believe the way we do. They think suicides go to hell."

"And divorce will get you kicked out of the church," Mom added.

"So?" I said, and my world crumbled. "You aren't getting divorced."

"No, but we don't believe in that church."

"What does it have to do with going over to the Franks?" I desperately needed to see Victor.

Duane straightened tall in his chair. "Because I'm the dad."

What about Victor? The Franks? What if they were waiting for us?

I had to see him. Find out if he felt the same about me. It was of utmost importance. I would sneak out. It was the only way.

Staying up after everyone else went to bed proved tricky. But my decision was made.

I let Sonja in on the plan. She'd been on a decline since her dad banned Amy Grant's *Unguarded*. I couldn't help but think it was my fault.

Because it was your fault.

I would ride my bike to the Franks. Ten miles. I timed it. It would take me an hour. Another back. Didn't allow much time to talk. It would be worth it though. Maybe he would even kiss me again.

The thought fueled my resolve.

I tiptoed down the stairs. At the bottom, Duane Sim in his underwear and white T-shirt, glowering at me. Distain oozed from every pore of his being. I wondered if he was thinking about what Malcolm did. My face got hot. Maybe he hadn't told anyone. He alone was aware of my shame.

Without a word, I retreated to my room. Phil Collins sang "A Groovy Kind of Love" softly on the radio.

The morning brought a three-page paper on honesty and no Victor.

We didn't go over to the Franks. Nor did they come to see us. I didn't know what they thought. Was Pearl hurt or did Victor miss me? After a while they would forget about me. He would forget about me.

Like the rest of my friends.

36

"We are the Borg. Lower your shields and surrender your ships. We will add your biological and technological distinctiveness to our own."

An alien race "The Borg" was introduced on *Star Trek Voyager*. The Borg assimilated thousands of species and billions to trillions of individual life-forms throughout the galaxy. A Borg infant was found aboard a Borg Cube. Children were placed in maturation chambers to grow quickly into mature drones. A drone's race and gender become irrelevant.

Malcolm made an attempt to put his hand up my shirt. "Your culture will adapt to service us. Resistance is futile."

I pushed him away. A once shameful submission now turned war, I had nothing to lose anymore. Victor or Keep Kool Kids. I wasn't taking it any longer. I for one, was not going to be assimilated.

He came at me again. "Don't close up shop yet."

"Get away from me." I clenched my fists and awarded him with a punch in his big belly.

He groaned, grabbing his stomach. "Ahhhh."

"Yeah right." I held my stiff pose.

"Seriously," he said, sweat beading on his brow. "I think I'm going to be sick."

I peered at him closely. "You're not joking."

Suddenly, George was there. His eyes shifted from Malcolm, to me, and back to Malcolm. "What's going on?"

Malcolm wandered away. "I think I'll go lay down."

"It's not my fault," I told George. "He grabbed me."

George cocked his head to the side. "Grabbed you how?"

I looked away.

George got in my face. "Has he been messing with you? Don't try to hide it."

Heat flushed up the back of my neck. "What are you going to do?"

"Don't worry about it," he said, his tone lofty.

During supper, Mom told us, "Malcolm has appendicitis."

I sat on my hands beneath the table. "Can you get appendicitis from getting punched in your stomach?"

"How long is he going to be in the hospital?" Sonja asked.

"Three days," Mom said.

Three days of freedom. Three to form a battle plan. I mentally rehearsed different scenarios. I would be the champion.

Upon his return, Malcolm moved about the house like a sloth.

I was secretly glad for the affliction. It meant I had my body to myself. At least until he healed. The next few days, I braced for war. A week passed and nothing. A month. And another. He was probably waiting for me to relax. Let my guard down. I was sure he'd try again. When he did, I'd be ready.

Mara and Malcolm went to the Franks. "Malcolm invited himself to Oliver's graduation," Mom said when I freaked out.

"The rules Duane made for us don't apply to his own wife and kids," I said.

Mom's gaze narrowed. "Tough."

Tears sprang to my eyes, spilling down my cheeks. "It's not fair."

"Wash your face and fix your hair pretty," Mom said.

"Who cares? It's not like anyone will see me."

She gave me the look of silence.

I retreated to the bathroom.

Mara cornered me upon their return. "Victor's girlfriend was showing off her promise ring."

"Girlfriend?" I swallowed hard.

"Yes, she never left his side the entire time." Mara gave a knowing smile. The lines around her mouth revealed bitterness. Deep valleys around her eyes, fatigue. An oversized embroidered sweatshirt, a prison cell uniform.

Mara was either lying to hurt me or she was telling the truth.

"She's lucky," I said.

Her features hardened. "Next thing you know they'll be engaged. You'll have to meet her, she's darling. They'll have cute kids."

The vision of a nameless girl having Victor's children overrode logic. "I don't know, Victor is ugly," I said. The ultimate betrayal.

A look of satisfaction settled in her eyes. "He's nice, though. Victor, I mean."

Nice one, Rosemarie. Now you have your enemy defending your friend against you.

Mara strolled away with a smile, humming a happy tune. Alone in my wretchedness, I couldn't figure out what happened. Mara was unhappy going in. Now I was the one most miserable.

One day I'd leave the country house. In my hands were the keys to freedom. God can save anyone.

A deeper realization: they don't want to be.

37

"I'm gonna get you with the Kodak Disc..." The commercial played on the TV in our room. We found a television in storage and got one and a half channels with the help of bunny ears.

Malcolm left for college. I got a new friend. A pen pal by the name of Jenny. Her picture and a letter about her came in the mail. She was from California.

Now for my picture. I feathered short hair in front and combed the back. A mullet of sorts, I suppose. I donned my favorite sweatshirt.

"You look nice," Sonja said.

"I do, don't I?" I fairly glowed with satisfaction.

"Now smile for the camera."

I had her take three to make sure one turned out and put the roll in the mail.

A week later, the package of pictures arrived. I shuffled through. At last, Jenny would be able to see what I looked like. I'd tell her about my records. We would be...I came across the first print. "That can't be right."

Sonja looked over my shoulder. "What do you mean? They all turned out."

"Yes, but..." The girl smiling back in the photograph looked nothing like me. She had horrible hair, a silly smile and was—

—ugly.

After staring for an eternity in horror, I threw the prints in the trash and didn't write back.

Graduation day. All had gone before me except Tommy. I knew what to expect. A month of work: cleaning, dusting, washing windows and every job in between.

Mom sipped her coffee at the kitchen table. "Greg Hamill graduated from Jamestown High School with honors." There was a long, dismissive pause. "Rosemarie, you're wearing too much makeup."

My hand came up. "Too much foundation or lipstick?"

She got real close, looking over my face. "And you're wearing mascara?"

"A little." I glanced away, wondering why I wasn't invited to Greg's open house. "My invitation probably got lost in the mail. What ever happened to Shelly Vanguard? Do you hear from her mom?"

"They moved to Minnesota," Josie said. Josie was home and the only one to get excited about cleanup.

"Where in Minnesota?"

"Brainerd."

"Weird she stopped writing."

"Probably grew up. It was a long time ago. Not like you were close."

"Don't say that." I could no longer hold back tears.

They exchanged looks, bursting into giggles. At last Josie said, "I don't know why you're making such a big deal about it."

"Besides, she would never have come over if you hadn't made the effort," Mom said. "It was a one-sided friendship."

Had I romanticized my childhood?

"You were always a better friend to her than..." Mom trailed off as Duane walked in. "Do you want supper?"

"I'm beat. I think I'll head upstairs."

Mom followed him. Josie got a phone call.

I retreated to my room, crying myself to sleep over my friends, real and imagined.

My open house was a picnic with half the county.

Afterward, Mom let Tommy and I drive over to the Frank's to celebrate Victor's open house. "He's going to Boston College for creative writing in the fall," Mom said. I wondered where she got the information, but didn't bother to ask. I'd get the details from Victor.

Pearl greeted us with a warm hello. "The boys are playing basketball. Why don't you go on over there?"

Aaron Demit, six feet four, all lanky and leggy, trotted over with a smile as Tommy and I reached the barn. Fred and Suzie Demit, Aaron's parents, lived a mile south of the country house.

Shaggy blonde hair, a powder-blue T-shirt and gym shorts, Victor was clean-shaven and all grown up. He saw me and propped the basketball beneath his arm. "Hey Rosemarie." His eyes caught mine.

A warm rush flooded me. "Hey Victor."

Oliver knocked the ball out from beneath Victor's arm. "I'll take that. Guys, this is Shawn Erickson." He motioned to a hairy guy in a red shirt and blue jeans.

Shawn winked at me. "Hey."

"Rosemarie and Aaron are on my team," Oliver said. "Victor, you get Shawn and Tommy."

Victor aimed and took a shot. Swish. "No fair. I wanted Rosemarie on my team."

Aaron was the star basketball player at Valley City High School. Tommy, although a farm boy and homeschooled, gave him a run for his money when it came to basketball.

Shawn must not be very good. Besides being paired opposite me, he wore blue jeans. No one wore blue jeans to play basketball. Soon, my suspicions were confirmed. He didn't make a single shot and hung on me the entire time. Every time I moved, he was there. Blocking was an excuse to cop a feel. By the time he put his arms around me to get the ball, I pushed him down with a forceful, "Get away!"

Victor high-fived me. "Good job, Mattson."

Late afternoon waned into evening with a bonfire. Afterward, tag in the dark.

I stayed by the fire. In the distance, I could hear yelling and excitement of the game. An occasional mosquito took advantage of my backside.

Victor returned early. Shadows danced across his face, firelight reflecting in his eyes. "I'd like to take you out to dinner sometime, Rosemarie."

Dinner! Could it be he felt the same way about me? My heart kicked up, pounding in my ears. "Really? You mean it?"

"Yeah," he said, tapping his chin. "I'd have to buy three meals, though. One for me and one for each of your faces."

"Oh." I suddenly wished the ground would open up and swallow me. Mara, the witch. I could imagine her delight. "What did she tell you?"

Pain twisted his features. "I didn't think looks mattered to you."

"I heard you were...Mara said you had a girl with a promise ring."

Victor's eyes widened with surprise, then recognition and he started to laugh. "Jill Pederson. Had to be."

She had a name. Hatred for the faceless female was forceful, blinding, and took my breath away. "Mara said you were pretty chummy."

"What else did she tell you?" Victor asked, clearly enjoying himself.

I stood. "Who cares? You can have her. Where is she anyway, if you're so in love with her?"

Rosemarie. Wow.

Victor shrugged with a grin. "Probably with Oliver. Jill's his girlfriend."

"Oh." I sank back down.

Victor poked the tinder with a stick. "Off to Valley City State University?"

"In the fall. Going into nursing."

"Huh." He set a roasted marshmallow between prepared Graham crackers. "I'm surprised."

"What's wrong with VCSU? All my family went there," I said, instantly on the defense. "Why, did you think I wasn't smart enough?"

"Not at all. I thought...never mind." He devoured the S'more.

"Tell me."

He licked his fingers. "I imagined you getting the world by the tail, pulling it down and putting it in your pocket."

"Saturday Night Live." I smiled. "Okay, Matt Foley, when do classes start?"

"Third week in August. My mom's brother, Dale, lives in Duxbury. I'll be staying at his place over the summer. My plane leaves in the morning." He held his hand out to me.

"Boston is a long way away from Valley City, North Dakota," I said, and to my horror, started to cry.

"Don't cry." He wrapped his arms around me. I pressed my face on his shoulder. If only today hadn't been so sweet. Then I wouldn't feel like I was drowning. At last, he pulled back and caught my eyes.

"Don't forget your friends when you're out there." I managed a smile through my tears.

"Not just friends, but dear friends."

"Sorry about the waterworks."

He gave me another, quick hug. "I won't say goodbye, but rather we'll meet again someday."

"Someday," I echoed.

38

Federal agents from the ATF went to the Waco compound to serve a warrant for illegal firearms and take David Koresh into custody. The raid turned into a four-hour gunfight. In the end, four ATF agents and six of Koresh's followers were dead.

My brothers and Josie were home for the weekend, which meant Monopoly around the table.

"The standoff lasted fifty-one days," Current Event Expert, George said.

Steve's eyes were on the board. "Daniel sounds nice." Daniel Spick was Josie's steady boyfriend. She met him on a cruise last spring.

"His parents work at the pasta plant," Josie said. "He's in his last year at the University of Minnesota Law."

"When are we going to meet him?" Steve asked.

"Soon. He said next time..." Josie picked up a community chest card. "Go to jail. Go directly to jail. Do not pass go. Do not collect two-hundred dollars."

"Speaking of a standoff, I was planning on having a chat with the folks before I take off," George said.

My heart leapt in my chest. "About what?"

George shook the dice. "About the Sims and what went on around here. Someone needs to do something."

"Let's forget it, huh?" Josie said. "All of them are grown up now. Why hash it over? Besides, not like it'll do any good."

A sliver of hope bloomed in my chest. "No wait, this is a good idea. That way we can clear things up. Assuming and imagining is enough to drive us crazy. Are you really going to do it George?" I asked eagerly.

George gave me a lofty look. "Of course. At breakfast in the morning before I leave."

"Why wait?" I said, all of my senses preparing for battle. "Why not talk to them at supper tonight?" Then he can't chicken out.

He sighed. "Rosemarie, let me handle this."

Someone was going to do something. George, not the one I would have picked to take a stand. No matter their response, I had a new regard for George. And on this, I would back him up to the death.

Duane sat in his usual spot at the head of the breakfast table.

All Mattsons were present, minus Steve and Tommy. They made themselves scarce lately. I worked away at a stack of pancakes, snatching occasional glances at George. He devoured his breakfast. If I didn't know better, I'd say he had plans to dine and dash.

Clearly, he needed a nudge.

I took a sip of water and cleared my throat. "So I have a question." No one acknowledged me, but I plunged ahead anyway. "Whatever happened to the Sims finding a cheap place to live and moving out?" I said, mortified at the volume of my inquiry.

Duane and Mom exchanged glances. Dad's eyes didn't leave the newspaper. Josie looked at Mom. Mara stared off into space.

"Right, George?" I said, raising my brow.

George somehow managed to shovel another bite into already stuffed cheeks.

Dad cleared his throat. "George, if you're not in a huge hurry I could use some help with the far east section. Should only take an hour or so."

"Yeah, I probably can do that," George mumbled through a mouthful.

Mom set her glasses on her head. "Josie, what are your plans?"

The phone rang. Josie answered it, speaking in low tones. She returned to the table, and said, "Grandma Degner was in an accident."

Grandma's funeral was a formal affair.

All the Sims attended. Many distant relatives mistook me for one of them. Greg was there with his mom. He shook my hand. None of it was real. Until Grandpa invited us for lunch afterwards. Her spirit was nowhere in her home or amongst her things. Reality was an empty chasm of sorrow.

My grandma was gone.

"She was definitely a product of the dirty thirties," Dad said as we went through Grandma's things in her kitchen.

Grandpa picked up a ceramic frog. I knew it well. Green with hand painted white spots, it once sat on the picture windowsill. "How about it, Rosemarie?" He held it up.

"Thanks, Grandpa." Although grass green and fat like a frog, the ceramic knick knack reminded me of Mr. Toad.

"Enough stuff here to start a bakery," Dad said. Scattered about the small space were boxes of baking pans, all shapes and sizes. Cookie sheets, a pastry cutter, spatulas, decorating tips, a cake wheel, and even a blow torch.

"You sure you're set on college, Rosemarie?" Grandpa asked. "Sally's Bakery is going out of business. We could go to the auction." He reached for the newspaper on the kitchen table and thumbed through it. "Let's see, a double wide convection oven, a proofing oven, a mixer...."

"Sounds spendy," Dad said.

Hope swelled my chest for the first time since they lowered Grandma into the ground. "I could get a job."

"You could put in a bid for the bakery itself," Grandpa said. "That way you could buy the works and not have to move a whole lot of equipment."

"I could see about a small business loan," I said with growing excitement. "If I went to college, I'd have to apply for loans anyway."

"I don't know, Rosemarie," Dad said, sifting through a drawer. "We'd have to talk to your mom. Running a business is a lot of work. Not to mention what your mother would say about you not going to college. And there are the other kids to think of..."

"No one besides me bakes. Pretty please?"

Dad paused and looked at me. "You're serious."

"Yes." A jolt of excitement filled my veins and my entire being came alive. "I'm going to open my own bakery."

39

Softball. Not my best sport, but Barb Anderson and Darla Adams were in Welcome Grocery and one player short. Their eyes sparkled when they saw me. I tried not to trip over myself saying yes. They wanted me to play.

Me.

Meaning there was nothing wrong with me.

Practice was six a.m. at Welcome Park. I showed up early. The majority of the girls huddled in a circle. Darla was there, petite with strawberry blonde hair and freckles. I slowed when I saw Holly Astringes. She wore Guess jeans and an Adidas shirt, her honey blonde hair pulled up. One of the few girls I knew who could pull off a fantastic ponytail.

Swoosh. Barb took practice swings. Barb's bleached blond hair was shaved on the sides and back. She was tall, close to six feet and muscular.

Eyes to the ground, Susan Sharp stood alone. Two dark-haired girls appearing to be twins sat on the bench. One had thick eyebrows. The other, a shadow of a mustache. They looked like they were my people. I made my way toward them.

Barb grabbed a bat. "Rosemarie, you're in right field."

Or maybe not. A few innings later I was dubbed catcher and Holly got right field. It was my turn to hit and I grabbed the bat.

"Rosemarie's up, I mean out," Holly called.

That got a few laughs.

Day two, annoyed glares.

Day three no one acknowledged me.

Monday was the first game and I was up to bat. I imagined hitting the ball deep left center. John Gordon would call a home run like I was Kirby Puckett in the 1991 World Series. The pitch. I took a wild swing. The actual ball landed in the catcher's mitt.

"Strike one," the umpire called.

I tapped the end of the bat on the plate, looked up and swung with all my might.

"Strike two."

"Keep your eye on the ball, Rosemarie," Barb yelled from the sidelines.

Heart in my ears, I focused on the pitcher and the ball in her hand. It sailed toward me.

Crack. The bat connected with the ball. The team went wild. *It's way back, way back. It's gone! Touch 'em all, Kirby Puckett!*

I ran fast as my legs would go, rounding first, second and headed for home.

Barb high-fived me when I got there. "Atta girl."

"Holy cats, did you see her?" Holly whistled.

Katie's eyes widened. "Man, you're fast, Rosemarie."

Darla thumped me on the back. "You can't hit but you sure can run."

We ended up winning the game. Afterward, Stacey said, "Hey girls, I have a table for us at Carlton."

"Girls" meant Katie, Darla, Barb and Holly. Susan and the twins, Ellie and Allie dashed for their vehicles.

"Nice hit, Rosemarie." Holly smiled.

"Thanks," I said, my face flushed. "You too."

A cargo van pulled up.

"Is that Pizza Face's mom?" Holly asked, watching Susan get in.

"Step-mom," Barb said, rubbing her nose with the back of her forearm. "Allie and Ellie turned out to be alright players."

Holly laughed. "Yeah, but I wonder if they ever heard of tweezers and a bottle of Nair."

I let out a nervous giggle. "Bottle of Nair."

Go home.

"Not quite as good as your sister, but you're not bad." Barb tugged at her gloves. "Sonja played last year."

Katie jabbed her side. "They're not sisters."

"That's right," Darla said. "What was it like to live at their house?"

"They lived at our house. Ours," I said.

All eyes were on me like I was a science experiment.

"We didn't really live together. They lived in the old house." First lie, guilt made its way into my gut. "Duane hit us." Second lie, it settled there.

Barb's wide eyes filled with genuine interest. "Really? I always thought he was a little off."

"How did he hit you?" Holly's eyes were skeptical.

"He lifted us by our shirt collars and pushed us up against the wall," I said. The truth felt much better.

Holly gave Barb a bored glance. "I thought you said he hit you."

"He came after me with a broom." I choked out a third lie, darkness worming its way in my gut. *Liar, liar pants on fire.*

"Oh." Holly covered her mouth with her hand.

"I can't imagine," Katie said.

Then the stories began to unfold. Half-truths, I corrected my conscience. But really, I lied like a rug. Until lying became easy as pie on a Sunday morning. Attention gained from every detail was a green light. While a voice inside my head said, *It's Duane's fault. If he wants to act like you're bad, you might as well be bad.*

Barb brought me a Coke the next day. "For good luck."

Rich Hamill's sports car pulled up to the curb after practice. All the girls turned to Holly. "Your ride's here."

"Burger night at the Carlton," Darla said.

My cue to head home.

"You coming, Rosemarie?" Barb asked.

Easy choice. "Coming."

The late July sun beat down, turning the humid day stagnant. I made my way over to the practice field. The girls were huddled in a circle with their backs to me.

My palms grew sweaty. I picked up the bat. "Good thing you weren't at my house this morning." I grasped for higher ground in the deep pit I was in. "Duane was..."

Barb turned around, her eyes filled with pity. "Oh Rosemarie, stop."

Hot shame swept up the back of my neck. "What do you mean?"

"Don't even." Holly glared at me. "My mom knew Duane and Mara Sim before they moved in with your family. I told her what you said about him. She says you're a liar. Duane Sim is incapable of hurting a fly."

Stupid, Rosemarie. You're pathetic.

I was dizzy with fear. "So you believed her?"

Barb crossed her beefy arms. "Some of what you've told us seems a bit far-fetched, Rosemarie."

"What do you want me to say?" I wrung my hands.

"The truth," Barb answered.

Duane was the bad one, not me. "I wasn't lying," I said, my face burning hot. "But I'm not playing with you anymore if you don't believe me." I took a step back, turned and made my way to the car. Slow at first, then with enough distance, I broke into a run. No one made a move to come after me.

Alone in my room, I couldn't even look at myself in the mirror.

You are a sneaky liar.

My palms ached with guilt and I couldn't think straight. Maybe if I explained the situation to my folks...no! But I would never, ever tell a single white lie again as long as I lived.

I needed to get it off my mind before my brain exploded. I plopped down on my bed, and reached between the mattresses for my diary. I flipped through the journal I'd started for Keep Kool Kids. A place to tell my side of the story and why I'd done it.

Mom and Duane were sitting at the head of the dining table.

"Rosemarie, we need to talk," Mom said.

"What about?" I licked dry lips.

Their eyes met and a silent message passed between them.

Mom rubbed the back of her neck. "I was gathering dishes from your room. I um, sat on your bed and ran my hands over the mattress. The corner of something caught my hand."

She picked up a laundry basket with the Harlequin novels I'd bought from Walgreens. On top of the stack was my journal. I made a grab for it.

Mom's arm shot out, blocking mine. "Sit," she said. I sat.

My mind raced, searching for all the incriminating things I'd written. I was so dead. I'd been betrayed by my journal. My confidante. I should never have started the dumb thing.

Then to my horror, she opened it, and began to read, "...I told them he hit us on the head with a baseball bat..."

I took another swipe at the journal, and she held it out of reach. "Okay, I told them!" It burst from my lips. "The softball girls."

Mom closed the tablet with a sigh. "Who else?"

"No one." I was lower than scraps in the slop pail. Dishonesty dragged me beneath a tidal wave of humiliation.

Dumb, dumb, Rosemarie.

Duane sat in cold silence. He didn't look at me. For the first time, I couldn't blame him for his disdain.

"Mm hm. Is this the first time?" Mom asked.

My cheeks were hot. "Yes. I'll never do it again."

Duane's eyes grew serious. "Lying is a bad habit. Satan is the father of lies."

"I know." I hung my head. Satan wasn't my dad.

Mom said, "Mercy bears richer fruits than strict justice."

Abraham Lincoln. Wait, what? My head came up. "But..." My voice cracked. "Thank you."

Duane stood and held his arms out toward me. "I don't know about you but I could use a hug."

The hug was awkward. I contemplated asking for my books and journal back. Then decided not to push it. I was glad it was over and the truth was out.

I took a step back and caught the gleam in his eye. A look that said I wasn't innocent Rosemarie molested by his horrible son. I was a liar. And this didn't make us even, instead I owed him.

Part II

The only thing necessary for the triumph of evil is for good men to do nothing.

Edmund Burke

40

Carlton Restaurant & Bar
Welcome, North Dakota
November 25, 1993

Thirty-three-year-old Maria Devi Khrystos, a self-proclaimed messiah, and her husband, Yuriy Kryvonohov, the White Brotherhood's mastermind, predicted the end of the world.

Yesterday.

Actually, Khrystos and Kryvonohov scheduled the apocalypse and mass suicide November 24, but the cult's teenage children gained attention of Ukrainian authorities and the media. The leaders bumped up the end to November 14.

Now it was Thanksgiving Day and the world was still going around.

"Next year, they should skip Thanksgiving and go right to Christmas," Stacey said. "A month before Christmas and all through the place, stockings are hung on the bar counter with care. In hopes St. Nicholas— might wait his turn."

I giggled. "Okay, Grinch who stole Christmas."

She shut the till. "I like Christmas as much as the next person, but twenty-five days is plenty."

"Did I ever tell you it's tradition at my house to carol and give groceries to the needy?"

She rolled her eyes. "Only like a hundred times."

"If you think about it, Christmas..." I trailed off as Rich Hamill walked in and sat down.

Stacey grabbed my arm. "He broke up with Holly Astringes. She's been crazy stalking him ever since."

I cut him another glance. "Mr. Two-dollar Tip?"

"I swear, Rosemarie you're as dense as London fog," Stacey said. "She's a woman."

A silly woman. "I'm a woman."

"Hardly," Stacey said. "T-shirt two sizes too big. No make-up and glasses. You do know they've invented contacts."

"I tried makeup. Mom said I caked it on."

"And there's your hair." Stacey reached for a curl.

My hand flew to my hair. "What's wrong with it?"

She twisted a lock around her finger. "Everything. The cut, the style...I bet you've never colored it."

"Why would I?" I took a step back.

"If you have to ask, forget it."

"Dyed hair isn't practical. I have to keep my head on straight. My bakery depends on it."

Stacey pushed the menu at me. "Yeah, yeah the bakery. It's your table. Unless you want me to take this one."

"I would if I didn't need this job."

"Good luck."

"Thanks." I headed to Rich's table. "What can I get for you?"

"I'll have the special."

"Ribeye, excellent choice. How would you like your steak done?"

"Rare."

"Baked potato, mashed, or French fries?"

"Baked potato. Extra sour cream."

"What dressing for your salad?"

He handed me the menu. "Ranch."

In the kitchen, Stacey asked, "What did you think?"

"I only took his order. We didn't get engaged or anything."

She laughed. "Oh, Rosemarie."

"Next time you can wait on him." I pulled out the salad tray.

Her eyes widened. "Why? What happened?"

I searched my brain for a reason and came up empty. "Hey, did I tell you the Walskys asked you to wait on them? Said they only come when you're working."

"They are our fussiest customers," she said, cheeks flushing.

A quick image of Rich flashed through my mind. I could think of one fussier.

Stacey cleared tables at the end of the night. It was my turn to do dishes.

"Jingle Bell Rock" in the background, I put away the last of the silverware. I took a step back to slide a rack beneath the sink and nearly leapt out of my skin.

Rich Hamill was in the doorway.

"Man you scared me." I laid a hand on my chest. For the first time I looked at him. Really looked at him. He was no more than an inch taller than my five-foot nine inches with a fitted shirt over defined muscles. "How long have you been standing there?"

"Not long. I was looking for Stacey."

"She went home."

"Okay, I get it."

I moved past him and my arm brushed his. Something akin to an electric shock raced through me. Before I could stop myself, I said, "What was that?"

He lifted his head. A lock of copper hair hung in his golden eyes as they caught mine. "The pounding of my heart."

Oh. Wow.

41

The Wilsons went to Hawaii for Christmas. Stacey asked me to house sit for the month of December. Mom said okay. It was the third day of Christmas. My evening plans consisted of homemade Chex mix and Russian Tea while watching George C. Scott's *A Christmas Carol*.

Nine o'clock and not a soul in sight. Not even the ghost of Christmas past. Stacey had gone home along with Bev, the cook. Soon, it would be me and the voice of Tiny Tim, "God bless us, every one." Wiping counters, I sang "Holly Jolly Christmas" until gooseflesh rose on my arms. I was being watched.

"A woman who listens to Burl Ives? I think I'm in love." Rich stepped up to the bar.

"I'm closing in fifteen minutes," I said.

He leaned forward, resting his forearms on the counter. "How about a hot cocoa?"

"I'm afraid I'm..." Hot chocolate was innocent. However, the way he was looking at me was everything but. "Whip cream on top?"

"Of course." He sat down. "Will you join me?"

"I'm good. I'm house sitting for Stacey."

Rosemarie. He doesn't need to know your business.

"I'm buying," he said. "Come on. I can't drink alone. You know what they say about people who drink alone."

"They prefer to be by themselves." I set a large mug in front of him, topped with whipped cream and a candied cherry.

"Gotta love a gorgeous woman who knows George Thorogood."

Gorgeous woman? "You can buy me a Pepsi." I filled a glass from the fountain. He was smooth, the most intricate of silk webs. "And don't think buying me a pop is license to get handsy."

He took a sip of his cocoa. "I was thinking of getting handsy, but now it's out there. I'll keep them to myself. Since I have to get my mind off what I'd really like to be doing, which of course is getting handsy, tell me what you're up to."

Charming too? "Not much."

"Do you like working here?"

"Yes."

"I hear you bought a bakery."

"Yes."

"Admirable. Sally's?"

"Mm."

"What got you interested in baking, if I may ask?"

"I've always enjoyed baking. Since I was a kid." My heart beat with anticipation until my insides were on fire. "When my grandma died she left a small fortune in baking utensils."

Rich held his mug up. "Merry third day of Christmas."

We sat in my favorite booth. Wall art: a poster of Barney Fife loading the single round into his revolver.

White Christmas lights draped over the pool table. "Baby It's Cold Outside" played on the restaurant speakers. I glanced at the clock. Midnight.

"I should be going." I slid across the bench.

"Don't go," he said. "I like talking to you."

"We can talk tomorrow." I yawned. "I'm an early bird. My brain doesn't work after eight o'clock."

"Me too," he said, leaning across the table toward me. "I get up and go to the gym at six every morning. Can't sleep past five thirty."

"Me either! I mean about sleeping past five thirty. Not the gym thing. I think it's because I grew up in the country." Okay, don't get into it for all the cheese in Wisconsin.

His golden gaze lit with interest. "Yeah, how was that?"

Bad news shouted from the housetop. "Fine. How should it be?"

"Okaaay," Rich said, pulling his wallet from his pocket. "You want to dance?"

I rang up his tab. "No thank you. I don't dance."

"Come on, it's Christmas. I won't tell if you don't." He held out his hand.

"I'd rather not," I said even as I took it.

"One dance." He pulled me against his hard chest.

My ears thundered, heart pounding in rhythm.

Christmas lights illuminated the dance floor. A passing vehicle created its own moving holiday disco. Cinnamon and scented candles lingered.

"Do you feel it?" His voice was low and all kinds of seductive. "The magic in the air? It's the kind a person could make a wish on."

"Like a star?"

"I don't know." He lowered his head until our lips were inches apart. "Are you going to make one?"

"I believe in God, not magic."

"Me too." We stood, a breath away from a kiss. "I made a wish. Let's seal it," he said in the time it took for his mouth to close over mine. His lips were soft, warm and thrilling. After long, drugging kisses, I became aware of every erogenous zone in my body.

When our lips parted, I could hardly breathe. "Slow down. Let's go back and talk."

"In a minute." He linked his hand with mine, drawing me toward the shadows. Reaching the far corner booth, he stopped and pulled me against him.

Alarm bells went off inside my head. "I need to be going."

"Hey don't tell me you're nervous."

"I don't get nervous."

"Then I'm flattered."

My ears burned hot. "I'm saving myself."

He laughed. "For what?"

"Marriage," I said. "I have to close up. I need you to leave."

"Serves me right. Of all the girls in Welcome, I gotta fall for the one with religion."

Alone once more, I dragged in breaths. Sting sang "Fields of Gold," nothing to do with the Christmas spirit, but a wistful touch to an unexpected evening. A surprising man. I had trouble focusing on my goal for the evening. Which was now bedtime.

42

Stacey set a tall mug in front of Greg at the bar. "My parents gave Dennis the manager position."

"You've done a heck of a job rearranging schedules," Greg said. "Haven't missed a day since you were ten. Dennis is Dennis." His carrot top turned auburn, Greg was tall and thick. A frequent flyer since I started waitressing at Carlton.

"Dennis isn't bad," Stacey said. "He went to Bismarck State College." Stacey had grown up as well, with a straight blonde bob, freckles, and perfect nose.

"Yeah, while you worked your butt off, waiting tables, Dennis drank and schmoozed with women."

Stacey folded her arms. "Rich is our new chef."

Greg belched. "News to me. Rich and I don't talk."

"You should have gone to college, Stacey," I cut in. "You too, Greg. Then we wouldn't have Dingle and Dangle running the joint."

They shared a laugh.

"Why don't you tell us how you really feel, Rosemarie?" Stacey giggled. "Don't hold back."

"Who's Dingle and which one's Dangle?" Greg asked.

I smiled slowly. "Take your pick."

After my shift, I sat at the bar with my supper. The rich scent of aftershave filling my senses, I glanced up as Rich strolled over.

"Mind if I sit next to you?" he asked.

"Okay." I ignored the thumping of my traitorous heart.

He glanced over at me. "I was reading the Bible. The part where it says to trade beauty for ashes. Strength for tears. Gladness for mourning and peace for despair."

"I didn't know you were a Christian."

"There's a lot you don't know about me," he said, his gaze heavy-lidded. "I attended the campus chapel in culinary school."

Icehouse's "Electric Blue" resonated through the bar speakers. "There's a song I haven't heard in a while." Rich smiled. "Funny, I used to think it was, 'I just breeze every time you see through me' but it's 'freeze.'"

I punched his arm. "Me too!"

"So, about last night. You were right. I was out of line." His eyes crinkled in a smile. "Can you blame me?"

"It's okay."

"You want to get married."

"Yes. I mean, not really. I'm more focused on getting the bakery up and running."

"Afterward? Kids? A house, I suppose, and three dogs?"

"I like dogs. I don't want kids."

"A house. Everyone wants a house." His eyes glittered with something I didn't understand. "You want a Pepsi?"

"Yes, please."

The way he took control and pursued me in spite of my desire for abstinence made me light-headed. And he was a Christian. The stars in my eyes dimmed the vision for my future.

43

The Dragon met with the Prince of Hell.

Riding on his steed—a winged lion with a dragon's neck—Asmodeus glided to a halt. Three heads, a bull, a sheep, and a man with pointed ears and a hooked nose crowded above his man-like chest. His abdomen turning into brightly-feathered rooster legs completed Asmodeus' appearance.

The creature was cunning, cruel and wicked down to the core. "Silly woman mistaking clever words for love."

"I want her slave-for-a-lifetime," The Dragon hissed. "She's one of *His*," he spat the word.

"Bossy snake." Fire breathed from the man-head's mouth. "If you talk nice to her and fill her head with sex, she'll see herself as a sex object."

Bull eyes glowed red. "Take it away and she'll get needy and desperate."

"Give her a few crumbs here and there, pat her on the head like a good girl, and she'll sit up and beeeeg." The sheep-head bleated.

"Won't be long before she'll do anything to get a man's attention. Women will loathe her. She'll call them haters. After that, its isolation and punishment," the man-head said.

"She'll fall quickly in line." The bull-head snorted. "Plaguing beautiful virgins with lust is my specialty."

"I'm going to enjoy her body," three heads said in unison.

44

The early afternoon sunset painted winter clouds a pale pink.

The Wilsons' house was decorated to a privileged hilt. Holly, garland, and twinkling white lights. A gigantic tree more real looking than anything from Grandpa's field, swallowed the large living room space. A white mantle lined with snowmen and wise men around a large gas fireplace. Silver and white balls teamed with large silver bows, high-class trimming.

Tommy showed up with rentals from Blockbuster. "I got *The Firm* and *Of Mice and Men.*" He stomped his boots and shed his coat.

"Stacey said to help ourselves to whatever is in the fridge." I hung up his coat.

Tommy made his way to the kitchen. "Wow, look at this spread." He popped a handful of cashews in his mouth. "Let's watch *The Firm.*"

"*Of Mice and Men,*" I said. "You only want to watch *The Firm* because you're not allowed to at home."

There was a knock on the door.

"I'll get it," Tommy mumbled through a mouthful.

It was Rich in a leather coat and blue jeans.

Tommy sized him up. "You lost?"

"Is Rosemarie around?"

"Hi." I made my way over. "We were about to start a movie. Want to join us?"

Rich glanced at Tommy. "Sure, if you don't mind." He removed his boots and whistled. "This place is nice. I always wanted to know what the inside looked like."

Tommy left when the movie was over.

Rich leaned back on the couch, stretching his legs. "Thanks for letting me crash the party."

"It was fun," I said.

"You know, the first time I met Tommy he was throwing up in the dumpster behind Carlton."

"What?" I gave an uncomfortable laugh. "Must have been the stomach flu."

He patted the cushion next to him. "Come here."

I felt his invitation everywhere in my body and sat down. Unsure what to do, I held a stiff pose. He moved over until we were thigh to thigh. "I don't bite," he said, glancing at my lips. "Much."

Russian Tea and conversation continued into the wee hours of the morning. I found myself telling him about my family. I gave a short version of the office door. "I don't really know why I was obsessed about it."

"He was alone for hours in close quarters with your mom," Rich said, scratching his chin. "I don't blame you."

"Let's change the subject." Suddenly, I wished I could go back and untell him. "Really, I'd rather not talk about it anymore."

"No problem." Rich picked up the *Of Mice and Men* movie case. "What did you think of this?"

"That I always win," I said, unease disappearing. "How about you?"

"Good, but no *Princess Bride*."

"I love that movie." I snuggled against him. "Favorite ice-cream?"

"Neapolitan." He slid his arm around me. "Favorite color?"

"Red." I was lost in his eyes, my thoughts scattered. "What about you?"

"Definitely," he said, and then his lips brushed mine. His mouth, hot and soft, shot an electric buzz through my body. Desire was a heady drug. When his hand slipped beneath my shirt, I was dizzy with anticipation. Then, warm fingers were beneath my bra. Warning bells sounded when his hand closed over my bare breast. I pushed it away. "Maybe you should go home now."

Naked heat gleamed in his eyes. "Maybe I should."

Rich showed up the next night, Bible in hand. "I was reading where it talks about fornication. I didn't see any place it says you can't make out."

It didn't sound quite right, but last night had consumed my thoughts. His eyes. His voice. His sleek abdomen that tapered to narrow hips. I imagined his hands on my breasts.

Desire drowned out reason. It would be okay as long as we didn't go all the way. We hit the couch, kissing. His hands came up under my shirt. Probing fingers skimmed across my skin and breasts until all coherent thought escaped my mind. I came to when he tugged at my jeans.

"I need you to go." I pulled away.

A quick surge of anger lit his golden gaze, then as quickly disappeared. "Of course."

The next night, Rich sat down on the far side of the couch.

"What's wrong?" I asked.

"Nothing."

But I felt it. Disappointment radiated from him. The look in his eyes said I'd hurt him. I counted to three and scooted next to him. He glanced over at me. Before I could chicken out, I pulled his lips to mine. He groaned low in his throat and his mouth devoured mine. I let him go a little further.

By the fourth evening we skipped conversation.

The act of intimacy fell vastly short of those painted in a Harlequin novel.

Afterward, the tears flowed. Rich held me for a long while. "I'm sorry, Rosemarie."

It happened again like a thrilling risk. The forbidden nature of it, addicting. I managed to push back the guilt until I was alone. I prayed, asking to be pardoned in a whisper.

Third time, I anticipated the next time.

And the next.

By Friday, I was peeling my shirt off and throwing my arms around him as soon as he walked in the door.

Saturday night there was a knock on the door.

It was Rich wearing a red sweater, dark blue jeans, and devilish smile. "Hello." His eyes shifted behind me. "May I come in?"

"Of course," I said, moving aside, the rich scent of cologne filling my senses as he walked past.

"No Tommy?" He handed me a red present wrapped with a bow.

"Thank you," I said. "Tommy snuck out last night. He didn't come home until two in the morning. I guess he was out with Aaron."

Rosemarie. Shhh.

"Aaron Demit?" A smile worked its way across his face. "That was the kid with him when he had the stomach flu."

He's joking, Rosemarie.

The doorbell rang and Tommy walked in.

"Tommy," I said. "I didn't think you were coming."

"Hey Rosemarie," he said, flicking a glance behind me. "Rich."

From the corner of my eye I saw my bra on the floor. A warm rush flooded my face. I shoved it beneath the couch with my foot.

"Get the movie started already." Tommy plopped down on the overstuffed chair with a bag of chips. "I have to be home by ten."

I shuffled through the movies. *"Nightmare Before Christmas."* I slid the tape into the VCR. "Are you going to help Oliver with the fencing?" Pearl was coming out of the hardware store when Mom was going in. After a brief exchange, Mom found out the Franks were expanding the herd, and that Victor was home for the weekend.

Tommy's brow lifted. "You want to come along?"

My heart gave a funny leap. "Sure," I said. I'd spent an intimate week with Rich. Then, at one mention of the Franks I was already planning what to wear.

"Where?" Rich asked, his eyes on me.

"Pearl Frank's place," I said.

"It's pretty boring," Tommy said in unison.

Odd. Tommy knew about my love for horses. I shot him a glare. "Horseback riding is not boring."

Tommy glared back.

"I used to ride all the time at my uncle's farm," Rich said. "Although, if Rosemarie doesn't want me to go..."

"No, you can come," I said.

Rich reached for my hand on the couch and Tommy scowled. My vision of Victor and a day of riding, sitting by the fire to catch up, and a kiss at the end turned into an awkward evening where Rich followed me everywhere. Suddenly, I felt I had no room to breathe.

45

"You cannot win him over," Amael told sleeping Rosemarie. "His heart is cold." He sensed growing darkness closing in and removed his sword. "Be gone."

A few scattered shadows of insignificance fled. Still, the oppression remained.

A rush of brilliant light and Michael swooped in, wiping out a cluster of shadows creeping beneath her bedroom door.

Amael chased the remaining fog with an order. "He turned her emotions up to maximum, dulling her intelligence and spiritual discernment," he said. "Having sex with him against her better judgement was the last straw. Now she's devalued herself."

"Her core value didn't drop. The way The Almighty sees her remains intact," Michael said.

"He adores her." Amael returned his sword to its sheath. "It's in her own mind she degrades herself. She's unable to see certain behavior beneath her. To the point of believing she deserves to be punished."

"She must choose the path set before her. Life and prosperity or death and destruction," Michael said. "We must go. The Almighty orders us to a stronghold in another region."

Amael gave Rosemarie a wistful look. "Will nothing be done to save her?"

"All has been done."

After a long, restless night, I gave up at four a.m. and reached for the Harlequin romance on the nightstand. Another benefit of housesitting: I didn't have to stash my books between mattresses. I never did find out what Mom did with the confiscated ones. I waited a decent amount of time, and slowly began rebuilding my collection.

Lost in a sea of heat and romance, it was seven a.m. before I surfaced. I reached over to the nightstand for the phone. "Hi Tommy. I wanted to let you know I'm not going to make it. I have a stomach ache."

Silence.

"Are you there? I said..."

"I heard you. Hope you feel better." Tommy hung up.

I dialed Rich's number.

"Hey." His voice was sleep-laden and I felt it in the pit of my stomach.

"I, uh. I'm not going today. Horseback riding, I mean." Talk much, Rosemarie?

"Everything okay?"

"Yes. My stomach bothers me a bit."

"You need anything?" He sounded wide awake now.

"No. I'm fine."

I hung up and went to the kitchen in search of everything to bake gingerbread cookies.

The doorbell rang. Before I could get it, Tommy walked in.

"Hey, Tommy," I said, closing the door behind him.

He whipped around. "Did he say you couldn't go?"

I frowned. "Who?"

He rolled his eyes. "Rich Hamill. Who else? The guy's been buzzing around you like flies on a manure pile."

I scrunched my nose at him. "Nice image, Tommy."

"You've got your head in the clouds, and the guy isn't leaving you alone." Tommy glanced around. "He isn't...here, is he?"

"No." I avoided his eyes. "I haven't done anything wrong."

Except have unprotected sex with Rich Hamill.

Tommy nodded. "Yeah, I told Greg you were smarter than that."

An uneasy feeling worked its way through my belly. "You talked to Greg about it?"

"Not really. He said his brother was moving in on you and I said no way in hell."

"Tommy."

"Sorry, no way in Hades."

"Don't worry. It isn't like that."

Tommy arched his brow. "I'm on my way over to the Franks now if you want to go without him."

My heart leapt in my chest. Then as quickly, the dawn of reality beat a steady rhythm. I couldn't sleep with Rich one day and kiss Victor the next. I slowly shook my head. "No, my stomach hurts."

"I'll tell the Franks you said hi." A pause. "Rosemarie, promise me you won't do anything stupid."

"Promise nothing counts." I crossed my heart.

He gave me a last look and walked out.

Rich stopped by early afternoon. "Holly told Stacey I knocked you up."

"Oh no," I said. The softball girls were talking about us? Summer lies buried deep resurfaced. I wandered over to the couch. What else had they told Rich?

Rich plopped next to me. "Those who spread canards enjoy manipulating others." His eyes rested on my mouth. "Making everyone think they are the victim, and the person they're pitting everyone against is an evil monster tormenting them."

"What?"

He gave me a lazy look. "Who cares what she says?"

"I don't." I sat on my hands. The last thing I wanted was to rehash "Softball Summer." But everyone knew Holly was still burned about Rich breaking up with her. If I had a chance to explain my side...

"There's something I have to tell you," I said. Then, carefully as I could without making light of Softball Summer, I told him about Softball Summer. "I don't know why I did it."

Rich sat in thoughtful silence. And then, "I can't blame you. The whole Malcolm-deal on top of everything else. Plus, they searched your room like you were a criminal and they were prison wardens. You were a pretty good kid if I remember right."

I blinked. "You don't think I'm awful?"

"Nah, I'd say you're pretty normal." His eyes took on a look of admiration. "In fact, I'd say you're pretty perfect."

"I'm far from perfect."

"You're honest and brave. In my book, that makes you perfect." He studied my face. "I like talking to you."

My heart thudded in my ears. "I like talking to you, too."

Monday evening, Greg sat at Carlton bar nursing a tall beer. "You and my brother are getting chummy. Rich doesn't buy the cow when he gets milk for free."

A quick shot of regret slammed in my abdomen and I was suddenly nauseous. "It's not like that."

Greg didn't answer, instead took another long swallow from his beer.

"Can you still see the future?" I pressed my lips together.

"Yes. The Rosemarie I know wouldn't pick Gaston."

"I love *Beauty and the Beast.*"

"It doesn't take a psychic to know he's a tool." Greg drummed the table. "I'm not giving you my rubber stamp of approval."

I frowned. "That's not..."

Colleen and Becky Walsky walked in. They scanned the dining area. I made a b-line for the back door of the kitchen and ducked out.

A few minutes later, Rich opened the door. I grabbed his arm and pulled him out. "Quick, shut the door."

He took advantage of our close proximity, bringing his body, muscular and hard, up to mine. "Why are you hiding out here?"

"The Walskys showed. I'm not up for twenty questions." I shivered.

He ran his hands up and down my arms. "I always thought they were strange. Someone said Becky was a lesbian."

The incredible way every one of my senses came alive was an exhilarating rush. "No. They are Christian ladies," I said, having trouble concentrating.

"I like making you hot and wet." His lips brushed my ear. His suggestive words were clever fingers on my naked thighs and between, made me ache in that very secret of places.

I licked dry lips. "We should go back inside."

"Yeah." Shifting his position until his large thigh was pressed between mine, he said, "What would you say if I told you I want you, right here, right now."

"Someone might see us." I barely recognized the sound of my own voice.

"Maybe, but it would be good. So good, you swollen and slick for me. Tight and ready." His leg rubbed mine.

"We can't," I said, the soft flesh between my thighs began to tingle.

His heavy-lidded gaze roved over my face, lingering. "Say the word and I'll make us forget where we are."

"But we're not married. You don't..." *Love me.* I frowned at the thought. "We can't," I said, scooting away from him.

He threw his hands up. "Then let's get married."

"What?" I couldn't possibly have heard him right. "I've got a bakery to open."

He grinned slowly. "I know a chef."

"I live with my parents."

"I own a house."

"You'd have to talk to my dad." I attempted to move past him.

He moved his body in the way. "I already did. He said to ask you."

The world tilted beneath me. "You asked my dad? How long have you been thinking about this?"

"Forever. Also, I figured since Tommy saw your bra on the floor, I better do something."

My cheeks burned. "He did not."

"I'm pretty sure he did. I'm surprised you left it there."

"I didn't leave it there." I searched my brain for the hundredth time. "I only wish I knew how it got there."

Rich gave me a wolfish smile. "How do you think it got there?"

"Y-yes but we hadn't been in the living room when we...and I wouldn't have..." An image of Stacey and her parents floated through my mind. They trusted me to housesit.

"Who cares, anyway? How about it, Rosemarie? Make me the happiest man alive and say yes."

"Yes." I threw my arms around his neck. "We will be able to make love all we want."

It was a perfect evening. A perfect man.

Perfect everything.

46

We were married the morning of Christmas Eve. A small ceremony in front of the Stutsman County judge. My folks and his mom along with Josie and Donny Gild were in attendance. I wore a dress of white silk. Rich, a charcoal sweater and blue jeans.

Christmas morning, I woke and stretched, admiring my wedding ring. A warm rush flowed through my body from the top of my head to my toes.

Rich opened his eyes, glanced over and gave me a sleepy smile. "Good morning," he said, his voice low and sexy.

"Holy cats, we're married." I giggled.

Rich began to trail kisses down my jawline. "You aren't upset we postponed the honeymoon?"

"A little," I said, tilting my head to give him access.

"Don't forget the bakery." His hot mouth found my neck, sending little shivers up and down my arms. An overwhelming surge of love, powerful and humbling swept over me. He lifted his head. The adoration I felt reflected in his eyes.

Rich took my hand. "Let's go see what Santa got us."

Rich's Charlie Brown tree was on the dining room table. I grabbed his present off the shelf. He tore it open. "A CD. Thanks, Rosemarie." He turned it over. "Michael English."

"I hope you like it." I rubbed my hands together. "Josie helped me pick it out."

"Sure," he said, setting it on the table. He pulled out a box wrapped in green Christmas paper. "Open yours."

A black sweater. I hugged him. "Thank you."

"Why don't you find a movie?" He made his way to the kitchen.

I sat on the floor in front of his entertainment center, and shifted through VHS tapes in the cupboard below the TV.

Rich returned with a bottle and two glasses. "Let's get this party started." He poured a glass and handed it to me.

"I don't believe in drinking. Besides, Mom invited us for Christmas dinner."

"One sip."

"Okay." I took a long swallow, coughing as it burned down my throat. Tears in my eyes, I held the glass away. "What did you say this was called?"

He plopped down on the couch. "Gentleman Jack. Whisky too fine for you to be hacking."

Sinking down on the couch next to him, I took a swig that resulted in a fit of coughing.

"Not like that. A quick swallow before it can burn," he said, taking a sip from his own glass. "Like that."

I complied. "Stuff's not terrible."

Holding his glass up, Rich said, "Here's to a hot wife, a good flick, and a bottle of booze."

He kept our glasses topped off as we watched *A Christmas Story.*

The credits rolled and the phone rang. "I'll get it." Rich stood.

I stretched as the room spun around me. The initial buzz, an inviting heat. Now I felt like I was on a carnival ride.

He returned. "That was your mom. She said dinner is ready."

"Okay." I stood, took a step and fell hard on my side.

"You aren't going anywhere. You've had way too much to drink."

I let my eyes fall shut. "My parents are way cooler than when I was growing up."

Rich snapped his fingers in front of my face. "Well?"

"What?" I slurred.

"I need you to clean up. My mom's coming for supper."

"She's coming here?" I crawled toward the couch to pull myself up. The room spun. I heard Rich say my name as the couch rushed up to greet me.

"I took you out over an hour ago and you're still frozen." I glared at the chocolate cake, bumping into Rich in the small space of the kitchen. "Is the pot roast ready? Holy crumb it's already four-thirty. Where did the time go? I haven't started the tea!"

It was a night for firsts: the first hangover, first Christmas, and first time having dinner with his mother.

Rich gave me a peck on the mouth. "Relax. The cake will thaw in time. I'll make tea. Why don't you go set the table?"

"You're trying to get rid of me." I tugged at the sweater he picked out. "Are you sure I'm dressed alright? You should have gotten a bigger size."

"You look great. Much better than those baggy sweatshirts." His golden gaze was fixed on me. "How's your head?"

"All right. I'm never drinking again, though." I grabbed a stack of plates, nearly dropping them.

"You're lit." Rich chuckled. "It's dinner."

"'Dinner,' he says." I set the plates around the table. "Are you sure you should have accepted this table? Sounds like a family heirloom."

"She'll be pleased as punch we're using it today of all days." He tossed a handful of popcorn in his mouth. "Asked if you were pregnant," he said through a mouthful.

"You set her straight?"

His smile was boyish. "You bet. Besides, what if you are pregnant?"

"If I were pregnant, which I'm not, I would want the discussion between the two of us. Before any outside family members got involved." The booze I'd consumed couldn't be good for a baby. Relax, Rosemarie. You're not pregnant.

"I was joking." He pushed a glass in my hand. "Here, drink this."

"What is it?" I brought it to my lips, the aroma of whisky made my belly roll.

"Hair of the dog." He tipped my hand, pushing the glass to my mouth. "Best thing is to have a glass of the same alcohol that made you drunk."

"Which was your fault." I took a sip, gagging.

"Hey, I didn't force-feed you half the bottle." Rich seasoned mashed potatoes. "Mom's not like your family. I mean, besides her boy-toy, she's pretty uncrazy for the most part."

"Seriously?" I cut him a glare.

There was a knock on the door. It was his mother. Hair dyed fire engine-red, she stood with a bottle of chardonnay. Her date was a chiseled blonde well over six-feet in his mid-thirties. Other than fake-baking, he was gorgeous.

"Come on in." Rich took the bottle from her. "I'm finishing dinner. Mom, you know Rosemarie."

I managed a wobbly smile. "Welcome to our home."

"My pleasure." She eyed me beneath heavy lids.

It was going to be a long evening.

The aroma of rosemary and basal wafted through the air. Rich poured four glasses of chardonnay. He sipped his while putting finishing touches on supper. Marjorie drank hers while perusing our small space with a critical eye. Robert downed his. I sipped mine in the kitchen close to Rich.

Dinner was divine. The roast was tender. Melt in your mouth good. My heart lifted at the thought of many more dinners like this. Chocolate cake was served with coffee. It was moist and delicious.

At last Marjorie spoke, "Rich tells me you're a waitress."

She made no comment about the table.

Rich stabbed a potato. "Rosemarie bought Sally's Bakery, Mom."

"Cool," Robert said.

"*Cool*, Robert dear, isn't the right term. Optimistic is what I would call it." Giving the fork in her hand a scowl, Marjorie asked, "Are you pregnant?"

"Mom, come on." Rich rolled his eyes.

I wiped my mouth with a napkin. "No."

"Nothing like adults wanting to play house." Her fine brow arched.

Robert took a sip of wine. "Cut 'em some slack, Marjorie. They're in love."

Marjorie dropped her napkin on her plate and stood. "We must be going, Robert." She waved a hand at Rich. "We'll let ourselves out."

After she was gone, Rich burst into laughter. "I guess I was wrong. Mom's totally crazy. Poor Robert."

"The bakery is happening," I said, willing away the sinking feeling in the pit of my stomach.

He pushed his chair away. "Of course it is. But now that they're gone, do you want to..."

"Yes."

Rich made his way over, sweeping me into his arms.

Laughing, I grabbed the bottle of wine from the table. "Now you can have your way with me."

His smoldering gaze caught mine. "Most definitely."

N ew Year's Day at the country house included a skating party.

Not at the Franks, but a pond Tommy had been working on. He didn't say much. Dark fog hung over him. I hoped it would hurry up and pass. Back at the house, the tree was fake and decorations, sparse.

At the dinner table, Steve announced he was going to farm in the spring. His bride was cute, kind of quiet. I wished for solitude to ask my brother what he thought of the whole me-getting-married thing. The window of opportunity never presented itself. I guess if he had a problem with me and Rich he would have said so. Before dinner was over Steve had another announcement:

Mary was having a baby.

47

Michael English singing "Holding Out Hope To You" on the stereo, I baked a cake in my new bakery. The first without a glitch.

Rich walked in and tossed his jacket on a chair by the back door. He cocked his ear. "What are you listening to?"

I turned the volume down. "Go sit down."

"Okay." He plopped down at the table closest to the checkout counter.

Black sofas and overstuffed chairs were scattered about. Large windows on both sides brightened dark walls. Twin oak shelves in the far corner held art for sale. The opposite corner was a six-foot statue of the Eiffel Tower.

"Ta da." I brought out the masterpiece: my first mini Fault Line cake.

"Nice, Rosemarie. Got milk to go with this?"

"Um, yeah." I brought him a glass and then sliced two generous pieces.

He was watching me. "You're not going to eat that."

"I was." I picked up my fork.

"Is it on your diet?"

"Well no. I know I said I wanted to lose twenty pounds, but..." My cheeks grew warm. "I thought...I mean, this is the first pretty one."

"I've never had the knack for baking. Drove one college professor nuts."

"You're a chef."

"Which takes an artist's mind. Baking is more of a science." He took a bite of the cake. "Not bad."

Not bad? I took a bite. Not only good, but melt-in-your mouth delicious. Wasn't it? I forked another mouthful.

"Go easy, Rosemarie. You want to get rid of that muffin top don't you?" He took another bite. "This is pretty good."

Hope carried me away on its wings. "Bread, baked goods, cupcakes. You name it, I'll bake it. That's what I'll call it."

Rich dug into his piece. "Name's too long."

"I can't call it Sally's."

A slow smile worked its way across his face. "We'll come up with something."

"You liked it?" I searched for a shred of validation.

He shrugged. "Cake was a little dry, but the frosting was good."

"Dry?" I touched the moist center. It wasn't a bit dry. Was it? I poked again. Didn't seem like it, but maybe it was. I pushed the plate away, willing myself not to cry.

He scowled. "It's not anything to blubber about."

A thought, quick and fleeting, popped into my head. "What do you think about soup and sandwiches for lunch?" I asked. "We already have the dining area for customers who want coffee and the local scuttle."

He tapped his chin. "I'm not sure if baking all night is conducive to serving lunch guests."

My heart began to race. "You can make the soup ahead of time and freeze it. We'll keep it warm in my roaster. I'll bake bread the night before and you can prepare the sandwiches."

Rich stretched his legs out. "Work for the wife, huh?"

"You can keep your job at Carlton. That won't change. You're shift there doesn't start until four. You could quit serving here around two. I mean, why not?"

He gave an easy grin. "Why not, indeed."

48

April 6, 1994, an aircraft carrying Rwandan president Juvénal Habyarimana and Burundian president Cyprien Ntaryamira was shot down.
The TV was on a Charles Manson special. Manson gave his people psychedelic drugs he didn't take. August 8, 1969, four followers killed without remorse. Manson got prison. His girls held hands, singing down the corridor while wearing eerie smiles. Manson uttered not one word in their defense.

"Greg's engaged to Susan Sharp," Rich said.

"I played softball with Susan. She's pretty nice."

"She know you two are tight?"

"Greg and I aren't tight. Even less now than when we were kids."

"Better not be lying." His eyes bore into mine.

Heat crept up my neck. "I don't lie."

"He's my brother and all, but Greg's always been a little different," he said with an air of superiority.

"Different how?"

"Like when he was five he had a fascination with dolls."

"He was a kid. Who cares?"

"Mom. She dressed him like a girl. Frilly pink dresses and patent leather shoes with bows."

"Ouch." Marjorie Hamill was feared in every women's circle for being the best at everything.

"Then he started seeing things."

"Ghosts." I got between him and the TV with a sultry smile. "There's only one Hamill on my mind."

Rich pulled his eyes away from the screen. "What are you wearing?"

"A shirt I got from Josie. I wanted to look nice for you."

"Does it make you look, I dunno—" he scrubbed his chin "—stocky?"

My hands flew to the red material. "Does it?"

"No." His eyes returned to the TV. "Did you ever hear about Nannie Doss? Went through five husbands before being caught and charged with a bunch of murders. All her husbands, a mother-in-law, her sisters and two of their children. Even her own mother."

"How horrible." I took a step back, thoughts of sex vanishing. My mind searched the dresser for a different shirt. "God's heart must be broken."

"God," he spat the word. "Who needs God when you got me, baby?"

He's trying to be funny.

"Nannie Doss was never put to death because she was a woman. Died 1965 in prison when she was fifty-nine."

"Not good," I said, because what else was there to say?

49

Mail in hand, I burst through the back door of Hamill's Bakery. Rich was sharpening knives in the kitchen.

"What's this?" I marched over to him, waving a credit card statement under his nose.

He looked up. "Looks like a bill to me."

"I know what it is," I said, fire burning in my veins. "What I don't understand is this charge for six-hundred thirty-two dollars."

"Oh that. I'll pay it off." He ran the blade across the stone. *Zip. Zip.* "I made pretty good tips this week. I figured it out. If I pick up two extra shifts a week at Carlton, I should have the gun paid off in three months."

"Gun?" I screeched. "You never said anything about buying a gun. Why do you need a gun?"

"For burglars. I'm going to keep it in the nightstand next to the bed." He lined up knives. "When I put you in charge of the checkbook, you said you'd be able to handle it."

"I can."

"Remember? You were mad because I suggested you hire Katie Marsh to manage the books at Hamill's."

"I could. I mean, I can." Truth was, Math wasn't my best subject. "I'll hire someone but not her."

"What's wrong with Katie?"

I shrugged. "She's been giving me a bad vibe ever since Softball Summer."

His brow arched. "I'm sure they've forgotten by now you're a liar."

"I'm not a liar." I gritted my teeth.

"If you can't manage a simple thing like a personal checkbook, I don't see how you can keep restaurant inventory and expenses. You even said it yourself. You were way off on your math."

"I'm not but if you don't..."

"Probably all the booze you buy."

"One twelve pack. Besides, what about the bottles of whisky you keep on the top shelf?"

"A six hundred-dollar mistake could hurt the bakery."

I watched him tuck the serrated blade in place, fingers of frustration poking at my backside. "We are supposed to discuss all expenditures."

"My bad. I thought you would freak out."

"I would not. I—" was freaking out. "I'm saying, let me know next time. Fifty bucks in the bank and still four days until payday."

He folded up the knife bag. "A good lesson for you, Flower Child. Keep a closer eye on it."

My eyes narrowed. "Flower Child? Now you're making fun of the country house?"

"No, you're beautiful like a flower."

The anger drained from me. "I really am good at math, but apparently really bad at communicating with you."

"It's a slump. We'll get past it."

So he said about sex. We hadn't made love since...I pushed it from my mind. We were good. "Seriously, let me know if you spend money."

"I will." He crossed his heart. "Scout's honor."

"You're not a scout."

"I know."

"I mean it," I said.

"Aye aye, Captain." He saluted me.

50

"Hey Rosemarie." Victor stood at the end of the isle in Walsky Grocery. He wore a light blue shirt. His hair had grown, a lock of blonde hanging in his eyes. He looked good. Really good.

"Hey Victor. I didn't know you were home."

"I had to take care of some business for Mom. I heard you're married." His blue eyes lifted, catching mine. Pain was reflected in their depths. I saw sorrow over the finality of the situation. Felt the punch in the gut when he couldn't breathe.

"I hurt you," I whispered.

He gave a sad smile. "Are you happy?"

"Yes," I said. Not that love was the same as in movies, but... "I'm very happy."

"I thought..." He shoved his hands in his pockets. "Doesn't matter what I thought."

Maybe the same as me. I wouldn't be able to go over to his house for horseback riding or marshmallow eating. It wasn't going to happen anyway since we were adults. "My bakery opens June 15. You should come check it out."

He nodded. "I'll do that. The cookies you made me for graduation were fantastic."

"Keeps me from talking non-stop."

"Shadow work." There was a smile in his response. "I'm happy you're making a future turning a weakness into strength."

"What are you...?"

"Rosemarie?" Rich came around the aisle. "There you are."

Victor held out his hand. "You must be Rich."

Rich shook it. "Guilty. And you are...?"

"Victor Frank. Rosemarie and I are old friends."

"Rosemarie and I are husband and wife." Rich released his hand. "Frank, huh? Related to Pearl Frank?"

"That would be my mom," Victor said.

Blood roared in my ears, and I no longer cared that I was in for it. "Good seeing you, Victor. Rich, we should be going." I pushed Rich to the car for the longest ride. To a house not home, and a man I didn't know.

"What did he want?" Rich asked.

"Nothing," I said, wishing he had wanted something and that made me bad. I was married to Rich Hamill. A tidal wave of misery crashed over me. How was it possible to have made such a colossal mistake?

"You aren't lying?" Resentment radiated from him, heavy and uncompromising. And then he chuckled. "Did I ever tell you the one about loyalty? If you lock your dog in the trunk of your car for a day, when you go to open it you'll see how happy he is. Your wife, not so much."

"Why would you lock your wife in the trunk of your car?"

"Lighten up. You wouldn't. It's a joke." His laughter stopped. "I trust you Rosemarie. It's the guys I don't trust."

At home, Rich sat in front of the TV with a blank stare. No smile. No frown. The empty void devoured living room space.

"What's wrong?" I asked, climbing onto his lap.

His eyes were fixed on the screen and he leaned his head away from me.

"You okay?" I asked.

Hatred resonated from him, familiar and damning. *It can't be.*

Not Rich. Not my husband. Everyone loved him. He was the life of the party. He enjoyed making love to me and wasn't holier-than-thou. He was feeling depressed.

"I'll clean up here," I said, slowly getting off his lap. "Are you sure you're okay?"

Angry silence.

I yawned. "Well nights are a killer. I'm going to sleep." I retreated to the bedroom.

"Rosemarie!" Rich's enraged shout came from the kitchen. I jumped from the bed, tucking the latest Stephanie Laurens' novel between mattresses.

"Where are you?" Rich's voice dripped with fury. I dashed to the kitchen. He stood at the sink piled with dirty dishes. There was broken glass at his feet. His eyes were black. "I came in here to make myself a sandwich, and the place is filthy. Dishes haven't been done since who knows when."

I blinked. "Is that all? I'll do them before I head to the bakery."

"What a pig." He scooped up a stack of plates, smashing them on the floor.

My mouth dropped. "What..."

He shot me a murderous look. "You see what you made me do?" He stormed out, slamming the door.

I stood for what seemed an eternity in shock. Then I began to cry. I made my way over to the sink, shame washing over me. Dishes clattered as I took my anger out on the nasty pile.

I was finishing up the silverware when Rich returned. Gone was the rage. He seemed almost cheerful. He eyed me a moment. "What's wrong?"

"Nothing." I blinked back fresh tears.

"Don't be so sensitive." Rich pulled me into his arms. I hugged him back and he started bumping his pelvis against my hip.

"Quit it." I scowled and pulled away.

"You don't think I'm funny," he said in his hurt voice. "Most women think I'm hilarious."

"I'm just tired. I'm going to try to get some sleep before work."

"Don't be mad." He dipped for a kiss. I turned my head and it landed on my cheek. He rumpled my head. "Such a serious wife."

51

Last night, Nichole Simpson and Ron Goldman were stabbed to death outside her condominium in Los Angeles. O.J. Simpson's attempt to escape was live TV, seen by ninety-five million viewers—and hundreds of fans lined the streets to support him.

Rich grabbed a can of beer from the fridge. "I don't know if I should be more impressed you bought a thirty-six pack, or that ten of them are gone already."

"Hardly," I said. "I only had two."

"You do know beer math, right? That means you had six." He cracked it open and took a long swallow.

Working nights had taken its toll. A beer before bed. When one didn't cut it, I upped it to two. "What difference does it make?"

"It doesn't." He shrugged. "Is all this beer in the budget?"

I yawned. "I'm going to bed."

I lay awake in bed. I didn't have a problem. One case of beer hadn't made a hole in the bank account. I could balance a budget. My eyes grew heavy.

Sleep, the elusive beast, took over at last.

The next thing I knew, Rich towered over me with a look of contempt. "You fell asleep during a fight. I would never have done that to you. What kind of person are you?"

I blinked. "What are you talking about?"

"Forget it." He stormed out, slamming the bedroom door.

Once again, I drifted to sleep before I could figure out what I'd done.

The late afternoon sun poured through the bedroom window. I tried to stretch away the groggy on-another-planet sensation. Then I remembered Rich's fury. Falling asleep had been thoughtless.

A high-pitched scream erupted from the dining area. Instantly wide awake, I bolted out of bed and ran.

The kitchen was empty.

The front door was open. Rich climbed the steps, leaning heavily on the railing. "You deal with it," he said, a wild look in his eyes. "I hate them."

"You hate what?" I glanced around. The sun was shining above a cloudless sky. Birds chirped. Grass, green as...there was a movement in the thick of it.

If it had been on fire, Rich couldn't have moved faster. "Get it away from me." He fell back on the steps.

"It's only a garter snake." I picked it up by the tail and flung it.

He gave a shaky laugh. "Show off."

Saturday night we went out for a drink. I brought the latest Stephen King and picked a quiet table at Carlton.

Rich stood at the counter waiting for drinks. Kiley Miller, a busty blonde, bustled behind it. She set a drink in front of him. "This one's on me."

"You didn't have to," he said with a broad grin.

Greg got up from his position at the end of the bar counter. "Mind if I join you, Rosemarie?"

"Please do," I said. "Do you remember Keep Kool Kids?"

A melancholy smile touched his lips. "Keep Kool Kids were awesome."

"It was a sad day when I learned about KKK."

"We were Keep Kool Kids."

"Duane Sim was afraid of snakes, right?" I took a sip of beer.

He gave a puzzled look. "Maybe. I don't really remember."

"Did we ever figure out what was wrong with him?" I drove a fry through the mustard.

Rich made his way over and plopped down next to me. "Okay, I'll bite. Mustard on French fries?"

Greg set his beer down. "I'll take another, Kiley."

"How about some water." She set a tall glass in front of him.

Greg slammed both hands on the table. "I want another drink."

Rich stood, puffing his chest out. "I think you've had about enough."

He held up a hand. "Wait a minute. Wait now."

"Greg, maybe you should go." Sweat tickled the back of my neck.

Greg pulled his wallet from his pocket. "Ah, you ain't worth it."

"He's got problems," Rich said after Greg left. "Did you hear what he said to you?"

"Me?" I blinked. "He was talking about you."

He shrugged. "I could have sworn he was staring straight at you."

I spent the rest of the evening trying to remember who Greg was looking at.

52

Soup and sandwiches were a big hit at Hamill's Bakery. Pairs were scattered about the dining area couches with lattes. A business man was at a table for two with a client.

Baked goods to order. A week passed, and there were no baked goods ordered. I caught Pastor Brady and Karen after Sunday brunch, and asked, "How was your lunch?"

"Great. Best in town," Karen said. "Your husband makes a mean soup."

"Thank you." I avoided Pastor Brady's eyes. I hadn't been to church since I got married. I had no excuse other than Rich would rather attend "The Bedside Baptist" with "Pastor Pillow" and I didn't want to attend alone.

I held up the bakery menu. "Have you seen we take orders? Cookies, muffins, doughnuts, Kuchen, pastries. I make a mean lemon tart. Something baked for all your special events," I said, my face flushed.

"We're stuffed." Karen patted her tummy. "Maybe next time."

"How are you doing, Rosemarie?" Pastor Brady asked.

Quick, sudden tears sprang to my eyes. "I..."

"Rosemarie?" Rich's voice brought me back to reality.

"Over here." I waved.

"Hang on," he said when the phone rang.

"You know, can I take a look at the menu?" Karen asked, holding her hand out. "There's a potluck coming up next week."

"Sure," I said, hoping she would pick something before Rich ended his phone call.

After they left, Rich asked, "What'd they want?"

I perused the ticket. "They ordered chocolate and vanilla popovers."

"I suppose now we'll have to attend church."

I looked up. "There were no strings attached."

"You stupid woman." Rich sighed. "There's always strings attached."

53

Holly and Rich were huddled around the stovetop when I arrived at Hamill's. I slowed down at the sight of Holly in tight jeans and a pink tee next to Rich.

Rich looked up. "Hey Rosemarie. I've got something for you to try."

I took a step back. "What is it?"

He flashed a boyish smile. "A burger." He turned the plate around. The hamburger patty was topped with melted cheddar cheese, onion rings and barbeque sauce on a fresh-baked bun.

"I gotta go," Holly said, flashing Rich a wistful glance.

Rich gave a nod. "You bet."

"What was that about?" I asked when she left.

He topped the burger with the bun and handed it to me. "Try it."

"Okay." I reluctantly took a bite. It was as delicious as it looked.

Rich's gaze was expectant. "It's good, right? So I hired Holly."

My ears began to buzz. "You what?"

"This way you could open for supper if you wanted."

"I don't."

"Alright, then it would be a chance to expand the menu."

"It's a bakery, not a bar and grill."

"I already hired her. She starts tomorrow." His cheerful tone was laced with annoyance.

"Then unhire her."

His expression went blank. "Fine." He turned and walked out.

It didn't feel fine. It felt bad. It was still dark at seven a.m. when I arrived home the next morning, prepared for battle. Rich didn't say a word. He sat in front of the TV in cold silence.

I blew out a breath. "I know you're upset, but I don't see how I can justify hiring her."

"I'm not upset," he said in a quiet voice.

"Also, I wish you would have asked me before hiring someone. You made me look bad."

Misery swallowed the space around him.

I sighed. "I don't know why I bother telling you. You don't listen anyway."

His eyes came up with murderous rage. "I was listening."

"What's wrong?" I cursed the tremble in my voice.

He got up and took a step toward me. "You're questioning me."

I took a step back, sudden, stupid tears burning my eyes. "I'm sorry. I..."

"Stop crying," he shouted, picked up Mr. Toad and threw him against the floor. The ceramic frog shattered.

My mouth opened but no words came out.

"Control freak," he muttered, turned and stomped out.

Alone, the tears flowed. I picked the fragments up off the floor. This was my life. There was no way out alive. Truth was a heavy weight in an oppressive afternoon.

I was in bed when Rich returned. He stood in the doorway. "You sleeping?"

"Um, no." I sat up and smoothed my hair.

"You sick?"

"My stomach hurts."

He leaned on the doorframe. "Join the club. My stomach's been killing me all day." A pause. "I need help for the lunch crowd. So hire someone or come in yourself."

Feeling completely drained, I scooted to the edge of the bed. "I suppose it wouldn't be the end of the world if she worked for us." My lip quivered. "I wish you hadn't smashed my frog. It was my grandma's."

"And I wish you wouldn't have disrespected me." His eyes studied me a minute more. "You want to call Holly and let her know, or should I?"

"You go ahead. I'm tired."

A sound worked its way into the deepest of sleeps. It took several rings to realize it was the phone. I answered it. "Hullo."

"Holly called in sick. I need you to come in," Rich said.

"What time is it?" My mouth felt like it was full of cotton.

"Eleven-thirty. You can go back to bed afterward." He hung up.

In a sleepy-fog, I stumbled to the bathroom and splashed water on my face. Donning the pair of jeans I discarded an hour before, I hurried out the door. He wasn't lying. Hamill's parking lot was full. Inside, there was a long line at the checkout counter. Every couch, stuffed chair and table was occupied.

"Who's next?" I asked him, grabbing a ticket book.

"I'll take orders. You serve soup and make sandwiches."

"What? I..."

"I'll mess it up. You make a mean sandwich." He winked.

"Fine," I said, pride reached up and grabbed hold of my heart.

The first order was burgers.

"Soup and sandwiches only," I told him.

"Come on, it's for Mark and Abigale," he said. Mark Dickerson was the new town police officer. Abigale his fiancé, was a stylist and opened "Hair by Abigale."

"I told them they could get a burger," he said.

"Then untell them."

"Have a heart. Mark gave me a ride home from the bar the other night when I was hammered."

I sighed. "Fine. But no more."

"We make a great team, right Rosemarie?" Rich said in his happy voice.

We. "Right."

54

"Sallaaay," Rich drawled the voice of Dr. Finkelstein in the narrow doorway of our bathroom. "You can come out now if you promise to behave."

"Hey, do you mind?" I stood, pulling my pants up.

Rich flipped on the faucet. "Why aren't you dressed? Costume didn't fit or what?" He lathered shaving cream.

"I don't feel like going out." I moved around him and stepped outside the bathroom.

"I guess I could whip something up here." He dragged the razor across his face.

And I could go to bed early. "No, we can go."

"We'll knock 'em dead."

We arrived at Carlton ten minutes after nine.

Spooky costumes: a perfect tradition for adults pretending to be someone else.

The sports lounge was decked in all the usual props: spider webs, witches and black cats. From behind the bar, smoke rose from a small steam maker.

In a black velvet witch costume, Kiley strolled over and glanced at Rich's blue police garb and my jailbird dress. "Cute. What can I get you two?"

Rich sat down. "Jack Coke for me please and thank you."

"Same for me." I took the bar stool next to him.

Holly made her way over in a nurse's outfit that had the eyes of every warm-blooded male following her. The form fitting white dress barely covered her booty. A zipper in front put her bountiful cleavage on display. Fishnet stockings, knee-high stiletto boots, and a 'come hither' look completed the costume.

I suddenly felt dowdy, wishing I would have worn heels. Then again, maybe not. I probably would end up falling flat on my face.

"I'll take whatever you got for sale on tap," she told Kiley.

Rich glanced at me. "Mind if I have one more?"

"No." I nibbled a fry, totally ready to go home. Etiquette said at least another hour to be social. I searched for a way to get rid of Holly. I didn't like her around my husband or my bakery.

After the third glass of whisky I tugged on Rich's arm. "I think I'm ready to go."

"In a minute." He leaned toward Holly. "Did you see the Browns? I thought they were going to kill each other for sure."

My ears perked up. The fight was about an undercooked burger the day Holly called in sick. When Adam and Janette Brown showed up and ordered a burger, I caved and made two more.

Holly snatched a glance at me. "I heard she was still yelling at him outside their car. Someone called the cop."

"They did?" Rich held his thumb to his ear. "'Yes, Officer? Could you tell my husband the burger was raw?"

She laughed. "He answers, 'Make it yourself next time.'"

"I don't feel good." I stood, caught my foot on the bar stool and landed rear-end up.

Rich helped me to my feet. "Enough whisky for you," he said, laughter in his voice. Outside he shot me a glare. "I told you to order water between drinks."

"I'm sorry. It was dark," I said.

Rich scowled. "You made a fool of yourself."

I patted his arm. "It was an accident. Wouldn't have happened if you had taken me home when I asked instead of drooling over Nurse Holly."

"Rosemarie," my name, a weary word on his lips. "You don't trust me. That hurts."

"Fine. Next time I'll hang with..." I searched my inebriated brain, "...Greg."

His face came right next to mine. "No you won't." Abruptly, he picked me up and dumped me in the passenger seat.

Silence ensued.

Rich pulled in front of our house and cut the engine.

The eggshell walk was old, booze, liquid courage. "I dunno, maybe we need a break."

"A break is what someone takes at work to drink coffee." He made his way around the truck and opened my door. "You are mine. Always and forever, you are mine."

A thrill raced up my spine at the possessive statement, chased by an ominous shiver of dread.

55

Carlton bar was decked in white lights, crowded with patrons wearing party hats waiting for Y2K and the havoc it was predicted to wreak.

"People panic. Swat they do," Rich said.

Kiley set a drink in front of him. "I hear it could be pretty bad."

"Massive power failures. Financial records, gone. Planes falling from the sky." I took a pull of my beer. "You imagine if a missile was launched by mistake?"

"Um hum," Kiley said, moving to the next table.

Rich scowled at me. "You're wearing lipstick."

My hand flew to my mouth. "Well, yes. It's New Year's and I thought it looked rather nice. You don't like red?"

"Not really." I leaned toward him. He leaned back. "Oh no. I'm not kissing you wearing lipstick."

I giggled. "You're wearing lipstick?"

"Ten...nine...eight..."

Voices filled with excitement, patrons ushered in the New Year with the countdown.

"Six...Five..."

"Getting kind of tired," he said, his mouth drawn in a firm line.

"Three..."

He stood. "Wipe that stuff off your mouth. I'll be in the car."

"...One."

"What?" I asked, but he was gone. Cheers, hoots and hollers ensued amidst couples kissing. The sky hadn't fallen. The world didn't explode. Nothing drastic changed. Not even me, sitting alone in light of a new millennium.

The For Sale by Owner sign next door was covered with *Sold.*

It looked like a young couple moved in. Our age probably. A toddler, maybe a year or two. I baked a cake. It didn't turn out. I dumped it in the trash. A "forever diet" is what I told people when they asked me my secret.

Cookies it was. They turned out perfect. I'd gotten really good at decorating.

"Not bad, Rosemarie." I caught a glimpse of my reflection on my way out the door. My hair had grown, humidity awarding wild chocolate curls.

I knocked on the neighbor's door. An eternity later, a woman with straight blonde hair coming to a perfect point below her chin eyed me through the crack. A baby started to cry and that's when I noticed the sign *Baby's Sleeping* taped beneath the door knob.

"I live at Rosemarie. My name's next door." I thrust the cookies at her, turned and hurried home. "Let me know if there's anything you need."

Rich walked in the front door. "You sure made an impression on the neighbors."

"Really?" I asked, my cheeks flushed from oven heat. Perhaps she liked the cookies after all. My belly warmed at the thought. They were pretty fantastic.

"Yeah. They caught me on the way in. Said you woke their baby and can't read."

"Oh man." I put my hand on my forehead. "I was a complete idiot. I went over there but didn't see the sign until after the baby started crying."

"Funny," Rich said.

"Maybe I should bake her an apology cake."

"I wouldn't, Flower Child. I didn't want to hurt your feelings, but she called you trailer trash among other choice words."

"Really?" I asked, feeling a foot smaller. "Why would she call me that?"

"Jealous. There's chicks for you. Hate anyone who looks better than they do."

"Do you think so?"

"I know so." His gaze dropped to my shirt. "Is that what you were wearing when you went over there?"

"Yes." I automatically glanced down at the cherry red top. "Why? What's wrong with it?"

"Nothing." His eyes came back up, a wealth of satisfaction in them. "You look real good."

I didn't like the way he said *real good like I was an option on a menu.*

"I have a few minutes if you want to..." He motioned toward the bedroom.

Any desire for sex went out with the trailer trash comment. All the time, money and effort to look good. Hours at the gym to achieve a body I could pour into tiny clothes only to look like trailer trash.

But I couldn't remember the last time Rich offered. And sex proved there was nothing wrong with us. There must be something wrong with the T-shirt if the neighbor called me trailer trash.

56

A rosy sunset peeked through skeletal trees. Ghosts, ghouls and goblins ran through the streets.

At Carlton, we met Josie and her husband, Daniel Spick, a well-dressed lawyer with a quiet manner. Now, Josie was well dressed too.

She squeezed me tight. "How are you doing?"

"Great. Swollen ankles, heartburn, and I crave ice-cream and bacon twenty-four seven. Not to mention being big as a house."

"She doesn't mean that." Rich reached over, rubbing the back of my neck.

I frowned. "I mean every word of it."

"You don't seem like yourself, Rosemarie," Josie said. "How are you feeling?"

"Other than being pregnant? Peachy."

"Josie and I were talking the other day," Daniel said.

"I suppose couples do those things." I sat up straight, pushing my hand into my lower back.

Josie drew a breath. "I told Daniel about Malcolm."

I scowled. "Really? That was so long ago. If you wanted to do something about it, why not back then?"

They exchanged uncomfortable looks. She laid a hand on my arm. "Women believe in going to the doctor if they're sick, but no one wants to admit when they need to talk to someone."

"Someone as in..."

"A counselor. They even have medication safe for pregnancy."

"I'm pregnant, not crazy."

"I didn't say you were crazy." Josie's eyes went from Daniel to Rich, and back to me.

Daniel cleared his throat. "So anyway, do you know if you're having a boy or girl?"

"Boy."

The ride home was silent. My gut said it was because I didn't act like a happy wife in front of Josie. I'd rather Rich yell from the rooftops and get it over with. His stonewalling made me feel like nothing.

At last he spoke, "Daniel is looking into taking legal action against Malcolm."

Dread slithered along my spine. "You can't be serious."

His eyes narrowed. "Why would you protect him?"

"Hmm, let's see." I held my chin. "They are my folks. The thought of dragging them through the mud doesn't appeal to me. He was three years older than me. Sixteen at the time so not a legal adult. Besides, it happened over a decade ago."

His eyes took on a sudden gleam. "You know, maybe you should stay with your folks for a while."

"Why? What would I tell them?"

He shrugged. "Whatever you want."

"You can't make me. The bakery's mine."

"I can. The house is mine. Close the bakery for all I care," he said. "I'll go back to Carlton. They lost half their customers when I started working for you."

"Please don't do this," I begged, hating myself for it but couldn't seem to stop. "I'll do whatever you want. Please..."

"You're the one who wants a break, a break you shall have."

The atmosphere said we were done talking. His stone-cold eyes said it was my fault.

He dropped me off at the country house.

"Hey Mom, sorry I didn't call. I'm working on something for the Bakery," I fudged my way through the front door. "Can I use your kitchen?"

"Rosemarie. Glad you're here." She glanced behind me. "Did Rich come?"

"Nope. He's got the lunch crowd tomorrow."

"How long can you stay?"

Um... "Until Sunday."

"You missed Steve, Mary, and their bunch. Baby Dana sure is getting big. And guess what? Mary's pregnant again."

"Nice." The baby inside me kicked.

"Josie and Daniel were here. Tommy is home. He got a dog." Mom opened the fridge. "Should we have hamburger hot dish?"

"Yum." I stuffed my pride to make the next request. "If I could use your kitchen to bake bread, I would appreciate it."

"Speaking of foodstuffs..." Mom handed me a pamphlet.

"What's this?" I turned the trifold over.

"WIC assistance. You should make an appointment and get on it right away. They give the mother beans, cheese, cereal, milk and eggs, I think. When the baby's born you can get formula."

"I was going to nurse."

"I mean when you go back to the restaurant."

"Bakery."

She gave me a funny look. "That's what I meant."

"I don't really want to be on welfare. I own a business."

"You pay taxes," Mom said. "It's for when you need it. Janette Brown works in the office. She's a bit of an airhead, but it's worth a try."

"I'll check it out," I said, suddenly exhausted.

Tommy strolled in the kitchen without a hello.

"What time are you going over to the Franks tomorrow?" Mom asked.

He mumbled something.

"Can you give the girls a ride?" This time there was an edge to her tone. "They'll be ready after school."

"I told Oliver I'd be there by seven-thirty."

"I guess I'll let Josie know," Mom said.

I wanted to go to the Franks more than a rare piece of steak, but not with Nosey Josie and Steve's gang. I caught Tommy at the foot of the stairs. "Can I go with you in the morning?"

"I don't care," he said. "Be ready by seven fifteen or I'm leaving without you."

57

It was still dark at seven when I arrived at Tommy's car. The ride was a silent affair. Not a Rich silence. Rather—early morning grouchy brother— quiet. I imagined the Franks' reaction when they saw me.

Pearl answered the door. "Rosemarie! You're in time for breakfast." She eyed my belly. "Your mother told me you were expecting. You look so beautiful."

A warm rush flowed through me. "Thank you."

The Grandfather clock bells began to chime. Seven-fifteen.

"Hey look who's here," Oliver said as I stepped into the dining room. "Rosemarie. How have you been?"

"Good," I held my breath, waiting for him to ask why I'd come.

He didn't, instead his two blonde girls came over. One sucking her thumb, the older had sapphire eyes. "I'm Emily. She's Toots." Blue Eyes pointed at her little sister.

Toots took her thumb out of her mouth. "I'm two."

"Her name is Paige, but Emily started calling her 'Toots' and it stuck," Lauren said.

Oliver's wife was tall and athletic with platinum hair. Their girls looked like her. Mom told me Oliver and Lauren met at Bismarck State College.

There was a spread on the breakfast table. A tray with maple syrup, strawberry sauce and whip cream. Sausage links and a plate of butter, all chocked full of calories. Orange juice in a clear pitcher, a carton of milk and ice water in clear glasses.

Pearl poured coffee. "Do you take cream and sugar with your coffee?"

"I'd love some, thanks," Tommy said.

She set an array of various teas in front of me. "Here you are, Rosemarie."

"Rosemarie." Victor walked in. A black cowboy hat, pearl button shirt and blue jeans brought me back to the day I asked him if he was a cowboy.

I was keenly aware of my puffy cheeks and swollen belly. "How have you been?"

"Real good." He swiped his hat off and plopped it on the window sill. "I didn't expect to see you." He sat across from me. "You know, I was out with Sheldon."

"How's he doing?" I took a sip of tea.

"Misses you." He leaned on his forearms, his eyes sparkling. "You want to go down to see him?"

"Is the snow white?"

"After breakfast then." He scooted up to the table. "You brought warm clothes?"

"Of course," I lied.

He scrubbed his jaw. "We have extra gloves and hats in case."

"Let's pray, shall we?" Pearl held out her arms. We grabbed hands next to us, and she prayed, "Lord, for what we are about to receive we are truly grateful. Thank you for Rosemarie, Tommy, and the time together. Amen."

"Amen." All eyes lifted.

"When is your baby due?" Pearl asked in her boisterous voice.

I drew a breath. "The end of April."

Victor's eyes caught mine. "Congratulations."

The phone rang. "I got it." Oliver got up and answered the wall phone. "It's for Rosemarie."

"Me?" My belly hollowed with fear. Rich. "Hey, what's up?" I said, moving away as far as the phone cord would let me.

"Who was that?" He punched out each word.

"It's breakfast. Waffles."

I could almost hear crickets chirping on the other end.

"I was about to leave anyway," I said, flicking a glance at the table of diners. "Plus, Josie is bringing Steve's kids over later on."

"Are you alone?"

"No. I mean Tommy brought me over. Pearl, Oliver and Lauren plus their two girls. Tommy and me."

"Uh huh. Why didn't you wait for Josie?"

"Because I was up and Tommy was coming over. I've got to go."

"How many waffles did you eat?"

"Ah, none."

"You sure? You used to put those things away by the dozen."

"I'm sure."

"You're not eating for two, Rosemarie. Baby weight is hard to shed."

"Okay talk to you later." I hung up and returned to the table. "I don't eat waffles."

"Without lots of strawberries and maple syrup." Victor grabbed the silver pitcher. "No one can out eat Rosemarie."

"What's that supposed to mean?" I felt the claws come out.

Victor held the syrup, poised for action. "We were fourteen and you challenged me to a waffle-eating contest."

"I'd forgotten," I said, our eyes met and my heart raced. "I suppose one won't kill me."

"Or two." He forked them on my plate.

"You okay, Rosemarie?" Pearl asked, reaching for the butter.

"I'm good." Except Rich was crazy jealous. What if he showed up? He wouldn't. He didn't even know the way. He could ask Mom.

He'll show up mad and everyone will know.

After a few forbidden bites and a dozen sorrys, I excused myself from the table. "Actually, I'm not feeling good."

"I'll be ready in ten to take you home." Tommy downed his milk.

Victor wiped his mouth on a napkin and stood. "I'll see you out."

"I'm sorry I can't go visit Sheldon," I said when we were alone.

Victor handed me my coat. "Me too."

I swallowed quick tears, tugging my tennis shoe on. "He's a really good guy. He's only worried about me."

Victor's eyes were on me. "The nobler a gal, the harder it is for her to suspect inferiority in others."

"I like it," I said, my toe staring up at me through the hole in my right shoe. I tucked my foot beneath the bench. "You make it up?"

"Nope. Marcus Tullius Cicero."

"Never heard of him." Suddenly, I was a girl growing up at the country house and he was Catholic. "I don't know if I can come back."

Victor gave me a sad, final smile. "I guess this is goodbye."

"Bye." I turned and walked down the hill.

Like Echo, destined to repeat a final farewell.

Rich came for me Sunday. In front of my folks, he drew me into his arms. "It's good to see you."

In the solitude of his pickup, he said, "Loneliness is a powerful enemy, Flower Child. Don't go over there again."

I flipped through radio stations. "Then you can't talk to Holly anymore."

He sighed. "Rosemarie, we've been over this. Unlike some people, she can fry a burger without giving customers food poisoning."

"Funny like the first, I dunno, fifty times," I said. "And no one got sick."

His golden gaze went dark. "I hate when you flip through stations."

I stopped on Everclear and "Wonderful." "...*I wish I could count to ten, make everything be wonderful again.*" "And I hate that song." He flipped the radio off.

58

"Going to church doesn't make you a Christian any more than standing in your garage makes you a car," Rich said for my ears only as the Welcome Lutheran Church congregation gathered in the foyer following the service.

Pastor Brady shook Rich's hand. "It's good to have you two here."

"We're having a potluck for lunch at our house. We'd love it if you guys could come," Karen said with a smile.

"Thanks," Rich said.

After they walked away, I whispered, "Pastor Brady used to live above our garage in town."

Rich shot me a look of disdain. "Duh. Everybody knows that."

"The parsonage is pretty nice. We could stop at Hamill's for the lemon tarts I baked last night."

Rich's eyes narrowed. "I didn't say we were going."

"Oh. Well I thought..."

"Oh great," he said beneath his breath. Shawn Erickson strutted over with a very pregnant Jill Pederson. Strawberry blond curls in a cloud about her face and sparkling sapphire eyes, she positively glowed.

Shawn shook hands with Rich. "How's it going?"

"Ooh, how old is he?" Jill reached for Peter.

"Six weeks," I said. "When is your baby due?"

"I've got another four." She sighed. "I signed up for the nursery. You should too."

My chest swelled. "I will."

Shawn nodded. "We'll see you folks."

I finished doing a mental inventory of my pantry on the way home. "Hot dogs for lunch?"

"You know my mom's coming next weekend," he said as we walked through the doorway. "Maybe you need to up the grocery budget."

"The grocery budget should work." I swallowed hard. "We could go over to Pastor Brady's for potluck."

"You can go. I don't feel like it." He flipped on the TV. "You never used to go to church."

"I want Peter to hear about Jesus."

"It's not like he'll remember any of it." His eyes were glued to the screen.

"I like going." I made my way to the kitchen.

"Huh. Did you know Shawn Erickson is a deacon?"

"Oh yeah?" The breakfast dishes and last night's supper dishes were piled in the sink. Yesterday morning's were stacked on the counter. "I met him once at a high school graduation, but don't know him very well."

"Shawn is a hot head. Starts a lot of bar fights when he's had one too many. He and Jill are living together. Mark told me he gave him a DUI last week."

"That's too bad." I opened the fridge and smelled what was left of the milk. Not bad. "Jill seems pretty cool."

"Erickson, the good ol' boy."
There were a few apples and some condiments. "It's church, Rich."

"You don't think good ol' boys attend church?" He glanced over at me. "You think they'll let you work in the nursery?"

"Why wouldn't they?"

He scrubbed his chin. "No reason."

The next Sunday morning, Rich propped Peter in the crook of his arm and shook hands with all those good ol' boys.

59

"What was your favorite thing about Mt. Rushmore, Peter?" Rich shifted his attention between the road and the map.

"Let me have the map. And maybe slow down." I gripped the handle next to the passenger window. "I guess I know why they call this the 'oh...'"

"Language, Rosemarie." He spread the map over the steering wheel. "Let the kid talk."

"The faces," Peter said.

My frown deepened. "You swear all the time."

Rich didn't look up. "Mom's going to get cranky if we're late. She gets cranky when anyone is late."

"Did you tell her about the dining room table?" I floored my nonexistent brakes, bracing both hands on the dashboard.

"I'm leaving it for you." Rich pushed the map aside. "She gave it to me as a gift. It's gonna be tough telling her I gave it away."

"I tried to tell you it was a bad idea." *Don't give away Mother's table, don't sit on precious magazines if you want to live.* "She made a big deal about it when she gave it to you."

"I didn't ask for it. I didn't want it." Suddenly, he slammed both hands on the steering wheel. His eyes wild, he shouted, "You're exactly like her."

The atmosphere vibrated.

"I'm not. I..."

He jerked the steering wheel. The truck crossed the center lane. I grabbed for the dash, uttering Jesus' name for help.

"You should see your face, Rosemarie." Rich chuckled.

"You're scaring me." I pressed my lips together.

"Oh yeah? How's this for scary?" He punched the gas, engine roaring, the needle crept past the hundred mark.

Peter started to cry.

"He's turning into a crybaby like his mom." Rich slowed down abruptly, pulled into his mother's driveway and cut the engine. "I didn't ask for the dumb table."

I breathed a sigh of relief, my whole body trembling. "Maybe not, but your mother went on and on about it when she gave it to you."

"You're such a drama queen." He got out of the truck and slammed the door. "I'm leaving."

"Wait, what am I supposed to tell your mom?" I asked, but he was gone. The seatbelt dug into my six-month pregnant belly. I unhooked it, turned around and released Peter from his car seat.

"You okay, buddy?"

He wrapped his arms around my neck. In my tummy, his baby brother gave a kick. A sudden sense of togetherness filled the cab. I felt a lot better this pregnancy than with Peter. No swelling, no heartburn. Even still, bringing another soul into this mess seemed wrong somehow.

I sat with my sons, and prayed. "Dear God, help us."

Rich returned a half hour later. "You're still here?"

Both relieved and disappointed, I said, "Where else would we be?"

"Inside?" He took Peter from me and headed for the door. Peter's face crumpled, and he held his arms toward me. Rich kept walking.

"You tried to kill us," I said.

He sighed. "Such a drama queen. If I wanted to kill you, I'd slip something in your food. Something untraceable." A pause. "You ever hear about Audrey Marie Hilley? She'd been married for twenty-four years when her husband started getting sick. A year later, he died. No one suspected a thing. Until her daughter came down with the same symptoms as dear old dad."

Gooseflesh raced up my arms. "Creepy, Rich."

"Joking, Rosemarie."

Dinner at Marjorie's was impossibly long. I breathed a sigh of relief when we arrived back home.

Rich plopped in front of the TV. "So you know, I would never do anything to hurt you."

A slither of unease crept through my gut, and I sank down on the sofa. "I know."

"I would never take Peter from you."

"Yeah." I didn't want Peter or his unborn brother to be without a father.

"All married people fight every once in a while."

"I know," I said, because I wouldn't let us be Duane and Mara.

"It's your drama I can't handle. I hate a nag."

"I'm sorry. It's my fault. I wonder if Josie's right. Maybe I should see someone."

"Josie's a little goofy. I've always thought that. Quit the booze and you'll be right as rain." Rich flashed the boyish smile that melted my insides.

"Okay." I sat on trembling hands.

60

I woke from a blood curdling scream. Rich stood in the bedroom doorway. "Can you get him? He won't stop."

Newborn Jim was red-faced and wild when I reached the nursery. I tried feeding him. He wasn't having it. I sat in the rocking chair. Back and forth, for two hours he wailed. At last, I fell asleep with him in my arms.

Baking bread was a sleepy task. Three o'clock rolled around and I could barely keep my eyes open.

At five a.m. the phone rang. "You need to get home right now," Rich said. Jim was howling in the background while Peter chatted away.

"You're kidding," I said. "I've got bread in the oven."

He hung up.

Rich met me at the door. "I'm going for a walk. I need a break before I do something stupid, like ram my fist through the wall."

The next day Jim screamed like the house was on fire.

A ding meant the dryer was done. I set Jim in the swing, Peter up with Lincoln Logs and went to change loads of laundry. Jim cried in the background. I pulled the wet clothes out of the washer, shoving them into the dryer.

At once, it was quiet. At last. He must have gone to sleep. Mental note: swing is key.

"Mommy." Peter walked in.

"Wait a minute. I'm..." I turned and Peter was holding Jim by his ankles. Four-week-old, upside-down Jim looked up at me, eyes wide.

I dropped the laundry.

Peter blinked innocently. "Baby wants you."

"Thank you, Peter," I said, taking Jim from my three-year-old's grasp. "You are such a good boy."

Peter smiled, satisfied. "Play toys?"

"I would love to." I abandoned the laundry.

61

Jim fell asleep at nine o'clock and I tiptoed out of the house. Hamill's kitchen was quiet, silence broken only by oven fans. Exhaustion poked at my back muscles and every last nerve. I filled the convection ovens with trays of cupcakes, sat down and stretched my legs.

Rich.

I couldn't leave the kids alone with him. The boys were more than a handful.

A sudden vision of three-year-old Peter and upside-down baby Jim brought a smile to my lips.

It was going to be alright.

"Something burning, Rosemarie?" Rich's voice worked its way into my dream.

My eyes popped open. "What?" I sniffed twice and shot out of my chair. "Oh no!" I rushed over and threw open the oven doors.

Peter was there. "Mommy burned cupcakes."

"Yes Peter, Mommy did." I sighed, turned a tray over the trash can, knocking cupcakes into it. "What time is it?"

"Almost eight," Rich said.

"Oh man. I fell asleep."

"Katie Marsh is here." Rich shifted Jim's car seat to his other hand. "She'd like to talk to you."

"Peter and I will clean up here. Tell her I'll meet her in my office."

Katie Marsh wore a tailored pinstripe suit and matching navy pumps. Her honey blonde hair was pulled to the nape of her neck in a tight bun. She stood and shook my hand when I walked in.

"What can I do for you, Katie?" I sat behind piles of papers scattered across my desk. Peter wrapped himself around my leg.

"I go by Kate now," she said.

"Okay."

"Cold out there today."

I rubbed my temples. "Look, Katie—Kate, I just burned six dozen cupcakes. My kids are here and I need to go home. So if you can get to the point, I'd appreciate it."

"I wanted to give you this." She handed me a folder.

Rich propped his shoulder against the doorframe. "Katie is interested in helping us with the books. She graduated from Bismarck State College with an accounting degree."

I glanced through her lengthy resumé. No thanks, came to mind but what I said was, "Tell me why I should hire you."

"To cost out products and sell at a profitable price. Then you can position products strategically within the marketplace. Also, where do you buy ingredients?"

"Here and there. I shop local when I can."

"You should avoid buying supplies at a retail level. Purchase stuff in bulk from distributors or better yet, from the source itself. Cut out the middle man. At the very least, compare costs." A pause. "What do you have for investment capital?"

"I don't have much to invest right now."

"Then you can't afford to buy the kind of equipment you need to achieve production efficiency."

"Hamill's is a family-owned bakery."

"Or afford to purchase ingredients and packaging in bulk. If you can't reach a low enough cost of goods then it's impossible to turn a profit at a fair market price."

"I'll think about it," I said.

Katie stood. "Thank you for your time. I look forward to hearing from you."

After she left, I turned to Rich. "She's confident, I'll give her that. Too bad I can't afford to hire her."

"You can't afford not to. We both know you suck at math. She could save us some real money."

I stood, fighting tears of exhaustion. "Okay."

Rich peered closely at me. "You can't keep burning the wick at both ends."

"Not much I can do." I picked up Jim's car seat.

"You could check out Ava Brown's daycare. Holly says Lil' Rascal's..."

"No," I cut him off. "I didn't have kids so someone else could raise them."

He shrugged. "Suit yourself."

62

The front door of Hamill's was green.

Not bright, hunter, or emerald. Pea green, as in the soup. All coherent thought fled my mind in an instant. I marched straight to the kitchen.

Rich leaned against the counter. Holly and the new hire, Darla Adams, stood across from him. "If you haven't failed, you haven't tried..." He glanced over at me. "Hi Flower Child."

"Don't you Flower Child me." I trembled with rage, spots danced before my eyes. "If this is your idea of a sick joke, it's not funny."

He held up both palms. "Woah Rosemarie, what are you talking about?"

"The door. What else?"

His eyebrows came up. "You said we could paint. You don't like it?"

"Don't like it?" I screeched.

He rubbed his jaw. "It's the same color as Mark's house."

I stepped back. "What do you mean?"

"Mark helped me with the door. It was his idea. He's here with Abigale having lunch if you want to ask him."

I turned and marched out to the dining area where Mark and Abigale perused menus. "Did you help paint the front door, Mark?" I asked.

Abigale hid behind her menu.

He shifted in his chair. "Yeah."

"Oh."

Rich came up behind me, laying his hands on my shoulders. "Are you okay? I can paint over it."

The wind left my sails. I muttered a deflated, "I'm fine," and made my way back through the kitchen in a slink of defeat. Past Holly and her silent stare and Darla's expression of discomfort.

Why didn't I hold it together? Count to ten or a hundred? Instead I waltzed in and made a fool of myself. Alone with my ovens and cookie sheets, I wished with everything inside me to leave the mess. Never look back.

Rich walked in. "Everything okay? Darla said she's never seen you so unglued."

"I'm fine."

He ran a hand through his hair. "So I talked to Mark. He knows a gal who does couple's therapy."

I stilled. "You're willing to go to counselling with me?"

"Of course. We're in this together." He flashed a smile. "I'll give her a call."

63

"I haven't read Harry Potter," I told Nancy Clemens while I drove trucks around with Peter on the church nursery floor. Six-week-old Jim slept in his car seat.

"Neither have I, but I've heard it's full of witchcraft. Kent and Rick won't be reading them." Nancy also had boys. She was slim with perfect makeup and stylish, jet black hair. She had a tree tattoo on the back of her neck just above her shirt line.

I didn't wear makeup and an oversized sweater hid my post-baby belly.

Nancy watched me for several minutes. "Do you always play with Peter?"

"Yep. It's fun."

"You should let him be. He'd be more creative and less clingy."

"Maybe."

Jill caught up with me after the service. "How was the nursery?"

"Good. Nancy Clemens was the other helper. Her boys were in there too." Should I tell her Nancy discouraged playing with my kids?

Jill's eyes lit. "She teaches first grade at Washington school in Jamestown. She's fantastic with kids."

Okay, I take that as a no.

Rich made his way over with a smile. "How was the nursery?"

"Good."

Pastor Brady walked up and shook Rich's hand. "Congratulations on getting the deacon position. You'll be a great fit for our ministry team."

Rich grinned. "I'm looking forward to it."

Marjorie and her newest guy were sitting in the living room when we arrived home. Ted was his name. I couldn't help but notice he appeared to be a little older than the others. Still, for a woman of sixty, the men she dated were at least half her age.

Lunch was red hotdish, Rich's favorite.

Marjorie moved it around with a fork.

"Sorry lunch is late, Mom," Rich said and flicked me a glance. "Rosemarie had nursery duty today."

"I don't care for goulash," Marjorie said. "I'm sorry."

"It's great. I don't know what you're talking about." Ted shoveled it in.

Marjorie sliced him with a glare. "Well, I don't date you for your I.Q."

I made a mental note: leftovers tomorrow.

Maybe she wouldn't notice the table was different.

"What did you do with the table I gave you?" Marjorie asked.

Or maybe not.

Rich winked at me. "Rosemarie gave it away to a needy family."

My mouth dropped. "I didn't..."

Her eyes filled with hurt. "I suppose it wasn't good enough for you."

You won't win.

Couple's guidance counselor Dr. Carrie Nelson sat with a ready clipboard and pen. Her office was windowless. One wall displayed her credentials, license, and various awards. A sign *This Too Shall Pass* on the opposite wall.

Dr. Carrie was in her early forties. She had inquisitive brown eyes behind black glasses perched on a thin nose. She made small talk with Rich. I picked at a spaghetti stain on the front of my cream sweater. Suddenly, I became keenly aware the room had grown quiet. I looked up.

Their expectant gazes were on me.

I frowned. "I'm sorry, what?"

"Tell me why you're here," Dr. Carrie said.

"Me?" I asked, a wave of panic rushing over me. I didn't know what to say, or rather, what not to. The truth. Maybe Dr. Carrie could get Rich some help. "He painted the door green," I said. "I mean, the door of my bakery."

Dr. Carrie studied me like a bug beneath a microscope. "Okay, let's talk about that."

Rich gave an uncomfortable look. "I still don't know what was going on behind the green door at the country house," he said, and glanced at Dr. Carrie. "I couldn't tell you why Rosemarie got mad about it. Something to do with her childhood. It's been years. She did say we could paint it."

The slap of betrayal was sharp and agonizing. He didn't understand? I suddenly felt small and alone.

"Is that true, Rosemarie?" Dr. Carrie asked.

"Yes. I mean, no," I stammered. "I told him he could paint the bakery, but...yes."

Rich appeared shame-faced. "I apologized and told her I would paint over it."

"Let's talk about the table," Dr. Carrie said.

"Not much to tell," Rich said. "Rosemarie gave away a family heirloom. I forgave her." He folded his arms across his chest. "She didn't have to say it was rubbish."

"How did that make you feel?" Dr. Carrie asked Rich.

He shrugged. "Honestly? It was the way she was raised."

"The end table and lamp belonged to my folks." I rubbed needles of frustration from my neck with a shaky hand. "Rich gave the table away and told his mother I got rid of it."

"Uh huh." Dr. Carrie wrote something on her chart. "Why do you think he did that?"

"Because I told him she was going to flip out when she found out."

"You have baby brain?" Rich asked.

"I...might have baby brain?" I sat on my hands. Truth was, it had been raining that day. The electric bill was three months past due and they shut off the power. Rich yelled about it for over an hour. I remembered saying I wanted to get rid of the end table and lamp. He gave away the dining table. Didn't he? I always prided myself in a good memory. I'd won 4-H awards for speech memorization. Something had to be wrong with me. But I couldn't remember.

"Baby brain?" Dr. Carrie asked.

"Rosemarie works nights at the bakery," Rich said. He pulled out his Bible, withdrew a photograph, and showed it to Dr. Carrie. "Cute little guys."

"Adorable." Dr. Carrie smiled. "How old?"

"Peter's three and Jimmy's six weeks." He returned the print and closed the Bible. "I'm afraid Rosemarie is exhausted."

I frowned. "You try sleeping during the day."

Dr. Carrie started writing again. "This is a prescription for Rosemarie."

"I don't need medication."

"Just something to help you sleep," Dr. Carrie said. "I'd like to see you both again in a few weeks. In the meantime, find the boys a daycare."

"I told you," Rich said, giving me a triumphant look. "Rosemarie insists on being the one who takes care of them."

"Admirable, but you need to do what's best for your children." Dr. Carrie tore the prescription from the pad and handed it to me.

Three days later, I dropped Peter and Jim off at Lil' Rascal's.

Ava's house was nice. She was the image of her mother, Janette. Soft brown hair, large eyes and long eyelashes. Her spirit was kind, and I knew the boys were in good hands. Still, I couldn't stop the flow of tears. Mine, Peter's and Jim's. Fifteen minutes later, I was apologizing while peeling Peter off my calves.

Lost in a gloomy fog, I went home and crawled into bed.

64

Texas authorities raided Warren Jeffs' ranch and took legal custody of four hundred sixteen children in response to a phone call.

Rich was on his recliner sipping coffee. "The men weren't allowed to have children with their wives. Only the seed bearer could. They were men Jeffs deemed to be worthy. Husbands were told to hold their wives hands while the seed bearer 'spreads his seed.'"

"What about the other men?"

"Which other men?"

"The non-seed bearing men. Surely they weren't going to sit by while a bunch of loons screwed their wives."

His eyes left the screen and caught mine. "What do you suggest they do?"

"You're the deacon, you tell me. Punch the seed bearers where it counts. Take their wives and get out. Gang up on them."

He gave me a skeptical look. "Gang up on church leaders?"

"They should do *something*," I said, heading for the kitchen.

"They did as they were told. There was nothing else they could do." He followed me, gathering me in his arms. "I love you, Rosemarie."

My heart galloped in my chest. "Love you too."

Here it comes. Merciless, it would demand its pound of flesh.

It stole everything. The sweet pleasure of a warm touch. A peaceful afternoon reading a book. My own quiet company. Even foreplay was like trying to enjoy prime rib in prison before the electric chair.

He seemed fine, but it was always the same. No amount of doing house chores, favors or climbing the moon would pacify it. I never knew what would set it off or when the explosion would occur.

But I'd been warned.

Part of me said bring it on. Enough hiding. Let it come if it must. The other part wanted to hide in my room under the covers until it blew over. That's where I was. Maybe this time it wouldn't happen. Maybe he was better.

God can save anyone, can't He?

"You stupid punk!" Bolted from a dream, I jumped up and ran to the living room. Rich had Peter against the wall by the scruff of his shirt. Peter, a good, quiet boy who didn't complain or sass back.

Five-year-old Jim was on the living room floor amidst toys. Crying, but not in a sad way. It was apparent by the fire in Jim's eyes he was furious.

What should I do?

I opened my mouth. Rich glanced back and saw me. At once, all the stiffness left his body. "Rosemarie, I didn't see you standing there."

Say something, Rosemarie. Now is not the time for silence.

Rich's face crumpled and he slowly released Peter. "What am I doing? Peter are you okay?"

Peter nodded, wiping his tears with the back of his hand.

I stared, frozen in shock.

Rich's gaze went black. "Whatsamatter?"

"N-nothing." My eyes fell.

He raised a fist. "You act like I'm going to hit you."

I shrank back. He turned at the last second, slamming his fist straight through the wall. "Pick this place up. It's a pigsty." His eyes boiled with rage.

I began picking up toys. "Peter, why don't you head to your room?"

Jim clung to my leg and wouldn't let go.

I should have said something. Easy, Rosemarie. Rich didn't hit him. He only yelled. Around and around the scene went until my brain felt like it was going to explode.

"Moooommmmiiiieee." Jim slapped my leg. "I'm trying to tell you..."

Peter marched up to his little brother and pushed him to the floor. Jim's face crumpled and he began to cry. Peter took one look at his brother and fresh tears flowed.

Out of nowhere, a sudden burst of anger hit me. I hauled back and kicked the wall. My foot went right through it. I stared at the hole.

"What did you do?" Rich bent down, tracing the damage with a finger.

"I'll buy plaster and fill it in," I said, and started to cry.

He glanced up. "Are you okay, Rosemarie?"

I was most definitely not okay.

Rich sat on the back deck, lighting his cigar. "Boys in bed?"

"Yeah."

"Headed to work?"

"Nah, I think I'll call it a night," I said, still reeling from the morning scene. "How was the lunch crowd?"

"Busy. I made Minestrone soup. It was pretty good. The Browns were there. They ordered ham salad. I had Darla run to Walsky's."

Darla was an employee I hired and was glad I did. Her bubbly personality and the speed at which she attended to patrons was a great asset to our team.

"...It was a stupid kiss. She caught me off guard. I stopped it almost immediately."

"Wait, who?"

Almost immediately?

"Weren't you listening? Holly. I had three shots of Jack after work. She came in, asking if there was anything she could do. I told her I was good. The next thing I knew, she was kissing..."

A vision of vivacious Holly kissing my husband sliced my heart to ribbons. It wasn't possible he was unfaithful. Not to me. I was a loyal wife, worked hard, took care of him and the boys.

"I'm going to have a glass of Port." I picked up the bottle. "Care for some?"

He held up his glass. "I've got my Jack."

Like a kaleidoscope of colors, images played in shades of brown and gold inside my head. I wasn't a weak woman ruled by petty jealousy. That was Mara and I was better than her, than Holly.

"It was just a kiss, I suppose," I said.

"Yeah?" His eyes widened with pleasure. "Here I thought you were going to flip out."

"Because I always overreact." I took a sip of wine.

"You do like to wear your heart on your sleeve."

"What was your dad like?" I ran a finger over the rim of my wine glass.

"Don't know. He left when I was a baby." Rich ran his hand over his head. "Why?"

"Something Dr. Carrie said about the importance of fathers," I said.

Rich took a sip of his whisky. "You're lucky you have a good one."

"Yeah, I am." I set my glass down. "At least you told me."

"Exactly why you don't need to make a fuss about some dumb kiss."

"Let's forget it," I said even as a vision of Rich and Holly went like a merry-go-round in my head. My husband would never kiss another woman, nor allow her to kiss him. Reality reared its ugly head. I didn't know this man.

I imagined waking from the nightmare. Relieved to discover my life was all a dream. I knew the man I was married to and he adored me. He wouldn't even entertain the thought of another woman in his arms. My real-life husband wasn't cold, unfeeling, or heartless.

65

A series of car and suicide bomb blasts rocked Baghdad and two northern Iraqi communities, killing dozens of people during a major holiday period.

A blast was on the verge of exploding in our home. Atmosphere crackled for those who had ears to hear, brimming beneath the surface.

The dreadful calm.

Sometimes it took weeks, or a day. Other times, an afternoon. I'd been sneaking beers all day. I started with the usual two before bed. Then two more before noon to sleep. I gave up sleeping at two p.m. and cracked open one more.

Rich strolled into the kitchen. "It's karaoke night at Carlton," he said, his phone pinged. "One drink."

Go along with it or something bad will happen.

"No thank you."

"Come on. Why not?" His fingers flew across the screen.

"Are you still attracted to me?"

"What?"

The thundering of my heart rolled on. "Do you think I'm pretty?"

"Why would you ask such a question?"

I sighed. "Your laptop was on the kitchen table."

"My computer?" The light came in his eyes. "I lent it to Mark. You know he's a porn addict."

"He is? Mark?" Okay that explained *Time to play with married women* and *Barely Legal*. The bad feeling continued. "Can you put your phone away for one minute?"

He slid his phone inside his pocket. "There. Happy now? You don't seem to appreciate all I do for this family." His pocket buzzed. He pulled his phone back out. "The hours I put in, every single one, I do for you."

"I'm sure. Like hiring Holly."

Rich lifted his brow. "She's your employee."

"No, she's your employee," I said, boiling with anger. "You know, I never wanted to hire her."

His lips flattened. "Can I talk now?"

"Go ahead."

He brought his face right up to mine. "Are you listening or are you going to keep interrupting me?"

I leaned back. "I didn't realize. I'm sorry. I only want to..."

"You make excuses for your unhappiness. You don't feel good. You have a headache. You ate too much." His attention returned to his phone.

I realized it was possible to be jealous of a cell phone. "What are you saying?"

"Never mind. Maybe it would be better if I was dead." He turned and walked out. The house shook as he slammed the door.

I cleaned, top to bottom and made a peanut butter and jelly sandwich. I ate it standing in the kitchen while scrolling through Facebook.

I glanced at the clock: three p.m. A half hour before Peter and Jim got home from school. Time for a small nap. Things would look better if I wasn't tired. I curled beneath the covers.

Bang!

A gunshot. It came from the basement. My heart leapt in fear. I crawled across the bed and opened the nightstand cupboard door. It was empty. An acrid taste formed at the back of my mouth. I checked my phone. A missed call from Rich. A text **Call me.**

Call me.

Where are you?

Rosemarie.

Hey.

Seven missed calls from him.

He shot himself.

I hurried out of bed and dashed to the basement. This was all my fault. What was I going to tell my parents? The boys? His mother? I barely noticed as tears streamed down my cheeks.

Rich stood at the bottom of the stairs holding a box of matches and a package of Black Cats.

It took a moment for my brain to process the scene before me. When it did, rage swept in. "You're lucky I don't kill you myself." I turned and marched back up the stairs.

He rushed up behind me. "Wait. I didn't mean..."

I held up my hand. "Not interested."

"Why didn't you answer your phone?" he asked in the little boy voice.

I stilled. A quick rush of compassion swept over me. I imagined a little boy and a mother he could never do right by. "I was taking a nap."

"Why was your ringer off?"

I rubbed my forehead. "I wanted to sleep."

He giggled. "You should have seen your face."

An image of a gaping hole in his chest played over and over in my head. Sanity slipped away until I screamed, "I can't believe you! Do you have any idea what went through my head? You selfish son of a..."

Peter was at the top of the stairs. "Are you okay?" he asked. "We heard Mom yelling."

I wasn't a yeller. I was calm, like my mom. "I'm sorry I lost it." All emotion drained from me, and I made my way to the living room. "I think I'm overly tired."

Rich scrubbed his chin. "Tell you what, I'll take the boys out for a burger. Give you some space. You want me to call Dr. Carrie?"

"I'm fine." I waved him off with a limp hand.

He eyed me for a minute. "You won't...hurt yourself while we're gone?"

I cut him a tired glare. "I'm not the one who lit a firecracker in the basement."

As soon as he walked out the door, I got up and headed to the fridge for another beer.

"The card was declined," Rich said in a chipper voice when they returned.

"At first I thought something was wrong with it. I checked the account and sure enough, it's twenty-three dollars in the hole."

Good one, Rosemarie. "I must have forgotten to check before we went out last."

"No problem." He nearly sang his pleasure. "I've got a knife set I don't use anymore. I'll put it on eBay."

I frowned. "You don't have to."

"What's mine is yours and what's yours is mine." A pause. "About earlier, I need to know where you are in case of an emergency."

"Okay."

Rich's lips thinned. "We'll keep this matter between us. No point in telling Dr. Carrie."

"I know," I said. Rest assured I wasn't telling anyone.

66

Becky Walsky, right out of 1985 with spiked hair and feather earrings, stood at the front door of the country house holding a bottle of wine and a basket of various cheeses, chocolates and crackers.

"You shouldn't have." I forced a smile.

"I didn't. It was sitting on the front steps." She held up the basket. "Says 'Compliments of Mecktal Law. Contact Mecktal before your spouse does.'"

I took the basket from her. "My brother-in-law's suggestion when I told him about me and Rich."

"What about you and Rich?" Becky asked.

"It's a long story," I said, making my way to the kitchen. Over coffee, I gave her the short version, anger boiling inside me like a volcano ready to erupt. "The whole thing sounds ridiculous to you, I suppose."

"What'd the attorney say?" Becky asked.

"Josie came to the complimentary consultation. Somewhere between assurance he would take care of me and Josie's twenty questions, I didn't get a chance to tell first class Drew Mecktal I couldn't pay him."

Becky sipped her coffee. "You say Rich is a beast. He doesn't seem beastly. Besides a few cruel remarks I don't really see anything too bad about him. I was expecting you to tell me he was beating on you. Cheating or doing something illegal. I didn't hear any of that."

"Okay." See? It's all in your head.

"You do seem pretty unhappy, though," Becky said. "Maybe you should talk to Pastor Brady."

"Maybe not," I said. "Rich told me Shawn Erickson put Jill Pederson in the hospital. Far as I know he's still a deacon at the church."

"Jill denied the whole thing. Last I heard she moved back in with him." Becky leaned forward. "What are you going to do?"

I topped off her coffee cup. "I don't know."

She took a sip. "At least you're smart enough to get a good lawyer. You're gonna need one."

"Yeah, well it's tricky. I scraped up all my loose change only to discover I can't afford him."

Becky set her cup down. "Find a lawyer you can afford."

"Rosemarie, so good to see you," Pastor Brady answered the door when I arrived at the parsonage. His face was weathered with age and years since he lived above our garage.

"Hey sorry to bother you. I came to see you about Sha..." I slowed down. Rich was sitting at the table in front of a monopoly board. Shawn sat next to him.

I turned around. "I'll come back later."

Karen laid a hand on my arm. "I've got the coffee on. We were about to start a game of Monopoly."

My heart thundered inside my chest until I was dizzy. "Okay."

"I didn't know you were coming." Rich smiled at me as I sat down.

Shawn flashed me a grin like a Cheshire cat who had just lapped up a saucer of milk.

At home, silence moved in. The kind that said I was bad and being punished. It was because I went over to the parsonage without telling him. Even though he hadn't told me he was going over there. The rule applied to me. He was going to have a cow when I told him about the lawyer.

Rich stood in the doorway of the kitchen. "I didn't tell Pastor Brady about your drinking."

My chest went cold. "What about my drinking? Why would you?"

"I wouldn't. That's what I said. I didn't tell him."

Silence.

"I looked into getting a divorce lawyer." Good one, Rosemarie.

A muscle in his jaw twitched. "You want a divorce."

"No."

He made his way over. "If you want one, Rosemarie, all you have to do is ask. I only want you to be happy."

Too easy. Something was wrong. He would fight for the boys. Prescription medication, drinking and paranoia wouldn't look very good in a custody battle. I rubbed my forehead. "I'm sorry. I haven't been getting enough sleep. I blamed a lot of things on you and I shouldn't have."

His eyes narrowed. "About what to who?"

"Not much. Becky Walsky. I'll set the record straight."

"Give me a hug." He held his arms out.

I stepped into them and thought of the tracks to cover. Make sure Becky didn't tell Rich exactly what I said. I'd told Mom, but she wouldn't talk.

Now he knew about the lawyer. Things should go back to normal. I took a step back and caught his grin. One that said he was happy about this and now I owed him.

67

Twenty-six-year old Reyhaneh Jabbari was executed for allegedly killing her attempted rapist. Jabbari was placed in solitary confinement for two months, tortured, and denied access to an attorney.

The sun peeked through scantily clad trees. Frost kissed the tips of dried brown leaves crunching beneath my feet.

Rich came out of the house in a T-shirt and blue jeans, color in his cheeks. "Rosemarie, we need to talk," he said in the dad-voice.

My palms began to ache. "It's cold out. You should put a coat on."

He pulled out my phone. "I checked your history."

My belly flip-flopped. YouTube, my new obsession. After talking to Becky, I searched for clues he was having an affair hour after hour, night after night.

"So?" Like a guilty lover, I always cleared history. Except, Rich called me earlier, upset I hadn't made the car payment. I might have forgotten to delete the most recent.

He tapped his chin. "I gotta tell you, some of your searches make me wonder."

I managed a bored, "Oh?"

"*7 reasons a man doesn't want to have sex with you? 12 reasons he's not interested in having sex?*" He looked up from the phone. "You're scaring me here, Rosemarie."

"Oh." I licked my lips. "I was upset the other night when you came home late. You told me you had a beer with Holly, and I guess I was jealous."

Otherwise, you're crazy.

"I see," he said. "This has to stop. Holly and I work together."

"And kiss together," I said underneath my breath.

His eyes narrowed. "What did you say?"

"Stop kissing other women."

Rich flashed me a quizzical glance. "I didn't kiss Holly."

"Yes, you did."

"I did not. You were the one who said we kissed." He scratched the back of his head with four quick fingers. "Isn't memory loss a side-effect of your meds?"

"You told me about it when you were smoking on the porch," I said with less fortitude than before.

Rich handed me back my phone. "Holly is a good friend who listens. She gets me. Like you used to."

Halloween night dipped to twenty degrees. Inside Carlton, things were beginning to heat up when Holly led Rich to the dance floor.

"Hey Rosemarie." Mark pulled up a chair next to me.

"Hi Mark. Didn't expect to see you here." I sipped my drink. "Abigale here too?"

"She's visiting her folks this weekend in Minot," he said. Mark did well keeping himself in shape. Auburn hair and neatly trimmed beard gave him an approachable look. His eyes caught mine. I flushed, and returned my attention to the dance floor.

"Quite the dance," Mark said. "Enough to start the bar on fire. Better keep an eye on them. You don't want to end up like John Lennon and Yoko Ono."

"Holly is beautiful, I suppose."

He shrugged. "Yeah, but she's not you."

"Thank you." My cheeks went hot.

"What are you drinking?"

"A Shirley Temple." I eyed his T-shirt and blue jeans. "Who are you supposed to be?"

Mark pointed at the label on his chest "Bob" written in blue marker.

"Funny."

Rich strolled over when the music ended. "Ready to go?"

"Yes." I gave Mark my warmest smile. "Bye."

"See ya, Rosemarie," he said.

"What did Mark want?" Rich asked when we reached his truck.

"Not much." I didn't want Mark on Rich's radar. He hadn't said anything inappropriate and he made me feel good.

"I don't want you talking to guys." Rich's eyes were hard. "Do I make myself clear?"

"Fine. I'll talk to myself."

Rich clicked his seatbelt. "I hear you there. I don't have any friends either."

An image of Peter and Jim brought a smile to my lips. "I have friends. Good ones."

Part III

Be silent in that solitude,
Which is not loneliness-for then
The spirits of the dead, who stood
In life before thee, are again
In death around thee, and their will
Shall overshadow thee; be still.

Spirits of the Dead; Edgar Allen Poe. 1827

68

Re: Sometimes dead is better.

Stephen King? I clicked on the email from Greg:

Duane Sim was born on March 19, 1955 to Jacob and Gertrude Sim of Glendive, MT. He married Mara Olson at Corpus Christi Catholic Church in Bismarck, ND in 1972 and had three children, Malcolm, Erica and Sonja. He abandoned his children Malcolm, Erica and Sonja after moving them to Welcome, ND. In 1991, he impregnated his brother's wife. He passed away December 18, 2016 and now will face judgement. He will not be missed by Malcolm, Erica and Sonja who understand this world is a better place without him.

Harsh, even for Duane Sim. I called Mom. "Hey it's me."

"Oh hi Rosemarie." She'd been crying.

"Josie emailed me the obit. I'm sorry."

"Are you coming to the funeral?"

I'd rather punch myself in the face. "Who's all going?"

"Everyone I think, except Tommy and Robin."

I heard Dad in the background. Mom said, "Look, Rosemarie, I've got to run. Service is at eleven, Monday."

I got on the elliptical and shoved in the earbuds. Unless it was thirty-five below actual temperature without the windchill in Hell, I was not going to Duane's funeral.

Absolutely not.

The shower with brass handles was divine. I wiggled my feet in the bath towel outside the door.

Brick walls painted white, nothing in our bathroom resembled Christmas.

No glittering snow, reindeer, stockings, mistletoe or lights. Rich agreed, gone was the Christmas spirit in today's society. The infamous holiday had become commercialized. A lot of set up and take down for twenty days.

Except for the Christmas Teddy hanging on the back of the bathroom door. It was complete with a hat. I'd seen the outfit earlier when I was shopping for gifts.

I brushed through tangled, wet locks, admiring my reflection in the mirror. One saying I was beautiful. My body, near perfect from working out. My skin showed youth and beauty. I reached for my hairdryer.

"What are you wearing?" Rich's voice rose over the noise.

Heart in my throat, I switched it off and turned around. "Do you like it? Oh wait." I donned the hat, sashaying toward him.

He scowled. "What are you listening to?"

"Burl Ives," I said, turning down "Holly Jolly Christmas." "I know we don't do Christmas, but I thought…"

His phone buzzed and he held up his hand. "Hold that thought." He turned away, speaking in low tones. "Mark," he said, ending the call.

I changed into yoga pants. It had been a long time since Rich made me feel anything but bad. A spark of eternal hope, always ready in my soul, gone with the Christmas spirit. An emptiness settled in its place.

69

Twenty One Pilots' "Stressed Out" played in my head. Rich sat in the living room reading Stephen King's *Rose Madder*. I'd never seen him read anything.

"Anne wants to meet for coffee Sunday. She moved back to town over this past Thanksgiving," I said.

"We'll see."

"Did you see the *For Sale* sign next door?"

"Hm."

"The Pedersons were nice. Not in your face, but gave me space," I said. "That rhymes."

"Hm."

"I wonder who we'll get instead."

"We'll see."

Another "hm" or "we'll see" and I imagined reaching over, wrapping my hands around his neck and squeezing slowly. "You're quiet."

"I'm reading."

"Well yes, but..."

"Then let me be quiet." His phone buzzed. "It's Holly."

"Huh."

"You knock her out of the water," he said. "You have something she doesn't. Holly is all sharp edges. You're soft and sweet. You sort of—I dunno—glow."

"You say it like it's a bad thing."

He shrugged. "It's a good thing in the right hands."

"In the wrong ones?" I tried a smile.

There was a gleam in his eyes. "Your soft center will be the key to your destruction."

Goose flesh rose up my arms. "Okay, not creepy at all."

He gave me a long, blank stare before his eyes returned to his book.

"Mark's the new manager of Holiday Inn in Jamestown," I said, putting the finishing touches on his turkey sandwich.

Rich leaned against the counter. "I heard that."

"Why did he get fired?" I handed him the sandwich.

Rich pinned me with a hard look. "Did he say he got fired?"

"No, I only assumed."

He took a bite. "Mark resigned. There was lying amongst other charges against him," he mumbled through a mouthful.

"He has little kids. Quitting his job before securing another doesn't seem conducive to caring for his family. Not like Mark at all."

"Yeah. I was shocked too. Mark's a good guy. Too bad, especially about him and Abby being swingers." He took two more bites.

"How do you know that?"

"I heard it from Bill Lane. Probably full of crap. Bill has had it in for Mark since he gave him a DUI last Christmas. Why, you interested in swapping?" He set the plate on the counter.

"Ugh. No." I put it in the sink. "How was the sandwich?"

He shrugged. "It was alright. Less mayo next time."

I drew a breath. "I'm going to Duane's funeral. It's my family."

"Since when are the Sims your family?"

"They aren't and I'd rather not make a case of it." I was planning on going to the funeral regardless. He couldn't stop me.

His eyes took on a familiar gleam. "You planning on meeting up with that Frank guy?"

"No." I folded my arms. "Why do I feel I'm being handled?"

"Bad past?" His phone pinged. "It's the restaurant. I'll be back."

Holly. Or some other woman. Big deal. Maybe he'll leave me. A sweet sensation shot through the core of my being. I could start fresh.

70

The sun peeking through skeletal cottonwoods, Meghan Trainor sang "All About That Bass." Rich pulled into the Welcome Foods parking lot and cut the engine. "Coffee, cookies. In and out."

"You don't have to come in," I said.

He unbuckled his seat belt. "I need to grab some shaving cream."

Rich didn't buy his own shaving cream. He didn't buy his own anything. He hadn't said I couldn't go to the funeral. We hadn't reached that point. A flat out no I didn't obey. Defying him meant questions and closer watch.

"In and out," I said.

That was the plan, but when Darla Adams waved us over, I scratched the idea. Darla loved to visit about everything and nothing.

"Hey Rosemarie."

I turned around. Holly was wearing a white sweater and winter-fresh smile. Blue jeans fit right. Suede boots to her knees.

My black sweater suddenly felt like I was in mourning. She had a breezy vibe as opposed to my funeral spirit. I wished I was having a better hair day.

"You got a haircut," I said.

"Yeah." She giggled, fluffing her chin-length curls. "It was time to do something."

"The Sims are in town. I saw Sonja yesterday," Darla said. "I heard they are burying him behind the country house."

"They are not," I said. Mom would have told me.

Like when she told you he died?

Darla squinted at me. "You know, you look like one of them."

"We look nothing alike." I thrust my chin forward. "It's not..." I was saved when the door jingled and in walked Rich.

No, not Rich. His clone.

Holly's son, Daren strolled up. "You almost done, Mom?"

"Tyler, Duncan! If you're going to kill each other, take it outside." Aaron Demit grabbed the boy closest to him. "Hey Rosemarie. Good to see you."

"You too. How've you been?"

"Can't complain. How about you?"

"Good," I said, not about to ask him why he weighed, couldn't have been over eighty pounds. Why his cheeks were gaunt and clothes hung on him.

"I suppose we better get shopping," I said.

"Me too," Aaron said. "Got the grandkids. It was good seeing you, Rosemarie."

"You too."

Darla pulled Holly close to her. "You missed your mother."

"Oh, did I?"

"Ya."

"Oh, that's a hoot."

Back in the truck, I scowled. "I look like a Sim? I'm so sure."

"She's jealous. Probably wished she could wear a sweater like yours." Rich set the groceries in the back seat. "Martin Kline lives with Darla. You know, the new guy at Greg's Auto Shop? Anyhow, she met him at Moorhead Auto Center last fall when she went to buy a car. After selling her a red Grand Am, he sold her on himself." He winked.

"Interesting."

"Looks like Aaron Demit's partying caught up with him."

"You don't know that."

"It's what I heard. I feel sorry for his grandkids. It's got to be tough having your grandfather in poor health. Anyway, it's idle chatter. Doesn't have to be false to be bad. There's a lot of truth which shouldn't be passed around. People do it when they hear something they like about someone they don't."

"I like it." I flicked him a look. "Where did you hear it?"

"I made it up."

It didn't feel like the truth, but not a big enough thing to call out.

But why lie about it?

71

Carlton was packed with fifty and unders. Overhead TVs played the Vikings' game. The special was written in colorful chalk on the black board as we walked in. Prime rib sandwich with choice of a side and boneless wings. Amy Grant's "Tennessee Christmas" accompanied the patrons.

Martin took a pull of his beer. "I could go for a tender Tennessee Christmas." He was a handsome blonde with broad shoulders and an Alan Jackson mustache.

Darla wore a pin-striped dress the color of sherbet. "I suppose you're going to the funeral," she said, her eyes on me.

"Yep. Frankenstein's funeral," Rich said.

Darla sipped her drink. "Shawn Erickson is in jail."

Rich's eyes lit. "Really? Rumor's true about Jill Pederson then."

Martin shrugged. "Must be. She married that investor from Fargo, Rory Newby."

Darla cupped her mouth with her hand. "I heard Anne Clark is pregnant and the father is Aaron Demit."

Rich stretched his legs out. "He looks like death warmed over."

"He was diagnosed with pancreatic cancer," Martin said. "It's terminal."

Rich whistled. "Ouch. Too bad."

Sorrow lapped my soul. I wished I'd kept up with Aaron, Vanessa, and their family. Now all I could do was feel bad.

"Stacey Wilson used to have a thing for Aaron," Darla said.

"Stacey's dating a rich lawyer in New York," I said. "I guess she broke up his marriage. Announced their engagement before the ink on the divorce papers was dry."

Rosemarie. Ugh.

Darla hiccupped. "Martin, I believe it's time for me to call it a night."

Martin stood. "I'll ask for the tab."

"See you two later," Darla said.

After they left, doubt twisted my gut, wringing out every insecurity. Why did I talk so much? What if Anne found out we were talking about her? And Aaron. Not only was he Tommy's friend, but was extremely ill with a wife to grieve his loss.

Rich yawned loudly. "I might skip out tomorrow. You're coming home right after the funeral?" He cut me a hard stare. A silent message saying there would be payback for disobedience.

"Of course."

Reverence of the Lord is the instruction in wisdom, for before honor must come humility.

The Bible verse was familiar. I learned it in Sunday school. The voice, original. Still and small. One reminding me things were not okay. I was not okay.

Be quiet, I thought. Please go away.

72

"He doesn't look like himself, does he?"

"No, he looks like a mannequin."

"He's been dead for over a week. They had to do an autopsy."

"Such a shame."

"How horrible."

Mourners gathered around Duane's coffin, speaking in hushed tones.

The funeral was open-casket. Mouth drawn in a death line, he was no longer the terrifying authority figure. Once a reigning king with a slew of people to control. Now a rather sorry-looking, shriveled up would-be man.

The processional walked its way toward the graveyard. The sky was cold and gray. Scattered fence posts topped with a hard crust of winter snow. Evergreens beyond gave an eerie backdrop.

Our backyard: the site of Duane's eternal resting place.

My feet were killing me. For the umpteenth time, I inwardly cursed the high heels. I defended my choice by telling myself they were boots. Regardless, silly for an afternoon on rough, snowy terrain.

Tom Jones was among attendees. A regular peeper of town catastrophe, like watching sandbaggers work to keep the river waters back. Doris Meyer and Myrtle Anderson, the ladies who reported every birth, death and divorce in Welcome. Pickles Johnson, who followed the volunteer fire department.

Malcolm and Mara. Erica with her arm around Sonja. Mom in a long black wool coat. Puffs of air emerged from her ruby lips. Dad and Josie alongside her. Steve and Mary and their seven kids and me. Like props in a play, insiders were supporters of the illusion at all costs. To make it real. As in life, at his death we wore drawn expressions of sorrow. Schooled in this game, I kept my head bowed.

Held by aluminum rollers, his coffin floated over the grave. An Ebenezer Scrooge ending.

No one shed a tear. Reverend Anderson wrapped up the graveside prayer. We moved as one toward the house for lunch. An odd tradition in my mind—food following funerals.

"Rosemarie," Erica called, jogging toward me. She wore a black suit coat and slacks, her graying hair closely shorn against her scalp.

Malcolm strolled over. His head was shaved, his eyes gaunt and shadowed with age. "Rosemarie. Bless you," he said, his voice had been taken down several notches.

"Sorry for your loss," I said.

Erica pushed her hands in her pockets. "I saw George and his wife at a basketball game. My nephew was playing."

I hadn't seen George since he got married almost twenty years ago. I only knew his kids from Facebook. "How's the oil field?"

"Slow going at this point, but a bright future," she said. "Supposed to start fracking early spring."

"Good deal." I took a step back.

"You know who I saw at the grocery store this morning?" Malcolm asked. "Victor Frank."

"Cool."

"I thought you two would get married. He's not married, and you married..."

"Interesting obituary," I said.

"You liked it?" Erica's eyes widened. "I wrote it for Sonja. I don't know if anyone told you, but Mom's going to be living with me."

I nodded. "I'm glad to hear it."

"Are you headed home?" Malcolm asked. "Supposed to be a storm coming in."

"Really?"

"Look me up if you ever make it to Glendive." Malcolm thrust his hand toward me. His handshake was firm, but not too firm. Not too long. A good handshake.

Sonja was waiting in the Chevy Impala, engine running. Children in adult bodies. They hadn't changed other than age spots and wrinkles. Still little kids seeking attention, approval, and validation.

"Tough to have him buried where he is," I said. "If I were you, I'd leave him there."

I walked away, and pulled my phone from my pocket, googling the weather. Huh. Malcolm was right.

After supper, I texted Rich. **I checked the radar report. State patrol advised no travel.**

Leave now. Where did they bury him?

The backyard.

Weirder than weird. I'll see you at home.

I headed toward the pickup and my phone pinged again. It was Greg.

Anne and I are at Applebee's in Jamestown. Swing by.

I started to type **I can't** and hit the back button. **I'd love to. Be there in a half hour.**

I'd never deliberately disobeyed Rich. A surge of power flowed through me, and I felt more alive than I had since the night I planned to sneak out and meet Victor.

73

Greg and Anne had a table saved when I arrived at Applebee's. Greg wore a brown sweater and matching scarf. For a second, he reminded me of the boy I'd met nearly forty years ago. Anne, beautiful as always. Her blonde hair curled in perfect waves around her face and a powder-blue sweater matching her eyes.

"This is like when we were kids." I sat next to Anne.

"Has anyone heard from Shelly?" Greg asked.

Anne said, "She married a taxidermist. Last I heard they live in Michigan."

"What about you, Anne?" I asked.

"I moved to Bismarck and went to school for medical laboratory science. I worked at St. Alexis hospital. Then two years ago, I needed a change and came back to Welcome and began Sunflower Anne."

She didn't mention Aaron Demit and the rumored baby, and I wasn't going to ask.

"What did Rich say when you told him you were meeting us in Jamestown?" Greg asked.

Heat crept up the back of my neck. "I didn't tell him."

Greg wiped his mouth with a napkin. "I stopped taking my meds."

I stirred my tea. "Don't you have to be weaned off those?"

"I was working on a car and the next thing I knew, Susan was standing over me. I'd fallen asleep."

"I fall asleep during movies all the time." Anne took a bite of her burger.

Greg was staring off into space.

"Who do you see?" I asked.

"Duane Sim."

"Truly?"

"Truly."

I blew a long sigh, letting my head fall back toward the ceiling. "Thank the stars. For a dreadful minute, I thought it was..." I swallowed. "Never mind what I thought."

Rosemarie. It isn't for him to consort with the dead.

"It isn't..."

Or for you to call him out.

He placed both hands on the table, leaned forward, wild eyes boring into mine. "Old Man Warter wants you dead."

"Sit down," I whispered, glancing around, an uneasy feeling making its way in my gut.

He went on in a loud voice. "I saw a dark figure follow you into the fitness center where you work out, and stab you over and over until you were dead."

Anne reached for my arm. "Oh Rosemarie."

The room closed in, conversations around me dimmed.

Zip. Zip. Rich sharpening his knife was crystal clear as a winter's day.

In a higher realm emerged a stronghold with massive columns, built brick by brick with dark thoughts of self-hatred, shame, and hopelessness.

Rosemarie was locked inside the thick walls. Her lifelong friends, Greg Hamill and Anne Clark, were no match for the haughty guards outside her chamber door, pride and justification. They remained unmovable, holding their position with a superior air.

A vast depth of insecurity reinforced the foundation. Surrounding the fortress, a hulking spirit of dread. Hateful beings crowded the southern portico. Origins of the territory, envy and lust, slithered about the gate.

"Earth to Rosemarie. Come in Rosemarie." Greg waved a hand in front of my face.

"Rich never laid a hand on me," I said.

"Like *Sleeping with the Enemy*," Greg said. "Only unlike Julia Roberts's character Sarah Waters, you don't have proof you're abused."

"I hate that word." I dunked my tea bag. "I'm the one who's got the issues. I'm needy and paranoid. I feel grouchy all the time."

Greg wiped his mouth with a napkin. "Sure is coming down out there."

"Maybe you'll get stranded, Rosemarie." Anne downed the last of her coffee.

"Rich would kill me," I said. "Not really, but you know what I mean."

Greg peered at me. "Just because you're paranoid doesn't mean he isn't after you."

"Did you see that in your crystal ball, Kurt Cobain?" I asked.

"No, but I'll tell you what I did see, Lady Lion. Why you ever married Rich is..."

Anne had the last word. "What you don't see with your eyes, don't witness with your mouth."

74

The National Weather Service interrupts this broadcast to bring you an announcement: *Urgent-winter weather message. Griggs, Steele, Foster, Wells, Grand Forks...Southern Stutsman, Kidder, Sheridan counties ...Heavy snow and areas of blowing and drifting snow will reduce visibility...*

A hint of scattered snowfall in the air clouded the black stubble field. The cruise set, I sped down Interstate 94, tiny flakes growing to gradual snow fog.

The prairie was lost in a cloud.

Brake lights emanated from the semi in front of me. Snow gathered on the windshield, melting in pools of slush. The ice-wrapped blades dragged watery paths across my line of vision.

Darkness fell.

A white-knuckled grip on the steering wheel, I said, "A little snow isn't a blizzard."

The wind howled, slamming bits of ice against the side of the truck. Needles of anxiety prickled my spine. I took the nearest exit and continued for several miles.

At the sound of rushing wind, the truck rolled to a halt. The engine chugged for several seconds before dying. I couldn't be out of gas. I filled up before I left. I glanced at my phone. No service. I popped the hood and got out. A blast of frigid air took my breath away. I trudged through a drift, shining my cell flashlight on the problem.

I knew nothing of engines other than the oil was good and the washer fluid was a little low. I climbed back in the truck and blew on my hands.

"God, help me."

While I waited for His response, I felt around the back seat. There was a duffle bag. I riffled through it and found a black case. Inside, Rich's knife set and *The Silver Chair.*

The cab grew uncomfortably cold and my fingers began to hurt. A song came to mind, *"I'm dreaming of a white Christmas."*

The pressure on my bladder from last night's binge drinking was unbearable. I crossed my legs and bit my lip before finally getting out. The cold cut through my jeans. I peed quickly and tried to jog around the truck. The snow was too thick. Jumping jacks? Nope. I got back inside.

The soft suede of my boots was a poor barrier, and my feet began to ache. I wiggled my toes and hummed "Amazing Grace" imagining a fire and hot cider.

My fingers screamed for mercy. I peeled off my gloves, wincing at painful fingertips. Needles of frozen agony stabbed my hands and feet. I tried to remember the words of "Holly Jolly Christmas."

Panic licked my gut. "I'm c-cold and s-stupid, stupid, stupid."

My eyes drifted shut.

Out of the blinding snow came a howling vapor of black. It shot away, freaked and squealing in horror, erupting a path of green fog.

Behind it, Michael sailed, light shattered the spiraling dark fog, leaving a glimmering trail. The black creature and Michael shot into the sky over the truck, twisting and turning like a rocket.

Then the fortress spewed out dark monsters, each one fleeing in terror, scattering in all directions. The first demon felt the heat of Amael's blade on his tail.

He shrieked over his shoulder, "Enough! I'm outta here."

The blazing edge of steel sliced through the air. The demon blocked the attack, shooting one of his own. Amael's well-aimed blows were relentless.

"Your time is up." Amael easily sliced through the hideous creature with a final blow. The demon faded, disappearing in a puff of black smoke.

"We'll go." A cluster screamed in unison.

In an instant, the seraphs slipped back to the realm where Rosemarie slept in the truck.

Michael watched the remaining hoard flee. "Look there." A blue Chevy truck approached.

Amael called an animal to his side. "Rosemarie knows scavengers such as these. It will be a warning to her." He eyed the coyote. "Stay."

I jerked from half-dead to wide awake. How long had I been asleep? Every nerve ending in my body cried out in frozen pain. I stilled. Something was outside the truck. I shut my eyes and counted to three. Then slowly opened them.

A pair of eyes glowed in the darkness outside my door. A coyote. Just then, dozens or more began to howl. They sounded close. I guess I wouldn't be getting out again. What are they waiting for?

You to die.

75

"Hey," a muffled shout woke me. A man pounded on my window. I rolled it down.

"Are you okay?" he asked.

"I think so." I wiggled stiff fingers and toes.

"A gal could freeze to death out here," the man said. Late forties, he wore a red stocking hat and a brown work jacket lined with fur at the collar.

"Do you have a phone I can use?"

"No sorry. My son-in-law's place is a couple miles from here. You could come and use the house phone."

"I don't know..."

"N-not likely to have a wrecker out here."

A stammer? Unusual for such an attractive man. "All right," I said, reaching for the duffle bag.

I tramped through thick snow to his pickup. He grabbed his checkbook off the passenger seat as I got in. Heat blasting from the vent, welcome warmth.

The silence wasn't really silent. His presence devoured the space. I sat on my hands, and his soul searched mine. My heart raced, believing some miracle brought me to him. It was me he'd been looking for all his life.

"Bad storm," I said. "I'm headed to Welcome on my way back from a funeral."

No need to share your life story with this guy.

"I'm Rosemarie Hamill," I blathered on. "I know you probably won't believe this, but before you showed up, there was a coyote outside my truck. Weird, right? In the middle of a blizzard, watching me."

He tapped the steering wheel. "C-coyotes form strong family groups. In spring, the female d-dens and gives birth to a litter of three to twelve pups."

"I didn't know." I pushed his arm.

"D-Don't usually see them when it's windy like this. I admire an animal willing to hunt in the middle of a b-blizzard."

My cheeks grew hot thinking about peeing in the snow. "Still, it could die in this weather like anything else."

"Name's Neil Johnson." He flashed a smile of even, white teeth.

A shiver rolled up my spine. *Dangerous.*

76

Yard lights emerged in the distance at the end of a cluster of cottonwoods. Every window lit the darkness. He pulled up to the front door. We got out, drudging through deep snow.

Mistletoe hung from the bright entrance. A real tree in the center of the living room with a toy train circling the base. Presents were stacked beneath the tree.

I glanced over to get a good look at him in the light. Straight out of a Nicholas Sparks film, his dark eyes caught mine and the world disappeared.

Two young women bustled about the kitchen. One, obviously pregnant. The other, maybe sixteen. Both, beautiful, cascades of dark hair past their slender shoulders. Suddenly, I felt old and frumpy. They dropped what they were doing and rushed Neil with hugs. "It's dark, Dad. We were worried."

"Okay, okay," he said.

The pregnant daughter released him and turned to me. "I'm Patty."

Neil shook his coat off. "Go on into the kitchen, Rosemarie. My daughters will get you something to drink."

"I'm good." I rubbed my forearms.

He washed his hands at the kitchen sink. "Might as well get comfortable. We already got fifteen inches. Supposed to snow until Thursday."

"Can I use your phone?" I peeled off my snow encrusted boots.

"Phone lines are down from last night's rain," Patty said. "You're welcome to stay until the plow goes through."

The younger one handed me a tall glass of pink liquid. "It's Christmas punch. I'm Heidi."

"Thank you." I took a swallow. Lemonade with a hint of orange at the end. Delicious.

A boy and a girl ran through the kitchen. "Mommy," they cried, flying at Patty.

"Did you have a good nap?" She rumpled the boy's head.

"Yes." He looked at me. "Who's dat?"

"I'm Rosemarie," I said.

He thrust his thumb at his chest. "I'm Damion. I'm three." He held up three stubby fingers, and pointed to his sister. "She's Samara. She can say mamma. She's two."

The door opened with a blast of cold air. A man in his late twenties, stomped his feet, and said, "Getting deep out there. Supposed to get another three feet."

"Hey, Logan," Neil said. "I found a gal whose vehicle broke down over by Forbes' old place."

"Good thing. It's going to be a bad one." Logan shed his coat and made his way to the kitchen. He kissed Patty on the lips, and whispered something in her ear. She blushed.

I blew on my hands. "I'm sure the highway patrol would have been along shortly."

A woman walked in wearing a blue sweater, her dark hair cut in a stylish blunt bob. She was in her early forties and unmistakable.

"Shelly? Is it you?" I rushed her.

Recognition lit her eyes and she smiled. "How are you, Rosemarie?" She drew me in a warm embrace.

I hugged her back. "I can't believe this. I'm so glad to see you, Shelly."

"I go by Michelle now."

Logan offered his chair. "Sit here, Michelle."

"Thank you." Michelle sat down. Neil took a seat next to her, hand resting on her lower back. Patty hurried over with a cup of coffee, nearly sloshing it. Heidi brought out a fresh loaf of bread and a plate of butter.

"I heard you were in Michigan, Michelle," I said, sitting down.

"I got a job transfer. We are staying with our daughter, Patty and her husband, Logan until they finish the closing process on our house. Patty and Heidi are our foster children," she said, and took a sip of coffee.

"Oh, okay," I said.

Logan took a seat at the table. "What do you do for a living, Rosemarie?"

"I own Hamill's Bakery."

"My wife is a stellar baker." Logan spread butter over a thick slice of homemade bread.

Michelle leaned forward, resting her chin on her hands. "Tell me about your family."

"I have two boys. Peter is a junior in high school and Jim is in eighth grade."

A girl around fourteen hung in the doorway.

Michelle waved her over. "Come in, Emma. Don't be shy. Rosemarie, this is Emma, our newest foster child."

"Hi," Emma said.

Like bees in a hive, all catered to Michelle, bringing her bread, filling her glass. Neil sat alongside her, back straight and proud.

I had imagined a much older, pudgier Shelly. An absent husband. Disrespectful children. Instead, Shelly—Michelle—became queen bee of a perfect life.

It felt a little too perfect.

We don't go by what we feel but what we know.

Shut up, Duane.

77

Emma led me to the spare room. The floor was hardwood. There was a poster bed with a patchwork quilt in the center. Next to it, an oval throw rug. A clock on the end table was a black cat's face.

"How old are you?" I asked her.

"Thirteen."

"Do you like to read?" Her eyes followed me as I reached for the duffle. I unzipped it, grabbed *The Silver Chair* and handed it to her.

She didn't move. "It looks like fantasy."

"When I was younger, my mom didn't let me read certain books. I got really good at hiding places." I made an obvious show of tucking the book between the mattresses.

After she left, I crawled beneath the covers. The last thing I wanted to do was get comfortable. Michelle was lucky. I envied her. A gorgeous husband devoted to her. Happy, successful children.

I wanted to go home.

Neil was in the kitchen when I woke the next morning. He wore a blue flannel shirt and a nine o'clock shadow. He had an easy smile and knowing eyes. Patty arrived and made breakfast. The ham quiche and lime sherbet drink were delicious.

I avoided looking at Neil for the rest of the morning.

Zero visibility along with blowing and drifting snow caused Interstate 29 between Fargo and the Canadian border to close. I-94 from Dickinson to Fargo.

All afternoon, snow blanketed the prairie.

Casual conversation with Patty revealed she was eighteen and Logan was twenty-four as of September. Young to be married but happy.

Logan came in while Patty was playing with Damion and Samara. He said something low under his breath and she followed him out of the room. I found out later it was to make supper.

Emma baked cupcakes with me because Michelle told her to. I sensed the entire time she'd rather be anywhere else.

The cupcakes were a hit.

78

It was still snowing at five forty a.m. on Wednesday. The weather report was on.

"Dangerous wind chill factors will continue to plague residents in the Northern Plains after a blizzard shut down a nearly 300-mile stretch of highway. The brutal cold will continue as sub-zero temperatures are forecasted in portions of the Dakotas..."

I was alone in the kitchen when the front door opened and Neil walked in. "Rosemarie. You're up early." His low voice played havoc with my insides.

"I made coffee."

"Smells good." He held up a flask and arched a brow. "Do you mind?"

My heart gave three swift kicks. "No." I poured two cups of the steaming, black liquid.

He added whisky and sat across from me. "Your husband must be worried sick."

"Rich? More likely ticked off he can't get ahold of me on my phone."

Neil studied his mug for a moment. "You're a beautiful woman."

"Thank you." Every fiber of my being came alive. "Can I ask you something?"

"You bet."

"How is it you're so good to your wife?" I found myself telling him the suspicions I had about Holly. He didn't interrupt or make faces. His silence was attentive and warm. When finished, I asked, "What do you think?"

"If it looks like a duck and acts like a duck, chances are it's a duck."

I couldn't straighten my thoughts. "My life was satisfactory. I was perfectly..." the 't' in perfect, clicking my tongue, "...fine with it. Now I feel so good, a little spinny, I admit, but mostly...delicious," I whispered. "And the fact I do makes me feel terrible."

He smiled and stood.

Taking it as my cue, I got up. "I'm sorry if I babbled too much."

"I enjoyed it." He came up behind me.

My traitorous heart slammed in my chest. It was wrong, the situation. Me, him. But I was alone with him. For a sliver of time, everything was good and right with the world.

His arms came around me and he whispered in my ear, "Is this okay, Rosie?"

Rosie? No one called me that anymore. Not even Steve. "My name's Rosemmmmarie."

"Light weight." He chuckled, his fingers brushed the soft skin beneath my sweater.

An indication life was good again.

The sound of others echoed through the hallway. I glanced at the wall clock. Eight a.m.

Michelle walked in and he stepped back. She appeared oblivious. I was sweaty with relief.

Keep to yourself, Rosemarie.

I retreated to the guest room and waited behind the door for Neil to come. He didn't. *Stupid.* I flopped across the bed, mulling over my situation. I hadn't done anything wrong, but the cloud remained.

Something was wrong with me.

79

Skies cleared Thursday, winds died down and temperatures dipped to thirty below. Patty played with Samara and Damion. Heidi and I baked cookies. Emma cooked and cleaned. Michelle was in her office doing paperwork. Logan was out with the cattle.

Neil's blue Chevy was running outside the front door. Patty sent freshly brewed coffee with us. Alongside him in the warm cab, I thought of all the things I wanted to say.

He handed me the thermos. "It's going to be lonesome around here."

"I know, right?" I twisted off the top.

"There it is." Neil slowed to a halt and exited the pickup. I drew a breath and followed suit. The frigid air bit my cheeks. My nostrils stuck together. Hard snow squeaked beneath my feet. We stood a minute and then he pulled me against him in a rough hug. He feels it too. Better leave now before something bad happens.

Headlights closed the distance. A tow truck and my red Toyota Prius.

A mixture of relief and disappointment churned inside me. I made my way over.

Rich exited the car and gave me a hug. "I came as soon as I heard." He turned to Neil. "I can't thank you enough for saving her."

Neil watched the tow truck driver hook a rope to the hitch. "Glad to help. We'll see you, folks." He got into his truck and drove away.

Rich handed me a thermos.

"Thank you." I unscrewed the lid and frowned. "It's empty."

"Is it? My bad."

"Also," I handed him the duffle to lighten the atmosphere, "Kind of hard to work without knives."

He unzipped the bag. "Oh, this is my old set. I got the Wüsthof Classic set."

"I don't remember them," I said.

Rich rolled his eyes. "You were with me when I bought it."

Shhh. You know this game.

"Oh right," I said. Game? The pieces began to fall into place, but it didn't make sense. He'd been playing with me this whole time? A sinking feeling in the pit of my stomach said that was exactly what he had been doing. But why? What was the purpose?

The void swallowed the miles it took to drive home.

80

Donald Trump became president. Experts didn't take him seriously. He was the first without government or U.S. military experience. It was the end of the world if you followed any kind of social media.

Rich sat on the couch scrolling through his phone. "I could use some coffee."

I headed for the kitchen. Soon, the aroma of freshly brewed coffee wafted through the air. I started the tea kettle, my thoughts drifted to Neil. I barely slept last night. The hole his absence left was terrifying. How could I have gotten wrapped up in a man so quickly?

"I got home half an hour ago and you were nowhere to be found," Rich said.

I handed him his coffee. "I went for a walk. I thought a little fresh air would do me good."

"Where exactly did you go?"

"To the post office and back." I sat down, dunking the tea bag.

"Next time, tell me where you're going. I had to ping your phone."

"Everyone in the post office stared at me when you did."

"Tell me where you are and I wouldn't have to," Rich said. "I thought you froze to death." He glared at me. "I was worried sick. Why didn't you answer any of my texts or calls?"

"No service."

"Landline?"

"Phone lines were down."

"If you would have come straight home after Frankenstein's funeral, you would have been way ahead of it."

"I told you, I had lunch with Greg and Anne."

"I'm glad you're alright. Truck had a busted belt." He flipped on the TV, taking two noisy whiffs. "Whatever you're slurping doesn't smell like coffee." I poured the rest of the Chai down the sink.

Netflix—the source of twenty-four seven cult-watch. Thirty-nine members of Heaven's Gate took their own lives. All wearing the same Nike tennis shoes, they believed an alien spaceship hiding in the tail of a speeding comet was coming for them.

"Castration." I shuddered, my eyes on the kitchen TV. "You'd have to be crazy to join a cult."

"Nope, but it sure helps," Rich said, sliding a knife into its place. "You don't have a thing for him."

"I don't, no."

"That's two no's. See, Rosemarie? This is my chef knife." He withdrew a six-inch blade and sliced through the air. "Slit your neck with one swipe. The one in my truck is from back when we were first married."

"They look the same to me. What happened to the set you bought online?"

"Sold a long time ago." He picked up a six-inch serrated blade. "This is used to cut bread or saw through any fare."

"Did I know you sold it?"

"Actually no. You were pretty mad about it. You remember the argument?"

I searched my brain. "Not specifically."

"I'm surprised. It was pretty bad." He held up a thick pair of kitchen shears. "These are used to cut bones."

"Ouch."

"Break chicken legs effortlessly," he said, snapping the shears open and shut. "You have your phone on you?"

"Yes."

"In case I need to get ahold of you. I still can't believe you don't remember." He returned the shears and pulled out a skinner knife. "Neil Johnson is a good looking guy."

"I hadn't noticed."

He flicked his thumb over the edge of the blade. "Keep it that way."

81

President Park Geun-hye, South Korea's first democratically elected leader was forced from office. Judges unanimously upheld parliament's decision to impeach Park over her role in a corruption scandal involving her close friend, Choi Soon-sil.

A moving van pulled up to the house next door.

Neil smiled and waved. A sweet gush of ecstasy rushed through me. Feeling nothing so long, my heart sucked up every drop of moisture like a thirsty desert. A coincidence? I think not. The universe was tipping in my favor.

I made popcorn for our Saturday night movie The Avengers and opened a package of Oreos.

Peter grabbed a handful as he walked by. "Are you sure you should be eating these, Mom?"

"Probably not." I shoved one in my mouth. I'd hit the gym an extra hour.

"It's only one cookie." Jim to the rescue.

"Exactly," I said.

"You have the body you've always wanted. Don't ruin it," Rich said.

"Right." I put the cookies away, thinking of the next door neighbor.

Emma returned The Silver Chair. We baked cupcakes for her birthday party Wednesday.

"My favorite part of the book was when they freed Prince Rilian from the spell cast by the Queen of the Underworld." Emma placed paper in the cupcake tins.

"Mine was the witch, green powder, and her magical mandolin." I licked my finger.

"I know," Emma said. "I shut the book when all four of them were hypnotized."

"Puddleglum saved the day."

"Burnt webbed feet sure weren't enchanting," Emma said, clapping her hands. "And the best part, the spell was broken and the creatures of the underworld were free."

"Want to lick the bowl?" I held it up.

Emma's eyes lit. "Yeah."

There was a knock on the door. Michelle stood in the entrance, watching us. "There you are, Emma. I thought you were going to clean the bathroom today."

"I have to be going, Rosemarie. See ya," she said, and was gone.

"Would you like a cup of coffee?" I asked.

Michelle sat at the table. "Sure."

"I'm sorry, I didn't realize she had chores." I set a mug and a fresh cupcake in front of her.

Michelle sipped her coffee. "When we were kids you used to tell me stories."

My insides warmed. "Echo and Narcissus were my favorite."

"The thing is, Emma already has a wild imagination. We're trying to help her get her feet firmly planted on the ground. She doesn't need you filling her head with silly stories."

"Okay. I'm sorry."

What are you sorry for?

Michelle took a bite of her cupcake. "Mm, this is really good, Rosemarie."

"Thank you," I murmured. "I made them this morning. I'll send some home with you if you like." I carefully placed the cupcakes in a Tupperware container and sealed it shut.

"I should be going. Thanks again." Michelle took the cupcakes and left.

82

The cupcakes were in the garbage.

It took exactly thirty minutes for me to realize Michelle left her purse at my house. I hurried over to her house and knocked on the door. There was no answer. It was open. I set her purse on the table. Then I noticed the sorry mess of frosting and crumbs in a heap of trash.

Maybe they were dry.

Because you and Emma were having fun.

Or maybe, because they weren't any good. I flicked a glance around. The kitchen was empty. I reached for the one at the top. Another glance around, I peeled the paper away. I pressed my finger in it. Soft. Only one way to find out. I took a bite.

Moist and delicious.

"Rosemarie."

I dumped the cupcake into the trash and wiped my guilty face with the back of my hand. "Hey," I mumbled through the forbidden morsel. "It's not what it looks like."

"I'm on my way out," Neil said.

"I came to return this." I held up the purse. "Michelle left it at my house."

"She's at her office." He flashed a beautiful smile. "I'm headed to the shop. You should come see it."

"I don't know..."

"Her office is on the way. Come on. It'll take ten minutes."

"Okay."

The new steel building reflected an iridescent sheen of violet and gold from the setting sun. Neil met me at the door. "Come on in. It still needs drywall, but they finished the insulation yesterday."

"Nice," I said, my heart hammering in my throat. "Seems spacious."

"Yeah, should be good." Neil took a step toward me, his heavy-lidded gaze fixed on my breasts. "Really good." The gravel-like sound of his voice was clever fingers stroking my flesh. I wanted his mouth on me.

My breath came out quickly, his hands were beneath my shirt, stripping my inhibitions until I was mindless.

There was a noise outside the door. He quickly stepped away and I straightened my shirt.

Flustered, I turned and left. Arriving home, I realized I still had Michelle's purse.

A thought made its way through my foggy brain.

Neil hadn't stuttered once today.

The boys left for school. Rich left for the restaurant. Heart pounding like a wild bird in my chest, I changed my shirt three times and ignored the persistent voice of reason. I'm returning her purse. He's probably not even there. Even if he is, it doesn't mean anything will happen. But he'll see how good I look. I'll see it in his eyes. It will be enough.

Neil was home. He smiled wide when he saw me. My heart hammered two hard strokes.

Easy Rosemarie. He's married.

He's lonely, like you.

He invited me to sit next to him with a pat on the cushion and a heady look. And then his mouth was on mine for the time it took to turn my brain into absolute mush. When he pulled away, his eyes were heavy and his smile, hot. "We need to talk."

"What do you mean?" I scooted away from him, both devastated and relieved.

Discomfiture in his eyes sliced deep. "We need to cool it. You're really pretty, Rosemarie."

Really pretty? "I was going to....you must know how I feel."

"This," he motioned between us, "Is going to blow up."

The truth slammed into me. "Right."

"I don't want to hurt anybody."

"I don't either." What was I doing? I scooted to the far end of the couch.

"I wanted to give you this." He handed me a jewelry box with a smile.

I didn't like his smile at all, rather despised it.

A ruby necklace.

"I didn't tell anyone." I closed the lid, passing it back. "I don't...I thought you wanted..." My voice was weak and my aspirations bled out.

"You're really hot, Rosemarie." Each attempt he made to soften the blow was painful and terrifying. Final. His eyes were on me like he expected me to explode. "Now I feel bad."

Regret in his tone was soothing ointment on my wound. "Don't feel bad." My smile wobbled, I lifted my chin and pushed the pain deep so he didn't see I was hemorrhaging inside. "I don't."

"Really?" He lifted a brow and caught my eye. "You really are smokin' if it's alright I say so."

The reality of his words reached my brain, but the rest of me refused them like a moldy piece of rye bread. Denial was morphine to the slow death of my dream.

83

Rich was at the bakery. Michelle invited me over for Emma's birthday supper at her new house. I didn't tell Rich I was going. Risky, but better to ask forgiveness than permission. Besides, I knew he would say no and I'd deliberately disobey. This way I could feign innocence.

The whole gang showed up. Heidi parked herself at a baby grand piano. Patty rested a twelve-string guitar on her swollen belly. Damion and Samara had toy drums. As for me, I drank in the concept of a close family. Samara brought her drum over and handed me a stick. She began banging on the drum.

"Do you play an instrument too, Rosemarie?" Patty asked.

"I guess I do now." I beat the drum.

"I'll get the board games out," Heidi said. "We can play after supper."

Neil walked in. The piano stopped playing, drummers quit drumming and the guitarist halted her strumming. Emptiness replaced merrymaking. Insignificance instead of togetherness. Shame rather than enjoyment.

Without a word, Patty followed him out of the room.

My mind refused to believe what it had witnessed. It was probably something Patty did. She'd done something she wasn't supposed to.

Patty returned, took the instruments away from her children and they started to cry.

I followed them to the kitchen.

Supper was a quiet affair with no Neil. The clinking of silverware and glassware, the only noise breaking the heavy silence.

Emma reached for the pitcher of punch and it slipped from her grasp. We all backed away as the contents spilled on our laps and the floor. "I'm sorry, I'm sorry," she said.

"Emma." Michelle sighed. "Go get a towel."

Tears brimming in her eyes, Emma hurried from the room.

There were no board games.

There was a knock on the bathroom door.

Neil stood in the doorway. My mind couldn't comprehend why he was there, but my heart jumped wildly. He shut the door behind him without a word. His eyes said he'd been drinking and he wanted me. Desire raced hot through my veins, wiping every conscious thought from my mind. There was no mistaking his intent. He was hopelessly drawn to me as I was to him. Heart pounding, I didn't say anything as he came up behind me. His body pressed against mine. "I love the sweater."

"It's new."

"I noticed." His arms came around me. "You're beautiful. You imagine how it would be if not for Michelle?" We stood in silence. I wished I knew what he was thinking.

He turned me around and kissed me.

Tentative at first and then voraciously. It was everything a kiss ought to be. Soft, yet demanding. Hot and bone-aching. Neil tasted like whisky, fruit and delicious.

I was powerless to deny him anything he wanted. My arms found their way around his shoulders. But he didn't stop. I didn't stop, and lost my head, who I was and why it was wrong to kiss him back.

After long, intoxicating kisses, Neil lifted his head.

A crash outside the bathroom door made me jump. Sanity returned in a rush. I stepped away. "I'm sorry." I turned to leave and caught his smirk in the mirror.

He was laughing at me.

84

The plow blocked me in.

Maybe the Johnsons had a rope. I grabbed the bottle of wine Darla gave me for Christmas. I hadn't seen Neil since Emma's birthday party. My stomach performing achy flip flops, I made my way over to their house.

He opened the door. Wine in hand, I smiled, taking a step toward him.

"Whoa." Both his hands shot up in the air and down behind his head. "What are you doing?"

I don't know what I expected, but not for him to throw his hands in surrender like I was...ugly. "I...they plowed me in. Do you have a rope I could borrow?"

A look of annoyance flashed across his handsome features. "Isn't your husband around?"

"He's at work." I didn't like the way he said "your husband." Formal and cold like I was no one to him.

You are no one to him.

"I don't know," he said. "I'm pretty busy."

My gaze dropped. "I'm sorry to have bothered you. I'll figure something out."

He sighed loudly. "Wait here."

Setting the bottle of wine on the end table, I mulled over the situation. What was his deal? Acting like he couldn't keep his hands off me one minute, and the next I had the plague. Deep feelings of worthlessness worked their way inside, eating at my confidence like a horse clearing grass in an empty pasture.

Neil returned in coveralls, a heavy jacket and ski mask. Dark eyes pierced mine. He was not trying to scare me. It was cold. This was not a threat.

Something's not right.

"The cupcakes weren't dry," I said, attempting to ease his fury. "The children loved them. They ate three each."

Silence.

"How will we get it out?" I asked, ignoring the unease creeping in my gut.

"Hook on the tow rope."

"To me?" I giggled.

"We could do that," he said. "I could hook it up and drag you around behind my truck. What do you think?"

He's joking. "I think I don't want to be dragged around. What do you think?"

"I think definitely," he uttered beneath his breath. "You have to be careful because it could snap and kill you. A guy was killed one time when the rope broke. The metal hook flew through the rear window. Took his head clean off."

"How horrible."

"Your husband would have to find a replacement wife."

"Too bad I'm not replaceable."

"Everyone's replaceable."

"Uh..."

"It was a joke, Rosemarie." Neil grabbed the tow rope from the back of his truck. Shoulders slumped, he made his way over to the hitch on my car.

I watched him hook his truck to my buried Prius. A wave of compassion swept over me. He was a good man, coming out to help me. But like Sonja and the hairdryer all those years ago, asking once was okay.

Not twice.

A rare night out with Rich and Neil was on his deck when we left. I wore my little black dress and caught his heavy lidded gaze as I climbed into the truck.

Chalk one up for Rosemarie.

At Applebee's, I sat in a confused fog and sipped from the tall mug in front of me. Working on popcorn, Rich was in a fantastic mood. "I know you probably think I'm crazy, but I think a move might be in order," he said. "I can't stand living next to Neil Johnson."

"Can't get away from bad neighbors. They have a way of finding you." I took a long swallow of my beer.

"Granny's in Grafton is going out of business," he said.

"What's in Grafton?"

"An opportunity."

"Sounds like you've got it all figured out."

"Only if you think it's a good idea," he said, his eyes grew serious. "We're in this together."

A surge of hope rushed through me. A fresh start for me to work on my career, our budget, my weight. Maybe I could make an appointment to get my hair done. I'd make new friends and hadn't failed.

I wouldn't fail.

85

Neil was on his deck smoking a cigar as I left for work.

"Rosemarie." He waved me over.

"What?" I checked my phone: eleven p.m. Rich and the boys were sleeping, but I spent the entire week thinking of the way he acted when I needed help. He could fly a kite.

"Can I talk to you?" he asked, sadness in his voice reminding me of the stutter when I first met him. He wasn't bad, only socially inept.

"Yeah?" I made my way over, stopping at the bottom step of his porch.

Embers glowed from a dying fire. He opened the cooler next to him. "Do you want a drink?"

"No thanks, I'm headed to the bakery."

He stared at me for a minute. Like he was lost, and I was the very air he needed to breathe. "What's this I hear about you leaving?"

"Yeah."

His eyes took on the firelight. "Sucks. I mean for us, not for you."

"Yeah." I scanned his tidy deck.

"You should come visit me." His eyes held mine once more. I'd never had anyone stare at me so intensely. My heart hammered riotously in my chest.

"Yeah. See ya." I waved, and made my way to my car. Inside, I leaned my head against the steering wheel, drawing a ragged breath. What was wrong with me? A snap of his fingers, and I was already looking forward to the next time I would see him.

The gym floor was dirty.

Planking: proof time is relative. I'd made it up to two minutes each. Three sets. Each, an eternity. I observed the black spongy floor around me. Dust particles, dirt and pet hair. How many memberships had a furry roommate? I exhaled, bits scattering. I checked the time.

Thirty-five seconds to go.

I blew the dirt this time. Everything around me flew, and I noticed something. The edge of my range where all the particles sat. A small feather waved when I blew at it, but didn't move. The edge of my reach.

That's where you need to be.

I smiled and knew what to do. Put enough distance between me and him where a blast couldn't move me. Ruffle my feathers. Not blow me away.

"I am not replaceable." I rolled onto my back.

86

We pulled out of McDonald's drive-thru in Jamestown. Peter wiggled his big toe through the hole in his shoe. "See? Told you I needed new ones."

"Man, I was at Walmart yesterday. I could have picked up a pair." I took a bite of a breakfast sandwich.

Peter dug through the bag. "School's lame, Mom."

"What about it is lame? The school work or the teachers, or..."

"All of it."

"What do you think about moving?" I asked.

Peter shrugged. "Not up to me."

"Of course it's up to you. You're part of this family."

"We'll move. I don't see Dad changing his mind."

Peter felt the same way I did. Uprooting and moving to a town where we knew no one was an oppressive reality spoiling the non-Rich moment. But like Peter, I didn't see Rich changing his mind.

I forced a bright smile. "How's your breakfast sandwich?"

"Pretty all right." Peter-speak for "delicious."

At home in his room, Peter sat in front of his computer.

"Games again?" I said. "I thought you were reading the Harry Potter series."

"Finished it." Peter started punching keys. "Mom, you would like this game if you played it."

"I'm sure."

"Really. There's even another dimension called the Void. I'll send you the link."

"Sounds interesting."

"You can read up on characters' back stories. For old peeps like you, Mom."

Out of nowhere, Rich stomped into the room, got in Peter's face, and shouted, "You ungrateful punk."

Shock widened Peter's eyes. He closed the laptop, hanging his head in shame.

My fists shook like a fighter in a ring. A gale force shot through the fiber of my soul, and without thinking, I shouted, "Leave him alone! Don't ever talk to him like that again!"

Peter got up and fled the room.

Rich turned on me in shock. "I was always taught to respect my mom. He was acting like a pathetic little punk."

"It doesn't give us the right to act like punks. We are the parents, he is the child."

Surprise lifted his eyes, quickly shifting to accusation. "You went to McDonald's."

Icy fear shot up my palms. "Were you following us?"

"I checked the bank account."

"Then you know I had money for breakfast."

"Do you know how many calories one of those pancake sandwiches has?" He gave me a look of disgust. "You're a terrible parent."

A surge of memories came flooding back. When I lost my temper and yelled. The day I kicked a hole in the living room wall. Every single time I was too weak to stand up for the boys. All said I was indeed a bad mother. But a deeper, quieter voice said something different.

"I'm a good mother." A feeling of power erupted through the core of my being. I was exhilarated. Before I could utter another word, his phone pinged.

He looked up with wide eyes. "Aaron Demit died."

87

Welcome Lutheran Church was standing room only. Every pew was filled along with a hundred folding chairs brought out by parishioners.

Aaron Demit, wild child, friend of Welcome, loving husband, and beloved father. Victor and Pearl were in attendance. Tommy, Robin with their girls, Ella and Sammy. Oliver and Lauren. Emily, all grown up with her husband and their two children.

Weird. My peers were grandparents.

Tears of joy and laughter were shed. By the time Fred stood and told a humorous story about Aaron as a kid, there wasn't a dry eye in the sanctuary.

Following the service, Becky Walsky approached me. "I heard you're moving."

"Yes, we are. Things are much better between Rich and me."

Her eyes brightened. "Really? Did you take my suggestion and talk to Pastor Brady?"

"Actually," I thought of the Monopoly game at the parsonage, "I did. Thank you for asking."

Steve strolled over, baby Robert in his arms. "Hey Rosemarie. Good to see you."

"You too." Steve and Mary never quit having kids. Grown up Dana and Hector preceded Chloe, Jessica, Helen, Gertrude and baby Robert.

My phone buzzed. Anne. **A bunch of us are headed over to Fred's place.**

Rich was passed out on the bed. I pulled my boots on, and shut the door quietly behind me.

Vanessa, Aaron's widow, answered Demit's door in a designer red dress and high-heel boots. "Fred and Suzie are in the kitchen."

Fred gave me a hug. "Rosemarie, thanks for coming."

"I'm sorry about Aaron."

Suzie's eyes filled with tears. "He was a good boy."

"Come on in and grab yourself a drink and something to eat," Fred said.

Stacey, Barb and Darla gave me hugs, tears streaming down their cheeks. Vanessa and Aaron's sister, Amber, went around making sure everyone had drinks and hors d'oeuvres.

Anne drew alongside me. "Look, there's Lynn and Laura. What good kids." Aaron's twins moved about the house, talking to anyone who needed to cry.

"Yeah they are," I said. "I see Donny Gild, but not Billy. I thought they were inseparable."

"They were until Don's twin boys were diagnosed with heart problems and ended up at the Mayo Clinic. Folks in Welcome put on a benefit for them, headed by Colleen Walsky. Raised over fifteen thousand dollars for bills and medical expenses."

"Hm." I took a sip of beer. "Billy and Donny hate the Walskys."

Anne sipped her wine cooler. "Don had a change of heart. Billy didn't."

After four drinks, I was between Darla and Holly on the couch, confessing my sins. "I'm sorry about all those things I said at the last funeral."

"What things?" Darla slid her arm around my neck.

"You know, gossip," I slurred.

Holly brought her face next to mine. "Who cares about gossip? I heard from the grapevine I'm going bankrupt."

"Isn't everyone?" I leaned forward. "I thought about going bankrupt. It started five years ago. I have a workable budget, but can't balance it to save a frog's life."

Darla patted my arm. "What's Rich think?"

"He's been good. He jokes about the fact I'm not great with numbers."

"I'll bet he does," Anne said from the overstuffed chair.

"Anne." I waved. "I forgot you were there. We're moving to Grafton. I wanted to move. Maybe not to Grafton."

Anne stretched. "I'm sleepy. Rosemarie, you need a ride?"

"Most definitely."

In her car, Anne shuffled through her purse in the center console and pulled out a packet of cigarettes.

I frowned. "I didn't know you smoked."

"Bad habit I picked up from my mom's boyfriend when I was fifteen. I quit when I turned eighteen." She lit a cigarette. "I never touched another until last week. Now I'm up to two packs a day."

"Ouch."

"You can't move away." She took a drag and blew it out the window. "He's changed you, Rosemarie."

"That hurts."

Her blue eyes were serious. "Lady Lion would never let her husband steal her bakery, hire women behind her back, and make out with them in her place."

"Leave it to the Club Cat to call me out." I giggled. "And he said I made the kissing part up."

"Crazy making." She grabbed a used envelope from the glove compartment and scribbled digits down. "I'm giving you the number to my therapist. Go alone."

I shoved it in my boot. "He definitely won't buff."

"Here we are."

"You're such a good friend." I patted her arm, stumbled into our bedroom and crashed on the bed. Boots still on, I fell asleep before my head hit the pillow.

88

December 2017

I flipped the radio station, stopped on Michael Bublé and "Have Yourself a Merry Little Christmas."

"It's got Alco. Rent is the same as Jamestown," Rich said, taking the long way around Grafton. "Cheaper even. I checked the Walsh County Record. Lined up three places for us to look at. Granny's restaurant closed. A bit of a fixer-upper, but the owner says he might let it go for ninety thousand."

"Is that a good price?"

"We'll see. I'm looking at it tomorrow. In the meantime, you could waitress. There's like six restaurants. I'd like to settle down."

"Yeah." Settling where I didn't know a single person. My best shot, a waitress sounded like the last nail in my coffin.

"Grafton has the Assembly of God church." Rich pointed out the building as we drove by. "There's no place to go to church in Welcome."

"Are you kidding? What about Pastor Brady and Karen?"

"Welcome Lutheran? I'm not a big Lutheran fan," he groused, flipping the radio off. "Not a big fan of Christmas music either."

"I could stay in Welcome and you could go to Grafton," I said as the idea came to me.

A switch flipped and his eyes went dark. "I never told you about my ex-girlfriend, did I? Her name was Lilly. She was sort of like you."

A jolt of fear shot through me like lightning.

"Look her up," he said. "Lilly Bacchant. Also could be going by Lilly Rahil. Lost her job as a paralegal for Smith and Ryan firm. Couldn't get another afterward. Lost custody of her kids. Last I heard she ran off with some guy and is living in her truck outside town."

It sounded like he was boasting. And still keeping tabs? Hopelessness was a giant wave. "Fine!" I exploded. "I'll go wherever you tell me and work as a waitress until the day I die."

"Rosemarie, are you okay?" he asked in the quiet voice. "You aren't going to do anything crazy, like spray paint the front door, are you?"

I made a mental note: call Anne's therapist when I get home. "I don't know anymore. I'm really tired."

"Join the club. I got like, two hours of sleep last night."

Rich was in the kitchen making coffee. Rich didn't make me coffee. He didn't make me anything. "Good morning," he said, handing me a cup. "Careful it's hot."

"Thanks."

He leaned against the counter, taking a sip from his mug. "I'm not a bad guy, Rosemarie."

"I didn't say you were." I stared at the black liquid. *I'd slip something in your food. Something untraceable.*

"What's the matter? Too strong for you?"

"No, it's good." I forced myself a small sip.

"If you want a divorce, I'll give you one."

I studied him over my mug, seeing no malice, feeling no ill-intent. He wasn't so bad. Sure he had a poor sense of humor, but was it criminal? I'd convinced myself he was out to get me. Perhaps I'd blown the situation out of proportion.

Like you always do.

I could handle his issues, but at what cost? I wasn't happy. Dr. Carrie had a togetherness approach. Anne's therapist said I'd be okay.

With or without him, I wanted to be more than okay. "I appreciate it."

"Of course," he said. "I'm a good guy. A bad guy would demand custody of Peter and make sure you never see him again."

My mouth went dry. "Sounds like a threat."

"It's not a threat. I'm saying, a bad guy would."

He's weak. Inside I mean, my ten-year-old self reminded me. "Peter's seventeen. If he wants to live with you, that's his choice," I said. Where the calm response came from, I had no idea.

"Right," Rich said. "I want you to be happy because I'm a good guy. A bad guy would send pictures of you to Pastor Brady."

The pictures. Ones he'd pressured me into taking. A nonconsequential point if someone were to see them. "It would only make you look like a bad guy."

"I told you, I'm not."

"Right. Since you're such a good guy, I'm sure I have nothing to worry about."

That's how you do it.

89

I crawled into bed feeling the hit I'd taken by Neil's silence. Like my soul had been ripped from my body. I resolved to stop making excuses to go over to their house. He'd made none to come visit me. I didn't know what I'd expected, but not indifference.

I woke to darkness and damp sheets, and grabbed my phone. A text from Rich. **Meeting with the owner of Granny's went late with a few too many drinks. Got a hotel room for the night.**

Thank God for small favors. I searched the web for side effects of the medication Dr. Carrie prescribed. *Nocturnal enuresis.* Great. One drug fixes your childhood problem, the next creates it.

I stripped the bed, slipping the sheets beneath. I'll wash them tomorrow.

Wash them now.

"I'm too tired." A spurt of laughter emerged from my lips. "And I'm losing my mind."

Just because you're losing doesn't mean you're lost.

I stuffed the sheets into the washer. On my return to the bedroom, I stopped in the kitchen for a package of Oreos. I imagined meeting up with Neil. Too bad he was married. No one would know. He wouldn't tell anyone, I wouldn't tell anyone. Michelle didn't get him. Truly love him for all his faults. I shoved a cookie in my mouth.

Get in the shower and fix your hair pretty.

A shower won't wash away fat cells.

Do it!

I got in the shower, scrubbed my face, and washed my hair. I put on my favorite T-shirt and pajama bottoms. On my way past the dresser mirror, I caught a glimpse of myself. Pajama pants? I looked pathetic. What if Neil saw me like this?

He's thinking about you.

My mind went to a dark, seductive place where opportunity presented itself. He would have found the opportunity if he wanted one.

But for Michelle.

A weak excuse.

You should come visit me.

Something was missing. A piece of the puzzle. An unhappy marriage was one thing, but...

...He was laughing at me.

There was a lot I wanted to know, but it could all wait. First things first. I needed a drink. Or two. Or ten because I was really thirsty. Then...I was going to do it all over again.

There was a bottle of whisky from Thanksgiving. Rich had two glasses and I hid it from him. Later, when he asked about it, I told him he finished the bottle. I didn't understand why I had done it at the time, but now I know. It was for such a time as this.

I turned my ringer off and crawled beneath the blanket.

My phone lit. Rich was checking up on me. Oh well. I'd deal with him tomorrow.

Tonight, I wanted to sleep and not wake up.

90

I am not afraid of an army of lions led by a sheep; I am afraid of an army of sheep led by a lion.

Alexander the Great

My phone said three o'clock. Wide awake, I lay staring at the ceiling, visualizing Narcissus. Living with a real-life version of the Greek mythological figure was a miserable existence. Cursed, I couldn't make Rich love me or Neil want me. There wasn't a single friend I could call. At least, not one I could be honest with who would still speak to me afterward. The joke was on me. Empty and void, like the men I loved, I couldn't even cry. I curled in a ball, my heart continuing its mournful toil. The wound was fathomless.

I'm here.

I can't breathe.

I'm near to the brokenhearted.

Who are you?

I am who I am.

I've been hearing a lot of voices lately.

My sheep know My voice.

My heart burned inside my chest and I rolled over. "I'm glad. If you leave I will surely die." My voice cracked, tears spilling down my cheeks.

"I've been lonely," I whispered, and then I was being held in ageless arms. In the stillness, I basked in His presence. He let me cry until the tears ran dry. His presence awarded me serenity.

I will never leave you or forsake you.

You are the air I breathe.

You are my beloved.

"Lover, I'm yours," I mumbled. "I don't want to fall asleep."

You'll be with Me when you wake.

Exhaustion began to take over and I yawned. "Wake me up. Tell me what to do."

Christmas morning came with no presents, boxes or bags. But then, Christmas didn't come from the store. I danced around the bedroom. Ebenezer Scrooge, light as a feather. I threw open the curtains and light poured in. If there had been a sharp young lad outside, I would have ordered the prize goose and sent it to Rich. Speaking of...I checked my phone.

Nine-thirty.

I dashed to the door, reached for the handle and stopped. I was about to walk out to any other day. Laugh off last night as an elaborate dream. Go back to life as usual. The familiar. Award a hangover to any other day.

The hangover was real.

The 'any other day' was obscure, like snow fog in a winter storm.

Whoever saves their life will lose it. I knew the quote but never understood riddles. I reached for the door, counted to three and opened it.

The smell of wood smoke lingered in the air. The sun shimmered off a fresh blanket of snow beneath my feet. Making my way toward the truck, I drank in the day like a five-year-old. Not a care in the world, I dropped to the ground.

Rich's profile cast a shadow over me, blocking the sun. "Rosemarie? Are you crazy?"

"I'm making a snow angel. Want to join me?"

"Not really."

Moving my arms back and forth, I said, "You're late."

"Ate breakfast with Deke from Grandma's. Which you would know if you ever checked your phone."

I stopped and pulled it from my pocket. Six missed calls and four text messages. "My bad." I squinted at him. "You seem different."

"Me? You're the one making snow angels in the front yard."

Fire rushed through me, from the tips of my toes to the top of my head. "You're never going to believe this, but God came to me last night."

He glanced at his phone. "You want to hear something funny? The new cop, Jake Linton, pulled a car over with Michigan plates. Husband and wife. I guess Jake mentioned the whole you stuck-in-the-storm thing. The wife said she used to work for Neil's wife, Michelle."

"A lot of information exchanged from one traffic stop."

"There's cops for you. Anyway, Jake was talking to Bill Lane later about the wife. Turns out Neil Johnson's doing her. Has been for years, I guess. Jake said she got a job here working at the high school—"

Whatever else he said was drowned out by the buzzing in my ears. A girlfriend? That explained almost everything nagging me about the relationship. It also ripped my insides open.

He wasn't yours.

It wasn't a relationship at all, more like a situationship.

You wanted the truth.

Logic: band-aide to a gaping wound.

"—you're not listening."

I blinked. "Sorry, what?"

"I said Granny's restaurant in Grafton is hiring. Maybe he'll consider you."

"For what?"

He waved a hand in front of my face. "Hello, McFly. For the manager position."

I frowned. "Wait, I thought you said they were closing. I don't want to be a manager. I own a bakery."

Something flickered in his eyes and quickly disappeared. "Deke wants to wait until his oldest daughter graduates high school. She'll be a senior next year. In the meantime, you could learn the ropes."

"Rich, I can't."

"Why not?"

Where the answer came from I had no idea. "I'm not going that way."

91

Rich was in the kitchen sharpening his knives when I walked in. "I found this today while I was looking for my wallet." He slid over the Michael English CD I bought him the first Christmas we were married. "You know Michael English had an affair with the singer from First Call. Knocked her up."

I shrugged. "Ancient news."

He dragged the knife blade across the sharpening stone, *zip*. "I never did find my wallet. Have you seen it?"

"No, I haven't."

Zip. Zip. "I'm only asking because I see you cleaned up yesterday. I left it on the table and it's gone."

"I didn't see it while I was cleaning up but I'll look for it."

"What's wrong? Why are you upset?" The quiet voice.

"Nothing's wrong." I spent the next twenty minutes and my last nerve looking for his wallet. It was on the nightstand next to my purse.

"See, I told you," Rich said. "You must have put it there when you were cleaning."

"I did not."

"You probably don't remember. Remember, you forget a lot."

"If I'm so forgetful, how am I supposed to remember?"

Rich laughed. "You don't even make sense."

"Maybe you put it there," I said, anger chasing away every ounce of fear.

He blinked doe-eyes. "Why would I? I'm not your enemy, Rosemarie."

"Okay fine, I put it there," I said, and began to cry.

"Oh, you've got to be kidding me. You haven't pulled that stunt in years!"

Don't cast your pearls before swine.

I turned away, wiping tears with the back of my hand. "I'm not okay with the way things are." I cleared my throat. "And I'm tired of fighting for your scraps."

92

Friday night, I headed to the bakery early. Weak and weary, I considered what Rich had said about Granny's going out of business. He met with the owner, Deke, drank too much and spent the night in Grafton. But Deke wasn't selling. Maybe I would walk in on Rich and her, whoever "her" might be.

There was no one in the office. The laptop was on the desk.

"Hey Rosemarie, I was just leaving." Katie walked in as I was trying to log into the computer.

"I don't know the password," I said, my tone edged with frustration.

She frowned. "Is there a problem?"

"No problem."

Her fingers flew across the keyboard and the home screen popped up.

"Thanks. I'll see you tomorrow," I said, my eyes on the screen. She hesitated briefly before leaving. I moved the cursor to the upper right-hand corner to click on history. The QuickBooks ledger was still open.

I scrolled to the bottom. That can't be right. I scrolled back up and then down slowly this time. I sat back in the chair. Numbly, I went through my desk, filling a bank box of old receipts and ledgers. I locked up and drove to Josie's.

My brother-in-law Daniel answered the door. Fighting tears of frustration, I handed him the box and a brief explanation.

Daniel nodded. "I'll get back to you."

Snow glistened in city lights outside the picture window at Carlton. Daniel was alone. I wasn't sure if it was due to the weather, or because he hadn't told Josie what I gave him. Either way I was relieved.

"Hey Rosemarie." He sat across from me.

"Snowing again." I dunked my tea bag.

Stacey brought a menu. He glanced at my cup. "Is that all you're having?"

"I had a big lunch." Truth was, I couldn't remember the last time I had an appetite.

"I'll have a turkey sandwich on rye and a house salad with ranch," he told Stacey. After she left, he scooted up to the table. "Your bakery is bleeding money. If you made a dollar, you spent two."

I felt my hackles rise. "I didn't."

Daniel popped open his briefcase and pulled out a folder. "Someone did. Numbers don't lie." A pause. "You look shocked."

"I had no idea. I thought Rich was having an affair." The spoon shook as I set it down, clanking loudly against the saucer. "What are your thoughts?"

"File a Chapter Seven."

"Bankruptcy?" My heart thudded in my ears. "I'll lose my place. The girls will lose their jobs."

"I don't see you have any choice at this point," Daniel said. "The court will appoint a trustee to liquidate the bakery and pay creditors. They'll divide up your assets."

The room grew smaller around me until I wanted to disappear. "This is my fault," I said, barely hearing my own voice over the buzzing in my ears. "I trusted Rich to handle it. I should have known better."

Stacey brought Daniel's food to the table. "Is there anything else I can get for you?" she asked.

"I'm good, thanks," Daniel said, pouring dressing on his salad. "There's good news. Certain assets are safe from creditors. For instance, you won't lose your home. Once the creditors get paid and the trustee receives their fee, sole proprietors receive a discharge."

"A discharge means..."

"Your debts are forgiven."

Just then, Victor walked in the door. He hadn't changed since the day I saw him at Walsky Grocery. He was still in need of a haircut. Still looked wonderful. There was a girl behind him with dark blonde hair, a yellow shirt and white sneakers.

When I got dressed this morning, I thought green went with my highlights, making me look like a holiday. Now I was keenly aware of my low neckline. I pulled on the snug material. It was too tight and I felt underdressed. It's a sweater, Rosemarie.

"Hey Rosemarie." He guided the woman at his side forward. "This is Jean."

"Nice to meet you," I said.

He ran a hand through his hair. "I'm helping mom settle affairs. She's getting out of the cattle biz. Oliver's got grandkids. Emily had her third and Paige has a guy."

I managed a smile. "Glad to hear it."

Victor's eyes searched mine. "We should be going. Take it easy, Rosemarie."

"You too." I turned back to my brother-in-law. "So now what?"

"You let your employees know," Daniel said.

I pushed my chair back from the table. "I appreciate you helping me."

"I'm sorry I couldn't do more," Daniel said, preparing to leave. "I wanted to tell you I gave your statement about Malcolm to a criminal attorney friend of mine. She died in a car accident last month."

"I'm sorry to hear that."

"Yeah, well I finished going through her cases and I couldn't find the Sim one. I'm afraid it's buried with her."

Let it go.

"Thank you for telling me."

"**Y**ou and the kids should go live with your folks," Rich announced when I dropped the news.

"For how long?" I sighed.

"Until I say you can come home."

Too tired to argue, I said, "Okay. What will you do?"

His eyes were cold. "Not much I can do. You lost the business."

93

The Christmas tree was shorter than me and artificial. There were no decorations to speak of. No stockings hung by the chimney with care. Where once laughter echoed through walls, cold silence. Desolate rooms, lonely as the souls raised here.

At the kitchen table, Mom poured coffee. "What about the bakery?"

"I hate to lose it." I took a sip of mine. "On the other hand, it will be nice to be able to sleep at night. Not worry about employees and taxes."

"You'll need a lawyer," Mom said. "I'm surprised Daniel helped as much as he did. He and Josie are officially separated now. Rich should pay alimony and child support."

My eyes welled with tears. "I don't want his money."

"Darla Adams moved to Jamestown," Mom said. "She works at the Truck Stop. Said they're hiring. Bill Lane is the manager there now."

Dad flipped through the *Welcome Chronicle.* "Beggars can't be choosers, Rosemarie."

"I'll pick up an application." I sighed.

Abigale cancelled a hair appointment I'd booked three months ago. A text, of course because no one calls anymore. Hey I'm sorry for such short notice, but I overbooked and I have to cancel for Tuesday.

It was Monday.

I was hoping to have my hair done for a New Year's Eve party.

What party?

Jill Newby's house party.

A party I was actually looking forward to attending. Theirs was the nicest house in town. I always wanted to see the inside of it. Plus, I was curious about how her life turned out.

When can I get in?

I'll get back to you.

My phone pinged. Abigale? Nope. Jill.

I'm afraid I have to cancel the party for New Year's Eve. I've got a terrible cold.

I drove by her house, to be sure. The lights were on. The party was on. My stomach churned. Among the cars parked in front was Rich's truck.

Making my way across the Truck Stop parking lot, I skirted puddles. Water dripped from the roof, promising spring.

Early March was such a tease.

Darla answered the phone as I walked in the door. "Truck Stop, Darla speaking." She held the phone away from her ear, the caller's voice, loud and demanding. She covered the mouthpiece. "Debt collector."

I shook my head.

"I'm sorry, Rosemarie isn't here. No, I don't know when she'll be in. Same to you, buddy." Darla hung up. "What a jerk."

"I'm sorry. I can't believe they would yell at you. What did they say?"

Darla shrugged. "Oh, the usual. They're coming for your first born if you don't pay up."

"Oh man. Every day this week."

"Maybe it's time to tell Rich about the calls." Darla folded her arms across her chest. "I thought the two of you were like Barbie and Ken."

"Hardly. More like the Hatfields and McCoys."

"Is it true about Holly?"

I forced a laugh. "You know rumors. If I want to know what I'm up to I have to listen to the local scuttle." The pizza oven tinged. "Better than the looks, I suppose."

"Looks?"

"The ones people give when they're talking behind your back." I grabbed the parmesan shaker.

"Maybe you're paranoid." Darla held up her hand when I opened my mouth to protest. "I'm like you. I need everyone to like me."

"I don't need—"

"It's a small town for sure," Darla went on. "But maybe you should consider not everything is about you."

"—everyone to like me." Okay, I get it. All in my head. "Yeah, you're probably right."

For the rest of the night, I pondered how my marriage, my bakery, *life*, had so not gone according to plan.

Whoever saves their life will lose it.

Okay Jesus, the riddles aren't helping.

The next day, I arrived at the Truck Stop to find a guy working my tables. "Who's that and what's he doing here?" I asked Darla.

"Talk to Bill."

Bill was in his office. He leaned back on his chair, resting his hands on his protruding belly. "Hey Rosemarie."

"What gives?" I asked. "Some guy's working my tables."

"Yeah, about that. I like you, Rosemarie. I really do, but you were late every day last week."

"Yes, but it won't happen again. I left Rich."

"There's the phone calls too."

"I'll leave my phone in my car. Bill, I really, really need this."

He sighed. "Rosemarie, I was talking about the debt collectors."

"Oh." Humiliation burned my cheeks.

"I'm afraid I'm going to have to ask you to leave."

My imagination took a roller-coaster ride. "Are you kidding? What did Rich tell you? Did he tell you to fire me?"

He swiped a hand over his balding scalp. "Of course not. Whatever trouble you're having at home isn't my concern," his tone, lofty. The look in his eyes, final.

There was no changing his mind.

"I see."

Bill stood, sucking in his gut. "My hands are tied. I hope the best for you, I really do."

94

April 2019

Rich texted **Hey.**
Hey.
How have you been?
Good and u?
Can we get together for coffee? I miss my friend.
My heart kicked up. **You in town?**
Yeah.
How about Nilsen's?
Be there at 6:30. Can't wait.

An hour later, my bed was piled with reject clothes. All my shirts were ugly. I couldn't even look in the mirror. "I'm going to meet with Dad," I told the boys on my way out.

"I got an extra controller if you want to help me battle the boss instead," Jim said.

"You know I'm not good at those games."

Peter's eyes were fixed on the latest George Martin tome. "Mom, if someone wants to leave, let them go. Don't force anyone to be in your life."

"For coffee. He wants to talk I guess."

"You don't have to talk to him anymore." Jim shook the controller at the screen. "Ah man, the Big Boss."

"Be good for Grandma."

Peter turned the page. "Grandma's lame."

"I'll be back. Love you, guys."

"You too," Peter mumbled.

Jim yelled, "Is that all you got?"

Seven-thirty. Rich was a no show.

I waited a half hour before texting, **Where are you? I'm leaving.**

There were two ways out of town. One by Hamill's Bakery and the other a straight shot. Don't do it Rosemarie. Don't...but of course I did. I went the bakery way. I slowed down before Hamill's. The storefront was a lonely, desolate place. Feeling foolish, I started to speed up when I caught a glimpse of his truck parked in the back. As was Holly's SUV.

I couldn't think straight. Couldn't see straight, only red. Spots danced before my eyes. I gripped the steering wheel with both hands.

What does she have I don't? Why can't he love me? What makes her special?

I rushed to the stupid green door and pounded. "Rich! Open up!" Each minute, an everlasting eternity. They were in there, the two of them...

Go home.

Defeated, I returned to the car. Several deep breaths later, a can rolled around the passenger side floor. It was the black spray paint Jim didn't need for his shop project at school.

Perfect.

Sweat beaded the back of my neck. I got out, shaking the can. The ball clanging around inside the metal container like images of Rich and Holly inside my head.

Rich will open the door now. Probably call the cops and have me arrested for vandalism, and...a bunch of other things. I don't care. It will be worth it.

Rosemarie, stop this.

"If you want me to listen, do one thing for me. One, measly little favor. Give me proof."

It won't help.

"Then we have nothing to say to one another." I wiped the back of my nose on my sleeve. "Who cares about trailer trash, anyway? Not like Holly. How long has he been doing her? At least three months. Before I left."

I pressed the nozzle and sprayed back and forth. I didn't major in art. Some of the black paint went on the side of the building. I attempted to rub it out. A song about a green door came to mind, "...*midnight, one more night without sleeping.*"

Rosemarie, have you lost your mind?

"Not yet, but close." I inched the nozzle right next to the pea soup surface and squeezed. It came out in a fizz, running in one big line. Intent on the bubble, I didn't even notice the lights from behind. A whoop of a siren and slam of a car door. I looked up.

A uniformed police officer got out and hiked up his gun belt. "Can I help you?"

I looked at the can in my hand. Oh boy.

The police station was a clean room with matching gray walls and carpet. There was a desk where Officer Linton, Mark Dickerson's replacement, punched away at keys on a computer.

Rich walked in. "Hey Jake, how's it going?"

Officer Linton looked up. "Thanks for coming in, Rich. I just needed to ask you a couple questions about your old bakery."

"No problem." He flashed a salesman smile. "Actually, it was my wife's place."

"Yeah? Well shouldn't take long."

"Sounds good," Rich said. "How are you liking the job?"

"Job's good. Pay sucks."

"I hear ya." Rich chuckled. "Excuse me while I talk to my wife."

Officer Linton nodded. "You bet. Just finishing up here."

Rich crossed the room and sat down on the chair next to me. "What happened? It wasn't because of anything," a sly grin slid across his face, "I said?"

I shot him an angry glare. "You didn't show."

He lowered his voice. "I was on my way when Holly called and said she left her jacket in the bakery."

"I lost my job at Truck Stop." Shut up, Rosemarie.

A look of pity softened his golden eyes. "I'm sorry to hear it. You got money trouble?"

"I've been getting a lot of collection calls." I handed him a stack of statements for credit cards he took out in my name.

He sucked his teeth, shuffling through the pile. "Next time you should keep the balances at twenty percent of the limit or lower. These are maxed out."

"They are personal credit cards not covered under Chapter Seven."

"Why not ask your mom for help."

I sat on my hands. "You know I can't."

"You get any more calls, give them my number."

"Really?"

He handed me the bills. "All you had to do was ask, Flower Child." He gave me a long look. "Did you quit your meds?"

"I'd rather not talk about that here." I flicked a glance at Officer Linton.

"Why not? I'm not your enemy, Rosemarie." Rich glanced over, switching to his loud voice. "I'm on your side."

Officer Linton pushed away from the desk. "Rosemarie, you're facing charges of trespassing and vandalism of private property. Are you willing to give a statement?"

"Yes sir."

He turned to Rich. "Would you mind giving one?"

"Not a problem." Officer Linton opened a drawer and pulled out two clipboards.

Rich stretched, muscles rippling easily beneath his snug shirt, he glanced at me. "You're beautiful as the day I asked you to be my wife."

I looked down at my paint-stained hands. "I was ugly."

"I saw it in you before you saw it in yourself."

Like a magnet to metal I was drawn in.

95

Kellan Jones would like to connect with you on LinkedIn.

An account I started based on Becky's recommendation.

Kellan Jones appeared to be in his mid-thirties with short brown hair. A navy blue suit coat, white collared shirt beneath. No tie. Dancing eyes. Easy smile. Familiar face. **How do I know you?**

We met at Mark and Abigale Dickerson's reception.

I paused. **Could be. Honestly, I don't remember.**

You were with your husband. Peach dress. White-wedged sandals.

My favorite. **Wow. You remember my shoes. Impressive.**

How could I not? Perfect.

What do you do?

I'm in investments.

Cool.

Can I take you out to dinner sometime?

Probably not, no.

That's two no's.

I'm married. Plus, I don't do online stuff with guys.

What stuff are you talking about?

Pics or whatever.

Thanks for the offer, but I hardly know you.

A sense of humor. **What do you want?**

A pause. **Friendship.**

My heart raced. Friends? Probably a line, but a good one. **Nah, I'm good.**

Too bad. Rosemarie is my favorite name.

Goodbye.

Hey, I respect what you said. Don't disappear altogether. Promise.

Promise nothing counts.

A week later, I texted Rich. **I'm still getting collection calls.**

Rich.

Hey.

Did you change your mind about helping me?

With trembling fingers, I called him. It went right to voicemail.

I hung up.

My phone buzzed. Rich. **Whatever you need to say, text only.**

Like I was the bad guy! Anger welled inside me. I tapped my finger on the phone. Don't react, Rosemarie. Don't…

Got another call, I texted Rich.

Did you get my text?

Hello?

Hey.

At last, my phone tinged. A number I didn't recognize. **Stop this craziness. You wanted separation, you got it.**

Fury racing through my bones, I dialed his number.

"...*we're sorry the number you've dialed has been changed, disconnected or is no longer in service. Please check...*"

He didn't mean it. He'll cool down and work things out. He always did.

Whoever saves their life will lose it.

My head began to pound. "What do you mean?"

Walk away.

Not much of a life to walk away from. My life with Rich, an illusion. I had no idea what to do. Except I was done chasing shadows. I was also done accepting part of a man.

I wanted my own.

Mom and I sat together at the kitchen table with morning cups of coffee.

"Did I tell you Bill Lane moved back to town?" Mom asked.

"He got a job at Walsky's shortly after I started," I told her. "I don't get it. He hates the Walskys."

Mom sipped her coffee. "The owner of Truck Stop fired him when he got a DUI. His mother is laid up. I was delivering bread to her, and the Café asked me to start baking bread for the lunch crowd."

"But you've always bought from Walsky's."

It's because you work there.

And then she said, "I really love your hair, Rosemarie. The dark brown looks so good on you. Like when you were little."

Suddenly I saw myself through her eyes: a little girl. She was different now. My heart reached out to her. Kids didn't come with instructions. Men either. Broken, we did the best we could with what we knew.

Mom topped off our cups. "I still think Rich should have taken responsibility for the bakery demise."

"I guess it's best to forgive."

"Oh, exactly. Not forgiving is like drinking poison and expecting the other person to die."

Mom filled me in on the local scuttle. I finished my coffee, oddly dazed at an intimate moment.

I took a package of Oreos to bed in the spare room.

Neil dominated my thoughts. Things he'd said, how he said them. How he made me feel.

You imagine how it would be if not for Michelle?

He has a girlfriend.

Says Rich.

But it made too much sense to ignore. The approach-avoidance game. The teasing.

You should come visit me.

He has a wife. I don't care anymore. I want to be left alone.

Get in the shower and fix your hair pretty.

He didn't want me. He never wanted me and I started to cry.

Quit your bawlin'.

"Okay, Rich, if it'll shut you up." I even sounded horrible. I flipped on the lamp and made my way to the dresser mirror. Red eyes and scrunched cheeks, I looked like a homemade cabbage patch doll. My nose ran and I cried even harder. So ugly.

So beautiful.

Worthless.

Priceless.

He rejected me.

I protected you.

From Neil or Rich? From...myself?

From evil.

96

My phone tinged. Kellan Jones. **You can't beat a person who never stops trying.**

Hey to you. I wandered to the bedroom.

I can't stop thinking about you.

I flopped on the bed, feet in the air. Almost a minute is how long I thought about it before texting, **I think about you too.**

Just friends. I promise that's all I want.

I'd like that.

I set *Outsiders* on the edge of the counter and got down on my hands and knees, rooting around the Lazy Susan. I located the package of Oreos I'd hidden, started to rise, and the tome fell on my head.

"Ow." I rubbed the spot. "That really hurt, Mr. King."

Hoarding food? Really Rosemarie?

"I wasn't hoarding. I just...don't want to be harassed." I opened the package and ate one.

You imagine how it would be if not for Michelle?

So he said, but his actions told me boo. I brought the rest of the cookies to bed. The pages of my novel blurred. I saw a little girl afraid of what was behind a green door. A used-up woman with a can of spray paint in her hand. Another desirable man concerned for her wellbeing.

And yet again, a different woman preferred.

"Enough! Who are you?"

Who do you think I am?

"My guardian angel?" I grabbed a cookie from the nightstand, searching my mind for a famous one. "Michael?"

Give me a little credit. A pause. *I'm you.*

"What a load of hogwash. Rosemarie, you're losing it." *They're coming to take me away, haha, they're coming to take me away, ho ho hehe haha to the funny farm...*

It's going to be lonesome around here.

It would just be sex.

A line I vowed never to cross.

You didn't cross it.

If it weren't for Michelle.

Think of how good it would be.

The sad truth. No matter how good I looked on the outside, I was rotten on the inside. I didn't feel good about myself. I felt desperate.

97

Rich's lawyer showed up to my door with divorce papers for me to sign.

I looked them over. The boys would reside with me. He wasn't going to take the kids. We shared a quiet lunch afterward. Had I been wrong about him? I lost the business, but I couldn't blame him. I should have been more involved. He made mistakes, but I did too. And he was acting agreeable.

The bad feeling continued.

A snap from Peter: a link to the game he played *League of Legends*. "There is a place between worlds....In Runeterra, it's called the Void. Cho'Gath: A voidborn creature driven by insatiable hunger..."

I scanned the website while folding clothes. "The land of Runeterra has no shortage of valiant champions, but few are as tenacious as Poppy. Wielding a hammer twice her size, Poppy spent years searching for the 'Hero of Demacia' a fabled warrior said to be the rightful wielder..."

I set the laundry down and went in search of Peter.

He was at his computer. "Hey Mom. What's up?"

"Did Poppy ever find the hero?"

Peter glanced up. "It's her. She doesn't know it though."

I peered over his shoulder. "I can relate to feeling alienated by the chaotic whimsy of others. I too, prefer stability and structure."

"Which brought her to the human, Orlon."

"She revealed herself to him, feeling a connection with a human for the first time."

Peter nodded. "Soon the two became inseparable."

"Thank you for sharing them with me, Peter."

Peter smiled, satisfied. "Want to play?"

"I would love to." I abandoned the laundry.

"Why don't you go back to baking?" Jim sat in the lotus position on his bed, controller in hand as he took down the Final Boss in Persona 5.

"Your birthday cakes were pretty alright." Peter's eyes didn't lift from George Martin's latest novel.

"No one in Welcome is going to buy something they can bake themselves for fifteen bucks."

Peter turned the page. "Bake for fun. Better than moping around."

"I don't think I have what it takes anymore. I was never good at cakes. Dad said they were dry."

Jim battled the Boss. "She'll buff."

"Don't you mean 'he'll'?"

"She'll buff," Jim reiterated with a grin. "He only has the power you give him."

"Maybe."

"Don't let him run the show," Peter mumbled.

Jim hollered, "Oh yeah. That's how you do it!"

98

Pearl Frank hired Peter and Jim for the summer. According to Peter, she intended to slow down on the cattle and concentrate on rental housing for single moms.

"Up Down" played on the radio. Green summer trees accompanied both sides of the winding driveway. Young trees had grown, forming a leafy path.

I arrived fifteen minutes early. Drove beyond Frank hill to the structure in progress. Victor's truck was parked outside.

I texted Peter. **Here.**

Peter. **Come in.**

Heart in my throat, I made my way inside. In the middle of the room under construction, Peter, Jim, and Victor sat around a table, each in front of a laptop.

"Hey Rosemarie," Victor said. "Want to play my spot?"

Don't get comfortable. Remember he's got a girlfriend. I peered over his shoulder. "Nah, you're Kai'Sa. I play Poppy."

Victor's fingers flew across the keyboard. "I think you would like Kai'Sa. She's an ordinary girl who got sucked into the Void after an earthquake."

"It's sad, Mom," Peter said. "For three days she could hear the faint cries of others from her village. She was the only one to survive."

Victor hammered away at the keys. "Kai'Sa stabbed a creature from the Void, and thought it was dead. When its skin grabbed her arm, she broke her knife trying to get it off. Soon, the shell became a part of her." He moved aside. "Here, you try."

I took his place.

Later at home, I readied for bed. Strange. I hadn't thought about Neil Johnson once all evening.

The following evening, I arrived and texted Peter. **Here.**

No response. I walked in and Victor was alone in front of a laptop. "Rosemarie, come on in. I was just setting up for game time."

A warm rush flowed through me followed by a vision of the woman at his arm the night Hamill's tanked. I steeled myself against silly fantasies. Still, I couldn't help wondering why Jean wasn't here. Not that it was any of my business.

"I can go." I jerked my thumb toward the door. "I mean, come back when you guys are finished."

"Don't be silly. Stay and play with us." Victor got up from his chair. "Take a look at this."

He had the universe of *League of Legends* pulled up on the screen. I sat down and scanned the biography. "Kai'Sa was trapped underground. Alone. With more than hope, she had a plan. She was transformed from frightened girl to fearless survivor."

"But at what cost?" Victor leaned over my shoulder.

I stiffened, smelling the clean spicy scent of soap, feeling the heat radiating from him.

"For years, she was between two worlds, attempting to keep them apart. The Void would devour Runeterra given the chance. She knows many of the people she protects sees her as a monster." I swallowed hard, flicking a glance back.

"Not everyone." His face, mere inches from mine. "Inside a daunting, sexy exterior of a woman beats the heart of a girl setting captive goats free."

My heart tripped, fell. He knew me. The real me, a quiet spirit. But he wasn't mine. A shot of fear burst through me and I pushed away from him, nearly falling off my chair.

"Rosemarie, I..."

The door burst open and Peter walked in. "Hey, Mom. You gonna play too?"

"Laying shingles is grueling work." Jim came in behind him.

"No truer words have been said," Victor told him. His eyes expressed disappointment, but resolve. I knew that look as he took the chair next to me.

He would keep his distance.

99

Becky stopped by to give me my paycheck. I invited her in for coffee and red velvet cake.

"How are you doing?" she asked.

"Good." Thanks to game night with Victor and the boys. "I stopped ruminating every possible scenario about Rich. I don't YouTube his condition anymore. It was rough when I discovered it was me who powered it."

"Condition?"

"Yes. I think he's a real life narc— well it doesn't really matter. I don't like calling people names. Dehumanizes them."

"Are you still seeing a therapist?"

"Sort of." I led her to the back door, and opened the freezer to my transcendent store of cakes. "All the self-help has made me fat."

Becky's eyes grew round as saucers. "Rosemarie, you made these?"

"Guilty. I gave some to mom for her work parties. The rest were too pretty to pitch, and I decided to freeze them."

"They definitely are too pretty for the garbage can. Do they taste as good as they look?"

"You tell me. The red velvet was one I baked yesterday. I thought about Hamill's. I don't have the money. Jim said he saw a raccoon on the roof.

It appears a few have taken up residence. The city wants to tear it down. I convinced them at the last council meeting to hold off."

Her eyes on the cakes, Becky said, "Looks like there's no one to stop you, but you."

The next evening, Becky met me at the door of Walsky's Grocery.

"Rosemarie, my mom wants you to bake a cake for my Aunt Marlene. My Uncle Clayton divorced her and she moved to Orlando."

I remembered Marlene. She was the librarian with the cat eyeglasses and helpful resources. I pinned my nametag on my shirt. "When's she coming to visit?"

"Mom wants it sent to her in Florida."

"Sent to her?" I glanced up. "Like in the mail?"

"Probably."

"I don't have a business anymore."

"Who cares, but get this. She'll be calling. Make sure you answer."

Colleen Walsky did call and discussed ordering a cake. The occasion: her sister loves cake.

Thanks to Becky's heads-up, I checked with Google to find out how to mail a cake. When Colleen asked me how much, I already had the estimate in my head. Cost of supplies plus time. I rattled it off, and held my breath for the what-are-your-cakes-made-of-gold speech.

"Too cheap," Colleen said instead. Then she told me how much I was going to charge, which was twice what I quoted. "Send the bill to my address."

Can I ship a wedding cake to Florida?

Turns out, you can. Providing the frosting is fondant.

Early bird gets the worm, Becky texted at five a.m.

Without a thought I texted back **Big incentive**.

You were the one who hooked me on this early exercise thing. Get your butt to the gym.

I closed my eyes again and my phone pinged. Kellan Jones. **Hey beautiful.**

Hey yourself. I love how you don't ask what I'm wearing.

My imagination is excellent.

Two seconds. The amount of time I thought about it before taking a selfie. I studied it. My black night shirt gave the right amount of leg and cleavage. Messed hair and sleepy look gave the right amount of everything else. I sent it before talking myself out of it.

No response.

Becky met me at the door of the gym, a twinkle in her eyes. "Guess what? My Aunt Marlene loved the red velvet cake. On and on to my mother, pleased as punch since her sister is super fussy."

"Nice," I said, my mind on the selfie. What if Kellan showed his buddies? Not a bad pic, but definitely suggestive.

"Happily ever after." Becky squared her hands. "A divorce cake? The bride at the top sitting among a pile of books. The groom at the bottom. Her favorite part was the cat eyeglasses on the bride. Where ever did you find her?"

"You'd be amazed what you can find on the internet."

"Uh, yeah." She grabbed a set of weights. "Now let's do this thing."

My phone pinged. **Okay, no one's imagination is that good.**

The corny line brought a smile to my lips.

100

Marlene's son, Devin, had a real estate business in Florida. Did quite well for himself. Devin ordered a cake for his colleague, Jerry's promotion. Jerry loved the carrot cake with the golfer and hole-in-one. He ordered a wedding cake for his daughter, Dawn, who ditched three previous grooms. The running shoes tickled Jerry and Dawn pink, and orders began pouring in. Anne Clark had a great following on Instagram and began to promote my cakes.

"Aren't you thrilled?" Becky grabbed me in a hug. "It's fantastic."

I yawned. "More like crazy. I got two hours of sleep last night. I have to go shopping in Fargo today for supplies. Which reminds me, I'm terrible at managing money."

Becky shrugged. "Simple math."

"Simple for you maybe." I was dealing with a three-day headache. Not a regular run of the mill pain, but on the migraine scale. *I'd slip something in your food. Something untraceable.* Good thing I wasn't living with him anymore. Still, how long does arsenic stay in your system? Something to check on Google.

"I could hook you up with someone. My cousin Delia is great with figures," Becky said.

"I can't afford to pay her."

"Not now maybe, but you will. Until then, I bet she'd help you out for a cake."

"What's her story?"

Becky shrugged. "Dunno. She's a lesbian. Her mom disowned her when she moved in with her girlfriend."

"Hmm. I'll see what I can come up with."

A vanilla cake with two girls holding hands and *Love Matters* in bright red turned out exactly right.

Delia accepted the job.

I got a text from Kellan Jones. **Hey sexy.**

A smile came to my lips. **I got 10 new cake orders. Not from local yokels, but from important people. I think things are finally looking up.**

I'm happy for you. You deserve every success.

He's married. The idea wormed its way into my head. **I know this seems sort of late to be asking, but are you married?**

I am, yes. Does it bother you? His response, a swift kick in my gut.

Of course it bothers me. Why wouldn't it?

I thought we were friends.

Dumb, dumb, dumb. I tossed my phone across the bed.

Well, Rosemarie, what did we learn today? Don't talk to men. I should have known. His thoughts on self-love were perfect. He adored strong women. His favorite book *The Shining?*

Something wasn't right.

I checked his LinkedIn pic with Google images. A fake profile.

That's two yes's. It was Rich. I'd bet my eye for decorative detail on it.

I thought back to all the things I said, really no big deal. But there were the pics I'd sent "Kellan Jones." Touché Rich. You always win.

He made you out to be a complete fool.

I made me the fool.

You have to do something.

Fine. I blocked both Rich and Kellan Jones on my phone and all social media sites.

101

Softly singing Twenty One Pilots' "Chlorine," I walked into the kitchen. Mom turned and pretended to do dishes. Dad picked up the paper.

"Hey guys," I said, searching my brain for what I'd done wrong.

Silence.

Okaaay. "I'm going to get started on today's orders."

Dad looked up from the paper. "How's the job at Walsky's?"

Mom rested her glasses on top of her head. "Oh, did we tell you about Colleen? First of all, hiring you was the smartest thing she ever did."

Oh boy. "What about Colleen?"

Mom's eyes grew serious. "Other than the astronomical amount she charges for foodstuffs, she fired Bill Lane."

"I was there when it happened. Bill showed up to work drunk."

Quiet.

Mom caught Dad's gaze. "We heard that too. It's sad though, about Bill. He lost his oldest granddaughter in a car accident. His daughter finally couldn't take it and killed herself."

I knew what happened and Colleen did too. She felt sorry for Bill, excusing his tardiness and absences. Until the morning Bill showed up drunk. Nearly running over Adam and Janette Brown's five-year-old grandson, Toby, playing outside the grocery store. "I know all that, but his drinking is out of control. Even before."

Dad folded the paper. "Mom and I aren't shopping there anymore."

"But I work there."

They're boycotting your livelihood.

Dad shifted in his chair. "Your mother tried to work it out with Colleen. In the end we decided to buy groceries in Fargo. It's nothing personal."

It sure felt personal. I felt the claws of betrayal rip my backside.

"Your choice, I guess," I said.

Now, let it go. Untie them.

"I want to thank you both for giving me and the boys a place to stay." I reached for the newspaper, still waters calming the rising tide.

Mom and Dad exchanged glances.

Mom said, "Of course."

I shuffled through until I came across the section "Houses for rent."

102

Nestled in a scenic river valley twelve miles northwest of Valley City on the Sheyenne River, Lake Ashtabula was smooth as glass. The reservoir created an opportunity to catch a variety of gamefish species in the manmade lake. But not today. I checked my phone. It was time to get back.

Tommy strode alongside me on the dock. "You got another pole for me?"

I reeled in the last of the line and grabbed the jig. "No, but you can use this one. Fish aren't biting."

"Thanks." Tommy cast the line, his eyes fixed on the lake. "How are things?"

"Good."

"You hear much from Rich?" He reeled in slowly.

"Let's just say I'm learning how to love my enemies."

Tommy reached down and opened the tackle box. "I guess if it were easy, everyone would do it." He baited the hook. "Maybe he's not your enemy."

"Rich? He sure acts like it."

"Do you still believe in angels?"

"Yeah."

"What if there's an army of them waiting for you to take a stand in this realm for a battle waged in another?"

Something inside me bloomed like a rose and my heart swelled. "I'm not much of a warrior."

"Standing up for Peter was a start. Raising your kids alone is nothing to sneeze at. Moving out of your parents' house was a step in the right direction. Now build your strength and character."

I sighed. "I can't fix him, Tommy. I've tried so hard."

"Don't fix him."

"But I'm supposed to forgive and forget."

"Yeah, the east from the west thing? That's God. You aren't God." He cast the fishing line. "Remember when Chester died? He was in agony and you couldn't go near him without him attacking you."

I glanced over at him. "You remember that?"

"How could I forget? You said it over and over, 'why would he hurt me when I love him so much?'" He scratched the top of his head. "If there was such a battle, I wonder what would happen if you didn't hold Rich responsible."

"I don't know. It sounds so…"

"Fantastic?"

There was a tug on the fishing line. I grabbed his arm. "Hey, I think you got one."

"Walleye. I've never caught anything in this lake except perch and bullheads." Tommy reeled quickly until a fish emerged from the water. He removed the hook and handed me the fish. "This reminds me of a story."

"Some days I think my whole life is a story." I pushed the line through the walleye's gill.

"There was a rabbit hopping through the woods. She was fuzzy and cute as a bunny could be. I'm talking melt-your-heart soft. She came upon a river. A crocodile offered her a ride across on his head. Now the bunny sensed danger, but being a trusting soul, she climbed up on the croc's head. The crocodile brought her across the river safely. When they reached the other side, he ate her up.

"A turtle saw the whole thing, and said, 'Why did you help her across if you were going to eat her?' To which he replied, 'Well, I'm a crocodile.'"

I laughed out loud.

"Thanks for the mercy laugh." After another tug on the line, Tommy reeled in a Northern. He handed me the fish, a twinkle in his eye. "I thought you said the fish weren't biting."

I blew out a breath. "They weren't."

After a peaceful hour and a handful of fish, he handed me the pole. "What do you say we take these fish and head to my place for a fish fry? Bring the boys over. Ella and Sammy are big into *League of Legends*. I bet Robin will whip up a salad."

"I could bring the monster cookies I baked," I said. "Give me a half hour."

"Cool. See you then."

"See ya."

103

Adam and Janette Brown, now in their early sixties, were tickled pink at the idea of renting to us. The rental house was small. Not near adequate kitchen space for my cakes and "Celebrate You."

It came down to being affordable and I signed the lease.

There was a small window with dusty curtains over the kitchen sink. I took them down and threw them into the wash. Scrubbing the sill, I saw a blue Chevy from the corner of my eye. My heart leapt in my throat, pounding a hard rhythm that left me breathless.

Neil.

I ran to the living room in time to catch brake lights as the Chevy turned the corner. I went back to scrubbing the sink, the sting of disappointment gnawed at my heart.

There it was again!

The Chevy drove past. Another quick jolt of adrenaline got my heart thumping in my ears.

Thirty seconds. The amount of time I thought about getting in my car to see if it was Neil. I couldn't drive around chasing shadows.

The dryer dinged, and I returned the curtains to their rightful place above the sink, peering out the window. I waited for a few minutes that lasted an eternity.

The truck didn't drive by again.

My phone blasted "Welcome to the Black Parade" by My Chemical Romance through a portable speaker. I finished unpacking dishes, imagining a place where ghosts, dead and alive, didn't haunt me.

I lay awake, staring at the ceiling. Neil and the blue Chevy came to mind. Now I understood Anne's addiction to cigarettes. One sight of his truck after months of not seeing or speaking to him brought me right back to fixation over intimacy he refused me. He was like a drug. I longed for the exhilarating rush he gave me. I traded my ideal for a bad trip. A man not even close to matching me. I adored him and he despised me.

Let it go.

I can't.

How long are you going to mourn a man I rejected as your king?

Rich, ideal in the beginning. Neil, a fantasy escape. I, a victim and ready to justify everything. I was willing to do anything to feel something. Even hurt a good friend to meet my own needs.

Quick tears sprang to my eyes. I'd become a crybaby.

Now untie him.

Barely able to keep my eyes open, I drifted to sleep. I would let it all go. My pride. The wrongs done to me. The wrongs I'd done. Myself. Most of all, myself.

"What a racket," The Dragon howled above the celestial uproar, "It can only mean one thing."

"I guess it's true," Asmodeus shouted back. "In the same way there will be more rejoicing in Heaven over one sinner who repents than over ninety-nine righteous persons who do not need to repent."

The Dragon kicked him like a dog. "Those words hurt my ears more than that ridiculous party. You can hear it all the way to Sheol. The pathetic little sap. I loathe her. Has she no pride? Vulnerable and weak. Who takes responsibility for their own actions anymore?"

"Apparently she does." Asmodeus moved away, licking wounds.

"I don't know how it's possible to have gone any worse." The Dragon held the sides of his head. "I can't believe I ever thought her to be of value. I want to punch her stupid face."

"I guess it's time to pack up shop. Move on," Asmodeus said.

"Not yet." The Dragon moved away. "It's over when I say it is."

104

The setting sun streamed paths of light, shadowing scattered clouds and coloring the sky brilliant shades of yellow, orange, and scarlet.

I texted Becky. **You going to the gym?**

No answer.

All those Oreos aren't going to burn themselves.

It was pitch black when I pulled up to the fitness center. I cut the engine and got out. The streetlight flickered. I glanced back. "Is anyone there?" The question, firm and calm in my head, came out a shaky squeak.

It's him.

My heart stopped, and started hammering in my ears, a postmortem news brief flashing through my brain:

Hamill. He's a real nice guy, so they say. Pillar of the community. Deacon in the church. Successful business. Stabbed his wife to death. No one saw it coming. She was unconscious by the time the ambulance got there. They managed to stop the bleeding, but couldn't save her. They say the gym mysteriously glows red ever since.

An ankle cracked. Black talons of fear crept up my spine. I turned and ran.

"Rosemarie, wait," Rich called.

Wait, nothing. I made a b-line for the door, pulling my phone out at the same time.

For a girl with short legs, you run like the wind.

First day waking in my own home was at noon. Groggy, I moved about the kitchen in a haze putting together a cup of coffee. I took a sip. Bleh. I poured it down the sink and made a cup of tea. There was a knock on the door.

Greg, with a crockpot of hotdish. "From Susan."

"Thanks."

"Everything okay?" he asked, concern etched in his brow. "Becky told me about Rich showing up at the gym."

"You once called me Lady Lion," I said, patting his arm. "Sleepy sheep is a far better description."

"Rosemarie..."

"If you ever see Old Man Warter again, tell him I'm too fast for him."

Second day, I downloaded the app Jim suggested. After a half hour of music, the song "Grace Got You" by MercyMe played. I cranked up the volume, dancing around the tiny living room like a little girl with a Tickle microphone. I didn't even notice the boys were home, until Jim said, "Hey mom. Got any food?"

Peter said, "School's lame."

I'm sure I looked like a fool, but neither said a word about my singing or dancing.

Third day was my day off from Walsky Grocery. I went to Fargo and bought everything red, including lipstick. Fourth day, I stayed home and read three Shari Lapena novels wearing a cherry sweater and fire engine lipstick.

Because I could.

Jim strolled into the kitchen. "Dad's here, Mom."

"Thanks." I rubbed his head. "Did you kiss any girls today?"

Jim pulled the liter of milk from the fridge. "Yeah, but they didn't like it."

Rich stood in the doorway.

"What movie are you going to see?" I asked.

"*It Chapter Two.*"

"Let me know if it's any good."

Peter came bounding down the stairs. "See ya, Mom."

"Be good." I took a step back. "Nice to catch up, Rich."

"Wait for me in the car, boys. I'll be right there," Rich told them. When they were out the door, he turned to me. "I know I made mistakes in the past, but God still loves me. I'm working on my relationship with Jesus. I'm sorry for all I put you and the boys through."

God can change anyone. "I'm glad to hear it."

Rich shoved his hands in his pockets. "I would really love another chance with you. Maybe a do over?" His brow lifted.

"Rich, I was this close," I pinched my thumb and forefinger together, "to calling the police."

He blinked. "What for?"

"What do you mean, what for? To get a restraining order."

"I didn't mean to scare you, Rosemarie. It's a public gym." His eyes pierced mine. "I thought I'd surprise you with a day pass." Then he chuckled. "You should have seen your face. I thought you were going to have a heart attack."

God can change anyone but you can't. "You know Rich, I'll bet God isn't thrilled with your crumbs either."

"What, now you're a Bible Thumper?"

"Goodbye," I said, and closed the door.

A Bible Thumper?

I didn't know but I knew where to find out. I retreated to the living room, searching the bookshelf. "Don't tell me I got rid of it. It has to be... here it is." I pulled out the Bible.

105

Belial regarded his own stunning reflection in the mirror hanging above the dresser before his attention shifted to the target.

Rosemarie was nicely rounded in all the right places. A bosom filling her shirt perfectly. He looked beyond outward beauty for signs of worthlessness and desperation. Recognized sad eyes. A stiff smile, rarely reaching her eyes. She was brittle. Nothing would stop him from destroying her.

Belial pandered to the needs of perverts, the worthless, and anyone with a disturbed soul.

It had begun. The duel between himself and his prey. He leaned over her and began whispering dark thoughts in her ear.

Fog settled over the house, dark, cold and thick. Michelle invited me to Heidi's birthday party. Heart galloping in my chest, I searched the closet for my prettiest shirt. Maybe a skirt to match.

You should come visit me.

No point in giving up my whole life. Nothing wrong or bad about a birthday party. A little fun. As long as no one knows.

A little sex you mean.

Sex is good and he is...yum.

Why even bother trying to look good. He probably won't even be there. He's with Ms. Michigan right now.

Familiar thoughts raced through my head: You're hot, but can't hold a man's devotion. Your youth will fade. Your body will sag, then no man will want you. Soon, you'll be the last any man notices. You'll die. Alone, like the worthless piece of meat you are.

Fear danced across my spine, and I whispered, "That doesn't sound like me."

Demons can't read your thoughts, Rosemarie.

That was true but...

Unless they give them to you.

God chose me. Pursued me, wanted me when I was at my worst. Protected me from making a really bad choice. I felt it in my bones.

We don't go by what we feel we go by what we know.

An idea planted deep in my belly, grew, until I had to say it out loud, "I don't have to listen to you."

A force flooded the room, blinding light knocking the destroyer into the next atmosphere. End over end, Belial sailed, knowing it could only mean one thing.

Amael.

I woke up, my eyes adjusting to the darkness. Next to the bed stood a seven-foot Nordic man, long blonde hair and six-pack abs. Arms folded across his thick chest, his head nearly reached the ceiling. His hair was braided at his temples, and he wore brown trousers held by a rope.

"How did you get in here?" I asked, mouth pressed into the pillow.

He didn't answer, but then I noticed his feet weren't touching the floor. He floated several inches above the rug next to my bed.

I fumbled around for the package on the nightstand. "Cookie, Angel?"

He smiled at me and was gone.

I rolled over and fell back to sleep.

I sent Heidi a birthday cake in place of me and took Peter and Jim to Carlton for supper. Fred and Suzie Demit were leaving as we were coming in.

"How are you doing, Rosemarie?" Fred asked.

Sorrow in his eyes brought tears to mine. "One day at a time. How about you?"

"Same."

"Divorce isn't anywhere near the pain of losing a son."

Suzie gave me a sad smile. "Loss is loss, whether a death or divorce. Makes no difference."

I laid my hand on her arm. "I'm sorry about Aaron. Everyone loved him."

"Thanks, Rosemarie," she said, unshed tears in her eyes.

Stacey was the new restaurant manager.

"Congratulations," I told her, perusing the menu. "I always thought you were the right choice."

"Oh, thank you. Both Dennis and I are happy with the arrangement."

Jean—Victor's Jean—walked in with a blonde man on her elbow.

"Who is he?" I asked Stacey.

"He's Jean's fiancé, Uwe. A South African who used to work for Pearl Frank. Jean is moving with him to South Africa after the wedding."

Well. That explained game night. "Poor Victor."

"Victor Frank? They broke up a while back."

My heart reached my throat. "Really?"

"Last I saw, he didn't appear too broken up about it."

Why didn't he say something? Who cares? Hope, stubborn and delicious, crept in. I pushed it out. Not that it would mean...well it meant nothing. I'm sure to him about me.

Oh boy. I lived in my head for so long, even my thoughts were confused.

106

Walsky Grocery was desolate when Colleen and Becky arrived at five thirty a.m. to have a coffee break with me.

Actually, they had coffee. I chose Chai Tea. "You look like the sort of people who might like a piece of cake for breakfast." I sliced two generous pieces of red velvet cake.

"You're having one too, right?" Becky asked.

"Okay you talked me into it." I sliced a third piece.

"Your cakes are fantastic. We are proud to have you as a part of our team," Colleen said.

A sudden vision of Rich carrying out his threat with the pictures, and I felt my face get hot. They believed me to be a good person. I'd been rotten.

You are not the sum of your mistakes.

Like Peter walking on water toward Jesus, I began to feel myself sinking. I was trailer trash.

You are royalty.

Rejected.

Beloved.

Not good enough.

Chosen.

"If there's anything we can do, don't hesitate to ask," Colleen said.

"Thank you." I licked my fork. "Let me know if you hear of anyone with a commercial kitchen or something adequate for baking cakes."

Colleen sipped her coffee. "You should talk to Doris Meyer. She signed a lease with Pearl Frank when her granddaughter came to live with her. Her granddaughter was in a foster home until her foster parents caught her sending risky photographs."

See what happens when the truth comes out?

"What's her name?"

"Emma."

107

It was mid-October, two months since game night ended and school began. Two months of an eternity. I envisioned going to Victor's place and confessing my feelings. Dozens of scenarios later, there wasn't an outcome I didn't end up looking like a desperate fool.

Late afternoon, I arrived at the house where Myrtle Anderson and Doris Meyer lived, a cozy cottage surrounded by various lawn ornaments. At the front entrance, a life-size statue of the Virgin Mary.

Myrtle answered the door. "Hi Rosemarie."

"Hi Myrtle."

"Did you hear the news? A gunman killed two people in an attack on an East German synagogue."

I frowned. "No, I hadn't."

Myrtle clicked her tongue. "Sad. It happened on one of the holiest Jewish days."

Behind her, Doris waved me inside. "Can I get you tea or coffee? Anything to drink?"

"Actually, I'm here to see Emma."

"She's in the spare room," Doris said. "Go up the stairs, last door on your right."

Emma's suitcase was open on the bed. "I'm leaving," she said.

"Interesting choice of items to pack." I eyed the sewing kit, complete with vintage needles along with silver and gold thread.

"You never know when you'll burst a seam," she said. "One previously used Kleenex. Crest three-D white toothpaste. One nearly empty magnesium deodorant with aloe and chamomile. Equate lens cleaning wipes. USB adapter. Crumpled up Saran wrap. One panty liner."

"A single panty liner?" I asked.

Emma grinned. "The older you get the harder you laugh."

"You are not old enough to pee your pants."

Emma shuffled through the remaining items. "One empty, slightly used Hefty Ziploc. Tylenol. A hair brush and hair pick."

"Um, Emma…"

"What?" she blinked innocently.

"I love you." I squeezed her tight.

Tears spilled down her cheeks. "I suppose you know."

"I suppose I do."

"I don't suppose you know how to get him to delete the pictures." Emma's eyes were hopeful.

"Afraid not. You won't do it again, will you?"

She looked at me like I'd grown two heads. "Not in this lifetime or the next."

"Then you didn't waste your pain." And I won't waste mine.

Emma's heart was in her eyes. "The guy was a nerd from school. I only did it to get Neil's attention." She chewed her lower lip. "Have you ever wanted someone so bad you did something crazy? Talk about backfiring."

My chest tightened. "Just because we want something, doesn't mean we should have it or that it's ours to take."

"I'm scared, Rosemarie. I wish I was brave, like you," she said, wiping her cheeks with the back of her sleeve. "You're never scared."

"Me? I get scared all the time," I said, rubbing my hands together. "But what we do when we are afraid determines our destiny."

"I can't even look at Grandma or Myrtle. I'm worried he'll show all his friends." She drew a shaky sob. "What am I supposed to do? I can't stop worrying about it."

"How about you don't? I mean, what would happen if you don't worry?"

Emma blinked. "Okaaay."

Whoever loses their life for My sake will find it.

Countless times I had heard the words. At last, my soul knew their meaning.

I had nothing to lose.

108

Two roads diverged in my life and I took the one less traveled. And that has made all the difference.

Robert Frost

I caught a glimpse of my reflection in the mirror on my way out the door. Red sweater, cherry lipstick, and eyes shining with courage. I like it, I thought for the first time since I was a girl with a Kodak Disc.

I drove west, the sun a hint on the horizon.

At the end of Frank's driveway, I slowed. My bravado disappeared amid vehicles in front of the four rental houses and the lawn around the castle. I pulled up behind the car parked furthest out and cut the engine. The bottom of the hill was still a distance. People moved about the property, hanging white lights around the barn.

I started to get out and stopped. This wasn't the right time for a confession of feelings. Not like he was holding his breath for me. The cake ... In the box next to me, a single-layer I made Victor. A rancher at the top, cows grazing, and edged with picket fencing.

I sat back in the seat and squeezed my eyes shut. I could go home and come back another day. Yes, that's what I'll do. I slid the key into the ignition.

"Rosemarie. Rosemarie!"

I looked out the window. Victor was running down the hill toward me. I got out. My legs took off on their own. When I was a breath away, my foot found a soft spot in the earth and I stumbled. He was there and caught me against his chest.

I opened my mouth. No words came out as I was laughing and crying all at once.

He held my face in both of his hands. "I was just coming to see you," he said, and kissed me, my neck. My tears.

At last he pulled back, laughing. "You're right in time for breakfast."

What could I say? There were no words to take back Rich. None to bring back carefree days or the girl in a red dress. A kiss between friends closer than lovers.

He was smeared with lipstick. "You got, you uh, got lipstick on you."

"Do I?" he said, grabbing my hand.

A woman with blonde hair, a brown sweater, and tall suede boots to match approached. "Uncle Victor, Dad said if you can't decide, he's going to pull out the Lutefisk."

"Tell him the prime rib," Victor said, his eyes on me. "Rosemarie, you remember Paige."

I blinked. "Toots?"

"Yes." She laughed. It was warm, friendly, and reminded me of Pearl. "We're having a celebration today."

"That is after horseback riding, games," Victor said. "Of course, S'mores will be in order." His eyes drank in my expression, my smile. "Our new paint, Kai'Sa is perfect for you. We have two more that will work for Jim and Peter."

"They didn't come."

"I'll go get them in my truck and guess what I was doing?"

"I've no idea." I searched my brain. "Making waffles?"

"There's even strawberry syrup and whip cream."

"I think..." I'll pass is what I should have said, but was feeling daring, reckless and more myself than I had in a very long time. "I bet I can eat more than you."

"You're on." He took my hand and turned toward the house.

The view of the setting sun, a deep orange flame against the earth, the day fading into a cream periwinkle behind Frank hill.

A feast was prepared. The guests reached nearly a hundred.

The occasion: a home for Doris and Emma. Delia Walsky, her girlfriend, and their two-year-old daughter. A woman, Katherine from Kansas, her three children. Anne Clark.

Tommy and Robin were there. Ella and Sammy sat with Peter and Jim at a table. Pearl and her laughter. Oliver and Lauren. Emily, and her husband, Emmet and their sons, Marcus and Thad. Their new baby, Sarah. Paige and her fiancé, Eli. My Aunt Jean.

The barn was fall festive. Pumpkins adorned a serving table and the entrance. Leaves of brown, gold and yellow were scattered about the room. White lights hung across the ceiling.

After dinner, I helped move tables, making room for the dance floor. Eli was the MC. Chairs were lined up against the far wall for non-dancing flowers. I mentally marked mine.

Victor came and sat next to me. "Your eyes dance, Rosemarie. I like to see it."

Little shivers raced through my body. "Thanks," I said, realizing I had yet to explain myself. But how? I drew a deep breath. "I've made such a mess of things. Of me. Whole conversations go on inside my head, and..."

"I like your sweater."

He didn't get it. "I only want you to know..."

The song ended and the room erupted in applause. Soon, Willie Nelson's voice vibrated through the speakers.

Victor stood. "Dance with me."

Heart in my throat, I set my wine glass on the table. I wondered how I would manage to be held by him an entire song.

I didn't have to wonder long. "You know how to two-step, Rosemarie?" he asked.

"Can you two-step to 'Always On My Mind?'"

A slow smile worked its way across his face. "We can do whatever we want. Follow my lead. To the left now." We moved left.

I started talking to keep my mind off the fact I was dancing. "It's been a long two months. I've missed game night." I caught his eyes. "I've missed you."

"To the right, Rosemarie," he said, guiding me right. "I couldn't stop thinking about you. It drove me crazy. I had to see you. I was on my way over to your house this morning when I saw your car pull up. Then you looked at me with those incredible eyes, and I knew you remembered."

"Remember what?"

"Who you are." He twirled me around. The song ended, and he was holding me in his arms. My eyes swam in the depths of his, making my heart pound in a way that had little to do with two-stepping.

Suddenly, the music kicked up. "I think I'll go sit down," I said.

"Oh no you don't." He grabbed my hand. "You can't possibly sit this one out."

Everyone got up from their chairs and entered the circle. Laughing, we joined the "Happy Dance" with MercyMe. All too soon, the song ended. The room broke out into cheers and applause.

He laughed. "I love that song."

Face flushed, my eyes caught his. "I've never had so much fun."

Marcus and Thad rushed us. "Uncle Victor, want to play with us?"

He rubbed Marcus' head. "Depends. What game?"

"Good guys and bad guys," Marcus said.

Thad looked at me. "Rosemarie can play too. Please?"

Easy choice. "Sounds like fun. Let's go see if Peter and Jim want to play."

Victor reached for my hand. "I want to show you something afterward."

"Where are you taking me?" I asked, getting into Victor's truck.

"You'll see," Peter said, shutting my door.

I rolled down my window. "Wait, you guys aren't coming?"

"We've seen it," Jim said with a smile.

Peter waved. "See ya back at the house."

"See ya," I said, closing my window. "I brought you something, Victor. It's in my car."

"Rosemarie." There was a smile in his voice.

He pulled alongside my car. I got out and grabbed the cake off the seat. Back in his truck, I thrust the box at him. "I made it for you. For your own place."

He opened the lid and his eyes widened.

I flushed in the dim light. "I know you don't have a place of your own, but someday. I wanted you to know I remembered."

He closed the lid. "It's perfect."

I could tell he meant it and I beamed.

Five miles north and three miles east, he turned down a road.

A newly-built house closed the distance. Rugged pine with an open porch and swing. Alongside, a three-stall garage in the same theme. Up the porch steps, on either side of the front door were black lanterns.

"Those are like the ones at our house growing up in Welcome," I said.

He opened the door. "Wait until you see inside."

The living room had a nine-foot ceiling, fireplace and a built-in bookshelf. There was a breakfast space with stools. Kitchen utensils hanging from racks over a bar. A gas stove was surrounded by dark marble countertop and there was a refrigerator to match.

"What do you think about the kitchen? Is it adequate for your baking needs?" Victor asked. "Peter and Jim said to ask you."

"More than adequate." I looked at him, startled. "I don't understand."

Victor leaned against the counter. "It was a summer of dreams, being with you almost every evening. I was thinking," his face reddened, "hoping rather, we could spend every evening together from here on out."

"Victor, I...am doing so much better, but I've got a long way to go. And you should know, I'm following Jesus."

"I'd expect nothing less." He took my hand, pulling me to him. "Do you remember the night of the Christmas cantata when I kissed you?"

"It was my first." I was breathless from his nearness.

"Mine too." He closed the space between his mouth and mine. His lips were soft and sweet, like coming home. He lifted his head. "I have a secret."

"Oh boy, I hate secrets."

"I've been thinking about the cake since we got here."

"Me too!" I punched his arm.

"First things first." He dug beneath the counter and pulled out a bottle of wine. He poured two glasses and handed me one.

He raised his glass. "To my darling friend who has come home."

"To my equal. In every way it counts." I clinked my glass with his.

We both took a sip. He reached for the cake and sliced two pieces, scraping extra frosting on both plates.

I rubbed my hands together. "Oh man, those are gigantic, Victor."

"The whole point." He caught my eye and took a bite. "You've outdone yourself, Rosemarie."

I took a bite of mine. "I did, didn't I?"

About the Author

Hazel Mattice grew up in an isolated community near Valley City, North Dakota. She lives in LaMoure, North Dakota with her two boys, two dogs and a cat who thinks he's a bird. Hazel is working on her next novel. Check out her website hazelmattice.wixsite\crashmoe, follow her on Instagram, Instagram.com/hazelmattice or visit her Facebook page AuthorHazelMattice.

Made in the USA
Monee, IL
09 November 2021

81746982R00225